PRAISE FOR SARAH McCARTY

"McCarty is a sparse, minimalistic writer, with a great ear for dialogue. She's a passionate observer of history, and manages to deftly and accurately weave her spicy stories through with important facts and issues of the epoch she invokes. She's also good at capturing that intangible magnetism surrounding dangerous, rugged men . . . I'm hooked." —*USA Today*

"If you like your historicals packed with emotion, excitement, and heat, you can never go wrong with a book by Sarah McCarty." —*Romance Junkies*

"It's so great to see that Ms. McCarty is able to truly take these eight men and give them such vastly different stories and vastly different heroines, all of whom allow us to see different aspects of what life was really like for Western frontier women, be it good, horrific, or simply unfortunate." —*Romance Books Forum*

"What really sets McCarty's stories apart from simple erotica is the complexity of her characters and conflicts . . . definitely spicy, but a great love story, too." —*RT Book Reviews*

"Readers who enjoy erotic romance but haven't found an author who can combine it with a historical setting may discover a new auto-buy author . . . I have." —*All About Romance*

Promises Decide

SARAH McCARTY

JOVE
New York

A JOVE BOOK
Published by Berkley
An imprint of Penguin Random House LLC
375 Hudson Street, New York, New York 10014

Copyright © 2018 by Sarah McCarty

ISBN: 9780425230701

First Edition: September 2018

Printed in the United States of America
1 3 5 7 9 10 8 6 4 2

Cover photo by Tetra Images/Getty Images
Dog by Justyna Furmanczyk Gibaszek/Shutterstock
Book design by Laura K. Corless

*For my mom. The one person I know
who will talk me back into sense whenever I come to her
foolishly brandishing the concept of "quit."
She is both my sounding board and my inspiration.
Always has been. Love you, Mom.*

One

H e'd be damned. Someone had been fool enough to buy the Bentley place after all. Jackson pulled up his horse and studied the betraying plume of smoke that rose above the pine trees in the hollow. Bentley had been trying to unload that place for years to no avail. And no wonder. The place was a living testament to Half-Assed Bentley's reputation for never completing any job that could be left half done. Heck, his reputation had even stretched the good twenty miles to Jackson's home of Cattle Crossing, Wyoming. It took a lot to stand out in that town of eccentrics, but Bentley had managed it. So much so that anytime a body did less than necessary, they earned the nickname of Bentley.

The mare tossed her head in protest. She wanted her oats about as much as Jackson wanted his bed. This last bounty had been grueling. Bucktooth Bart had led him a merry chase through some of the roughest country, but in the end he'd caught him and hauled his ass back to Dover's sheriff for trial. In retrospect, the bounty didn't seem near fat enough for the amount of effort he'd expended. But it was always that way. Once he got on a trail, it didn't matter what the payoff was, only that he got to it. Jackson sighed and patted the money pouch in his shirt pocket. He really needed to work on that too-tight focus. He wasn't as young as he used to be. Crossing the line to twenty-eight last month had made him introspective in regard to a lot of things. Including the fact that the thrill of the chase wasn't clinging to his smile the way it used to. Instead of feeling victorious after this last bounty, right now he was just damn tired and looking forward to a couple days' rest and then getting back to working the McKinnleys' stock. Something he rarely got to do anymore. For reasons that had more to do with that inner restlessness than lack of time.

Jackson sighed. Truth was, he should be working his own stock on the Lazy M, but the life seemed to have left the place upon his mother's death. As if it, too, mourned the laughter that once had been the heart of their home. He didn't blame his father for leaving to chase a new love. Jackson had done his own running. It'd simply been easier to hunt bounties and work the McKinnley ranch than to reshape the Lazy M around the hole left by his parents' absence. Oh, he paid for someone to care for the house and did what was needed in basic upkeep when he was in town, but he didn't stay long. Part of him kept expecting Big Jake to come back and pick up where he'd left off, but lately Jackson was beginning to wonder how much longer he could let the Lazy M languish. There was an impatience gnawing in his gut to take it out of mourning, to separate his stock out of the McKinnleys' and . . . go home. Really home. If

Big Jake had found happiness in California, then Jackson had to make a decision: sell the Lazy M or follow the lead of his friends and neighbors, the McKinnleys, and return the Lazy M to prosperity.

Patting the mare's neck, he asked, "What do you think, Little Lady? Would you like to help me make the Lazy M shine again?"

The toss of her head could have meant anything. He chuckled. "As long as you get your ration of oats, you don't care, do you?"

She dismissed the comment with a dip of her head. Once the thought entered his head, though, it wouldn't leave.

The McKinnleys were earning quite the reputation for having not only well-trained horses but also a knack for turning wild into workable. No small feat with some of the horseflesh that came through. The army had them on retainer, which provided a good job for Jackson when he wasn't bounty hunting. And, truth be told, there was nothing Jackson liked better than working horses. But he could be doing it for himself. There was enough demand for everyone to make a good living. And before his mother's death, he'd planned on doing just that.

He pushed a narrow branch out of his face as he urged Lady on and corrected himself. Making love to a woman ranked right up there as a favorite pastime, but right now neither training horses nor loving women was of paramount importance, because he who brought the gossip of Bentley's fiasco having a new owner was going to be in high demand in Cattle Crossing. Heck, Jackson might just get a free pie at Millie's restaurant for that tidbit. A man didn't pass up the opportunity for free pie. Especially one of Millie's.

The mare tossed her head again when he turned her off the trail. He patted her shoulder. Dust flew up to dance in the late-summer sunbeams.

"I know, Little Lady, but there's no way we can pass up the opportunity to get a gander at the fool who swallowed Bentley's line of bull."

Laying the reins against Lady's neck and pressing in with his right knee, he directed her down into the hollow. The mare snorted, shook her head, and balked, keeping her nose pointed in the direction of home.

"Don't be temperamental, honey. You know there's an extra scoop of oats in it for you."

As if she understood the crooning reprimand, the little mare pranced, adding a jig to her get-along. It was the spirit in that jig that had caught his attention when she'd been dropped off at Clint McKinnley's as part of a broken-down remuda. There had been nothing particularly eye-catching about the little bay. She'd looked no better than any of the rest of the poorly cared for horses delivered to Clint as payment on a gambling debt owed by a local cowboy. That was, until the wrangler had tried to use his bigger gelding to shoulder Little Lady into the corral. Then that pretty little head had come up and her tail had swished one disdainful sweep before, neat as a pin, she'd tattooed the bigger horse's nose with her hooves, driving him back. And then with another toss, she'd pranced right into the corral like a princess. A tattered bit of royalty, for sure, but a princess nonetheless. Jackson had made up his mind to claim her then and there.

The only thing standing between him and his goal had been Clint's cantankerous nature. Clint was as tough a son of a bitch as his cousin Cougar. Jackson had nothing but respect for both. They were deadly fighters and honest men, and over the years they'd formed a deep friendship, but that friendship was spiced with some good-natured rivalry. Part of that rivalry was seeing who could finagle the best deal out of the other.

Clint hadn't wanted to sell the spunky mare. He'd planned on breeding her to his blood stallion, but Jackson wasn't one for giving up on what he wanted. That being the case, when Clint had rejected his initial request, in the form of "Not a prayer in hell," Jackson had waited Clint out, refusing payment for favors, until the debt had gotten high enough between them to weigh in Jackson's favor and Clint had gotten tired of hearing the inevitable "So, about that mare . . ."

Jackson's tactics might have been a bit underhanded, knowing Clint's bone-deep sense of honor, but Little Lady had been worth the twinge of his conscience. The mare had heart. The kind that wouldn't quit. The kind that could drag a man out of hell. Jackson patted her neck again, smiling. Now, if he could only find a woman as sweet as Lady with that same spit-in-the-devil's-eye jig in her step, he'd snatch her right up and to hell with his bachelor status. Fortunately, such a creature didn't exist. He smiled as he cut through the woods. Being a bachelor had some mighty fine side benefits, like the widow in Cheyenne who enjoyed the sense of danger she claimed clung to him.

The wind blew up from the home site, bringing the stench of smoke with it. Too much smoke. The kind that came from burning green wood. Which didn't surprise him. Anyone who looked at the Bentley place and saw promise had to be a tenderfoot. Oh, it was a pretty enough spot, but the ground was too rocky for farming, too wooded for grazing, and the house didn't have a right angle in it. While all of that was bad, it wasn't the worst of it. What made the Bentley place an unsellable disaster was that it sat square in a wash that took the runoff from the mountains. One big storm in the highlands and the unsuspecting new buyers could wake up one night to find a flood knocking at their door.

Jackson sighed, wondering just how dumb the new owners had to be. One look at the well should have clued them in to the trouble they were buying. It was too shallow to be good water, and making it deeper in the rocky soil was going to take more muscle than most wanted to put into the job. It was certainly more than Bentley had wanted to put into it. The so-called well was only twenty feet deep and was fed more by runoff than from a clean, underground supply. Jackson shook his head and pushed another branch out of his way, shaking it again when his long blond hair got in his line of vision. The best thing that could happen to the new owners was for the well to be dry, because otherwise, they were likely to take seriously sick from any water pulled from it.

He released the branch. It swished back in place behind him, rustling as it collided with another. Reaching into his vest pocket, he pulled out a leather tie. Lady twitched as the knotted reins dropped to her neck. With a quick gather he tied his hair back. He really should cut it. The comment that had started him growing it all those years ago had long since stopped stinging, but amusement could be as inspiring as resentment, he'd found. And he did get a chuckle from the surprise on the faces of the men he laid out who'd thought he was more pretty boy than threat.

The high-pitched sound of panicked children's voices rode piggyback on the wind and smoke. He grabbed up the reins. What the hell? The fool who'd bought the land had children? Shit. That was going to complicate his get-a-gander-and-run plan. Jackson had a lot of things riding double on his conscience, but leaving kids as sitting ducks for disaster wasn't one of them. With a curse, he urged Lady forward.

As soon as he cleared the trees, Jackson saw the source of the commotion. Two boys and a very young girl were milling around the rough stone wall above the well. As he watched, the little girl clambered up the side, the clunk of something metal in her hand against the hard rock carrying in the late-afternoon quiet as she leaned over the edge. A heartbeat later, the boys were in the same position, peering into the well. No doubt they'd lost a toy down there. Jackson shook his head. They ought to know better than to lean over like that. No telling how stable that wall was. No matter what the prized possession, it wasn't worth a broken neck. Even if they escaped broken bones, there were other dangers. Snakes loved a dry well, and for sure any well dug by Half-Assed Bentley wouldn't hold water in the recent drought.

Jackson nudged Lady into a lope. As he did, the boys grabbed the girl by the ankles and, to his utter horror, lowered her over the edge.

"Son of a bitch!" Were they crazy?

There was a cry.

"She's slipping!"

Jackson's heart leapt into his throat as the girl's skirt flew over her head, exposing her skinny legs. The boys made desperate grabs for the back of her faded blue dress. Jackson prayed the material held. Something that little shouldn't tumble that far. Lady charged across the clearing. Jackson leapt from the saddle as soon as he got close, scooping all three of the precariously perched children away from the edge of the well. The tinkle of broken glass followed his roll. He let the boys tumble to the ground, their squeals of surprise ringing in his ears. The little girl he clutched to his chest, protecting her from the brunt of the fall. He braced himself for the little girl's wail, but instead, unbelievably, she giggled.

Damn.

He stood, brushing off the seat of his pants with his free hand, keeping a tight hold of the girl with the other. "What the hell were you doing?" he barked.

All three children blinked at him, then the middle child, a boy of about seven or eight, glared at him through a shock of bright red hair. Pushing up onto his elbows, he stuck out his lip. "I'm going to get the soap!"

It took Jackson a minute to figure out what the kid meant. And when he did, it took all he had to bite back a smile. "You'll be wanting to get a bit bigger before you go threatening to wash my mouth out with soap."

The kid's belligerence didn't budge as he got to his feet. The little girl dangling in Jackson's grip whispered too loudly for a secret, "Mimi will do it."

The dark-haired boy stepped closer, tension and frustration humming off him. "Hush up, Melinda Sue," he ordered in a surprisingly deep voice.

"Mimi?" Jackson asked, setting Melinda Sue down. She immediately went to stand by her brothers.

Melinda Sue nodded, her long blond hair a tangle about her face. The smudge of dirt on her cheek only made her eyes seem bluer. He frowned and glanced at her brother. His eyes were green, and the older quiet one's, brown. They were a mismatched bunch, for sure.

"She can make anyone do anything," Melinda Sue declared righteously.

Interesting. "Where is Mimi?" For that matter, where were their parents?

All three children looked to the well.

Shit.

"Mimi is in the well?"

In unison the children nodded. The lower lip of the blond urchin trembled.

"What is she doing in the well?"

"She wanted to see where the water was."

The water was a good thirty feet farther down and likely somewhere else entirely, but Jackson didn't say that. He studied the area surrounding the well, his mind working on how best to get the child out.

"And she fell in?"

The older boy nodded. His skin and hair were darker than his much fairer siblings. Jackson guessed his age around ten. "What's your name, son?"

"Tony."

Jackson held out his hand. "Nice to meet you, Tony."

Tony ignored his proffered hand, countering with, "What's yours?"

"Jackson Montgomery."

Tony cocked his head to the side. "Is that name supposed to mean something to me?"

"Nope." Not if a body wasn't from around these parts. Jackson changed the subject back to the relevant. "So, Tony, did Mimi get hurt when she fell into the well?"

He shrugged.

The urchin piped up. "She didn't cry."

Hell, that could mean anything from she was dead to just terrified. "I guess she's a brave girl, then."

The redhead with the pugnacious attitude chimed in, "No one's braver than Mimi. She dares anything."

Which was probably why she'd landed in the well. Where the hell were the parents? Feigning nonchalance he didn't feel, Jackson wiped his hands together. "Well, good, then we shouldn't have any trouble getting her out."

Melinda Sue looked him over from head to toe. "You're going to get her out?"

Damned if he didn't detect skepticism in her look. "Yup."

"You're not very big."

It wasn't the first time he'd been told his five foot ten inches of height didn't measure up.

"Big enough."

She cocked her head to the side. "You've got pretty hair."

Was that supposed to make him feel better or worse?

"Thank you. What did you put down the well when I rode up?"

"A lantern so she could see."

"See what?"

"Where the snakes were."

Double shit.

"There are snakes down there?"

The little girl nodded and leaned against her older brother. For the life of him, Jackson couldn't see a family resemblance.

"Really ugly ones."

"Snakes aren't ugly," the middle boy retorted. "You're just scared of them."

"Are not."

"Are too."

"Shut up, Kevin," Tony said without inflection.

Jackson cut Kevin a glance as he headed to where Lady stood waiting patiently for instructions. "Anybody would be smart to be cautious about snakes around here, boy."

"Mimi hates snakes," Tony said in a quiet statement devoid of emotion. "We were giving her the lantern so they couldn't sneak up on her."

Jackson remembered the sound of broken glass just before he'd scooped up the kids. He glanced again at the well. No smoke billowed out. "You didn't light it?"

Melinda Sue shook her head. "I'm not allowed to touch sulfurs."

And a good thing that was, too. Dropping a lit lamp down the hole would have been like tossing raw fire. Everything down there would have burned when the kerosene spread. "Good to know you can follow some rules."

Tony cut him a glare. He ignored it. Pointing to the off-kilter porch steps, he told the pixie, "Go sit over there."

Her lip stuck out a bit, but she did move away from the well. One tiny step. He looked to the oldest boy as he took the rope off Little Lady's saddle. "I'd appreciate it if you took Lady over to the stream and got her a drink."

The boy didn't move, just stared at the mare. "We don't have a horse."

How the hell did anyone not have a horse out here?

"Well, I'm sure Lady will enjoy being the center of attention." Jackson held out the reins. He was trying to keep from looking in that well as long as possible. He hated snakes, too. The boy came forward. For all the excitement in his face, he was cautious taking the reins. Inexperience with horses or a bad experience? Jackson guessed it didn't matter. The boy would have to conquer that fear. A man was dead out here without his horse.

"Don't worry. She doesn't bite. As a matter of fact, if you scratch the spot above her nose, she'll be your friend for life."

"Will she be my friend, too?" Melinda Sue asked.

"Don't answer that unless you want her bothering your horse all the time," Tony warned.

Jackson looked at the little girl. She personified knee high to a grasshopper. And he most certainly didn't want her anywhere near the horse without him there. Little Lady was gentle, but any horse could spook. "Well, now, if you let me introduce you, I imagine she will like you just fine, but until you grow a bit, you'll only be able to pet her when I'm around."

She immediately nodded her head. "All right."

He didn't buy that ready agreement for a second. First chance she got, Melinda Sue would be over at Lady's side. Jackson reached in his pocket and pulled out a thick stick of peppermint. It was his last one, but sometimes a man had to make sacrifices, and this was one of them. "Why don't you take this and go sit on the porch."

Her eyes grew big as dollars. "That's candy from in the jars!"

Had she never had penny candy before? "Yup."

She all but snatched it from his hands. Before she could pop it in her mouth, Tony said, "You mind your manners, Melinda Sue, and say thank you."

His eyes lingered on the candy in her hand, but he didn't ask for himself. Jackson felt the heel. The kids' clothes were threadbare, and whoever was taking care of them had fallen—hook, line, and sinker—for Bentley's pitch, which didn't speak well for their business sense. The family had likely never had a penny to spare. Hell, had any of them ever had penny candy?

Melinda Sue frowned at her brother, took the candy between her fists, and grunted. Only half paying attention,

Jackson tied a hitch in the end of the rope. With a huff, Melinda Sue poked him in the arm and shoved the candy at him.

"You don't want it?"

She frowned at him. "Want you to break it."

He didn't have time for this.

"Just suck on one end."

She folded her arms across her chest. "Can't."

He had even less time to argue. He took the candy. "How many pieces?"

The older brother looked uncomfortable, the middle one hopeful, and the little girl determined.

"Two will do," the oldest said.

The middle kid's lip came out. "Three's fair."

Jackson approved of the elder child's sense of sacrifice and of the middle's sense of fair play. Whoever had raised these children was doing a heck of a job. "Three it is."

He broke the stick into three pieces, which was a good thing, because the study the little girl gave him was nothing compared to the study she gave those pieces. He had a feeling he'd have been in for a lecture if they hadn't come out roughly equal. "What about Mimi?"

The little girl shook her head. "She doesn't like candy."

There wasn't a body alive that didn't like candy.

Was she the oldest, then?

"Fine, then. Go sit on the steps there and eat that while I get Mimi out of the well."

As if he'd tugged her chain, the little girl's lip quivered. The stick of peppermint caught in the corner, smearing her cheek with red. "It's a long way down."

"But I'm a grown man with a long reach."

It was a measure of her age that she fell for that nonsense. She plopped down on the steps and smiled at him.

The oldest boy called from the stream, "You're not that big."

"You got a last name, kid?" Jackson asked, heading over to a suitably thick maple.

Instead of a surname he got a shake of the boy's head. Not an unusual response out here. Lots of people moved west to hide their past and a man respected that. But most of them had a few more years on them than this boy.

"Well, Tony, you're right." He looped one end of the rope around the trunk and tied it. "Size isn't everything, but you back it with a bit of smarts and a pile of muscle and I've found you can accomplish just about anything."

"Even getting Mimi out of the well?"

He checked the knot. A man could accomplish anything with a bit of applied intelligence and brawn. The trick was not to get fancy. "Yes," he said, heading for the too-quiet well, playing the rope out behind him, a sick feeling in his gut. "Even getting Mimi out of the well."

He just hoped to hell the child was still alive.

Leaning over the rough stone wall surrounding the hole, he looked down. The well was shallow enough that a little light reached the bottom. He could barely make out a shadowy form huddled to one side.

"Mimi?"

Silence greeted his call.

"You don't need to be afraid, Mimi."

Still no answer.

"Mimi doesn't like strangers," Kevin offered.

Well, she was damn well going to have to like him. At least for the length of time it took for him to get her out. He uncoiled the last of the rope and called down, "I know I'm a stranger, but I'm here with the rope and the muscle to haul you out."

"I'd appreciate it more if you had a gun and a knife."

The voice was shaky but unmistakably feminine. Mature. That was no child in the well. An inner sigh of relief went through him.

"They got you surrounded, huh?"

"Yes." The soft syllable shook with fear.

"Well, rest easy, I'm packing both."

"Thank God." Another harshly indrawn breath quickly followed the exclamations. Jackson didn't speculate on what inspired that gasp. His imagination already had enough of a leap. In his experience, just focusing on the immediate facts kept a man on course better than looking ahead. "You hurt?"

"Not really, although my foot seems to be quite attractive to the residents here."

Shit. "Can you elaborate on that 'not really'?"

"My arm. I don't know how badly."

With his luck, it was probably broken.

He could see the remnants of the wooden ladder leaning against the side of the well. The sides were riddled with rot. Only a greenhorn would have thought that was sturdy. More to keep her distracted than from a need to know, he asked, "The ladder break when you stepped on it?"

"Yes." Then, "Hurry."

It might be his imagination adding color to the moment, but that much fear added up to more than one snake down there. As if to prove his point, the rattles started, first one and then another, until they rose from the depths in nerve-jarring chorus. He slipped the noose he'd tied at the end of the rope over his head and shoulders. For once he was glad Bentley's well-digging skills were so half-assed. He had enough rope to reach the bottom.

"Don't move. I'm coming down."

Jackson looked to the kids as he swung a leg over the wall, putting as much threat as he could in the glare, because damn it, there was something about the way they watched that made him nervous. "No matter what, don't you try to come down here. Stay over there."

As one they nodded, but the jangle in his gut didn't settle. "I mean it."

"We hear you."

Tony's flat agreement didn't settle his nerves at all. "Good."

As he went over the side, his last impression was of all three children moving forward. So much for his threatening manner.

"I told you to stay put," he hollered up.

Only one of the children bothered to reply. In a voice as sweet as the candy he'd handed her, Melinda Sue called back. "You have very pretty hair."

Damn it, that settled it. As soon as he got home, he was visiting the barber. He lowered himself hand over hand into the darkness, skin crawling as the light faded and the dank smell of mold grew right along with the sibilant warning rattles. Maybe then he could strike terror into the hearts of three helpless kids.

Two

About six feet down, he wrapped the rope around his wrist and carefully braced his feet against the wooden wall. Dirt slid down into the depths behind the flimsy barrier. The rattles took up the staccato tempo that every living creature instinctively recognized as a warning.

A hushed "Be careful" snapped out of the darkness.

He injected a bit of calm amusement into his voice. "I'm always careful, honey."

The next sound could have been a snort. He wasn't sure, but the possibility amused him.

"If that were the case, you wouldn't be dangling over a snake pit."

"That might have more to do with my mental state than my cautious nature."

The next sound was definitely a snort, followed just as quickly by a gasp. "Snakes getting feisty?" he asked.

"Yes."

Definitely time to get the woman out of there. He continued lowering himself. "Well, hold tight, help is on the way."

"Hurry."

He was trying. A glance down revealed nothing. His shadow blocked whatever light there was. Which meant Mimi had better have Tony's stable temperament, because he was going to need her cooperation.

"Let me know when my feet are just above your head."

Her "How?" was shaky. He pretended he didn't notice, just kept his voice quiet and steady as the dank smell of the well surrounded him.

"Did the kids throw you any matches?"

"I don't know where they landed."

That might have been a blessing, considering the broken lamp. "Not a problem."

He went deeper, hoping against hope the lamp hadn't been kerosene fueled. "Very carefully put your good arm above your head."

"Why?"

"I'm getting to that." He stopped when he'd judged he should be just above her. The odor of old lard penetrated the musty stench of the well. He never thought he'd be grateful for Bentley's cheap ways, but lard wasn't as flammable as kerosene. That was a blessing. They could strike a match. He stuck his foot out in the direction of her voice.

"Is your hand up?"

"Yes."

"Good. Now, I want you to feel around, very carefully, above your head for my boot."

He heard the rustle of cloth as she shifted position. It was accompanied by a raucous renewal of rattles.

It took everything he had to keep his voice calm when he wanted to curse and retreat. Fucking snakes. "Don't move anything but your arm."

"I can't feel anything."

"Hang on."

He lowered himself a little more. "Try again."

This time, he felt a tug on his foot. The pull was to the right.

"Good. Just hold on, now, and don't let go until I tell you to."

"Not a problem."

He smiled at the feminine imitation of his own dry response. "Where am I in relation to you?"

"Out and to the left a bit."

Roughly where he'd estimated. "Well, that's just about perfect."

"For what?"

"For a game of catch."

"Insanity isn't what I prayed for when I prayed for rescue," Mimi muttered so low he bet he wasn't supposed to hear.

"Now, that's a shame, because I do some of my best work in my less stable moments."

"As if you'd be in any condition to judge."

She had a quick mind. He liked that. "You can judge for yourself in a minute."

Her grip on his shoe tightened. "You're joining me?"

"Nope."

"Oh."

The softly whispered exclamation pricked his conscience. He reached into his pocket. "I'm going to toss you some sulfurs."

"And upset the snakes?" she gasped.

"Well, the way we're going to do this, we're not going to disturb a rattle on their scaly posteriors."

"I don't understand."

"I'm going to toss these sulfurs in your lap."

"But the snakes . . ."

"Are going to sleep right through the whole thing."

"I don't see how."

Obviously. "That's because you think you have to do something."

"And don't I?"

"Nope, you just need to sit there pretty as a picture while I toss the sulfurs in your lap."

"You can see?"

"No."

"Then how do you know I'm pretty?"

"The same way I'm going to know where to toss these sulfurs. From your voice."

"My voice could be the only pretty thing about me."

"Well, now, finding out that truth is going to be my inspiration." He shook the tin. "You ready?"

Her hand on his boot jerked with her fear. He had to admire her ability to fake calm. There wasn't even a quaver in her voice when she ordered, "Don't miss."

"I never miss."

"Well, don't make this the first time."

His chuckle caught him by surprise, as did the spurt of interest her sass inspired. "Wouldn't dream of it. Now, just hold still and let me drop these. If I miss, don't grab for them."

"You said you never miss!"

He lobbed the sulfurs down. "I don't."

He had to give her credit. It had to be damn hard to sit

in the dark with snakes slithering around and not grab wildly for those sulfurs.

"Do you have them?"

"Yes."

"Told you I never miss."

"It's impolite to brag."

"So I've heard, but if I don't blow my own horn, who will?"

"If you get me out of here, I will. For the next fifty years, at least."

"Well, then, for sure I'm getting you out." The sulfurs rattled in their tin as she picked them up. Bracing his feet against the wall so he'd have a good view of the situation when the match flared, he ordered, "Now, I want you to carefully strike one and hold it up high. Away from my foot," he added quickly. The last thing he needed was for his pants to catch fire.

There was a scratch and a hiss, and the hole was flooded with a weak light. What it revealed wasn't pretty. Five snakes coiled nervously on the ground around a young woman. Obviously rattlers, and all big enough that one bite could probably kill off a man his size. For sure they could take out the fine-boned woman who stared up at him with big eyes and a stubborn set to her delicate jaw. He wondered what color her eyes were. The flickers of light from the match danced across her features, giving an illusion of impermanence. A chill went down his spine. Forget that. He wasn't letting her die.

"Well, hello, Miss . . . ?"

She blinked. "Banfield. Mimi Banfield."

"Nice to meet you, Miss Banfield."

"Call me Mimi."

He scanned the space. It was tight. So much so that there

was no way he could lower himself farther without creating chaos. Those were some mighty nervous serpents. He glanced at Mimi. "You can call me Jackson."

"Thank you."

It was an airy, wispy nod to propriety. She was as nervous as the serpents. One wrong twitch and snake and woman looked ready to launch. That could not happen.

He noted her left arm rested awkwardly against her side, obviously injured. He added that complication to the threat of the snakes, the distance back to the top, and the match's dying sputter. Getting her out wasn't going to be as easy as he'd hoped.

"You've got yourself in a bit of a tight spot here, Mimi," he started conversationally.

"I know."

That extra shimmer in her eyes might be tears.

"Lucky for you, I'm good in tight spots."

Her smile wavered along with the match flame. "Lucky me."

"Yes. Is your arm broken?"

"I don't think so."

"Good." But it was likely going to slow her down. He nodded to the near-burned-down match. "Blow that out and light another."

He didn't need to tell her to be careful. The warning rattle of the nearest snake did that for him. For a few seconds the well was plunged back in darkness, leaving Jackson with nothing to focus on but the memory of her face and the harsh reality of her breathing. For sure her voice wasn't the only attractive thing about her. She had a pretty face, oval in shape with a cute nose, a slight pout to her lips, and beautiful round, expressive eyes. He'd bet those eyes would be even prettier when not full of worry. The match flared. She was still holding herself together. Admiration cozied up to interest.

He kept his voice easy as he said, "I've got some bad news for you."

Her chin dropped a notch. There was a long silence. She looked at the nearest snake. "You can't get me out."

Hell, she thought he'd leave her? "Oh, I'll get you out, but I need to leave you for a second to do it."

She licked her lips, looked up to the daylight shining so far above, and then back at him, her gaze traveling down until it settled on the knife sheathed in his boot.

"Leave me the knife at least."

"I am coming back, Mimi."

The sulfur was burning dangerously close to her finger-tips. She didn't blow it out. It was as clear as day she didn't believe him.

"Please."

"First, blow that match out and light another."

She hesitated. He knew why. There weren't that many sulfurs in the tin. "Damn it, woman, I swear to God I'm coming back down and dragging your ass out of here."

A trio of gasps filtered down from above. Did no one follow orders?

"I told you kids to stay back!"

"But—" Kevin protested.

"Do as you're told!" Mimi snapped.

A snake hissed. Another gasp, then the faint thuds of retreating footsteps filtered down as the match blew out. Darkness returned in an oppressive blanket. Jackson untied the knife sheath from around his calf as the next match flared. Mimi's anxious gaze met his. He nodded toward her lap. "Just like we did with the matches. Let me drop the knife to you. It's going to be heavy. Whatever you do, don't jump."

He dropped the sheathed knife in the center of her skirt. She squeaked as it landed, but she didn't jump. The slither of a snake over loose rock sounded unnaturally loud in the tense silence.

"Don't use it unless you have to," he warned. "You're a bit outnumbered."

She clutched the knife in her hand and nodded.

"I'll be back in five minutes, then we'll get you out of here."

"Promise?"

"On my mother's grave. Now, stay calm and start counting."

Her "To what?" pulled him up short.

She wanted something concrete to hold on to. He glanced up and did some quick calculations. "To a thousand."

"Fine, but you'd better be back by the time I get to nine hundred and ninety-nine."

He smiled at the threat and started back up the rope. "Or what?"

"Be late and find out."

He grinned. A sweet little thing like her didn't have much to back up a threat, but he bet she'd be inventive in the trying. "You do tempt a man, honey."

Smiling at her groan, he started back up. He'd made it only halfway when another rattle, too close to be just an echo, sounded. He stopped. The dark made it impossible to tell where it originated, but it was a pretty safe bet there was a ledge nearby and there was a rattler coiled up on it, pissed at having its afternoon nap disturbed. Shit.

Mimi called from below. "Are you all right?"

As right as anyone expecting a snakebite could be. "Right as rain."

Taking a breath, he kept climbing, expecting to feel a lethal bite any second. It didn't come. With a lunge he cleared the last foot and dragged himself over the edge. He collapsed on the ground, fear and relief roiling in his stomach.

The kids jumped him before he could take a breath. "Where's Mimi?"

"Waiting on me."

"You didn't get her out," Tony stated flatly.

Jackson pushed himself to his feet. "My original plan needs adjusting."

"You said you'd get her out," Melinda Sue accused, her lower lip wobbling. Beside her Kevin stood, his expression stony with the effort not to cry.

"And I am." Going to the tree, Jackson untied the rope. He motioned to Tony. "Bring Lady over here."

Tony didn't hesitate. As he handed Jackson the reins, he said, "You will save her."

It wasn't phrased as a question and Jackson didn't take it as one. "Yes, and Lady is going to help me."

He tugged the rope over his shoulders. The other end he tied off at the saddle horn. He tested it twice, putting all his weight behind it. Mimi and he were both buzzard food if the knots or the chest strap gave. When he was satisfied, he patted Lady's neck and handed the reins to Tony.

"This is very important, Tony. When I yell go, I want you to walk her away from the well, slow and steady. No stopping for anything. Just keep a steady, even walk. Think you can do that?"

Tony nodded.

He motioned to Kevin. "Come here, son."

He liked the way the boy didn't hesitate. "Stand right there by the well. When I say go, I want you to make sure to tell Tony to pull. If I say stop, fast as lightning you're going to tell Tony to stop. All right?"

Both boys nodded solemnly.

The pixie piped up. "What about me?"

"You, I want to watch and make noise if anyone comes."

The little girl nodded. He didn't trust her for an instant.

"It's very important that you stand up on the porch and watch for help. Just in case we need it."

She nodded with the same determination as her brothers and sprinted for the porch. He should have thought of giving her a job sooner. Lady turned her head and snorted at him. He scratched her nose just above the bridle. "A good time to show me that sass would be when I tell you to pull." Rubbing her velvety nose, thinking of Mimi sitting amidst those snakes, he muttered, "This is too important for you to be contrary."

Lady tossed her head and did the prancing thing she did with her feet when she was feeling good. Tony jumped.

"Don't worry, kid. That just means she's set to go."

Tony didn't look convinced.

Jackson ignored his uncertainty. "Everybody ready?"

From their respective positions, they nodded. Jackson clapped Tony on the shoulder.

"Then let's get Mimi out."

The weight of the children's expectations followed him as he eased the loose rope back over the edge and then swung a leg over the wall. He hoped like hell the stone wall didn't crumble, the snakes didn't bite, and the rope didn't break. As if sensing his doubt, Kevin asked, "Are you sure this will work?"

He forced a smile as he grabbed the rope and lowered himself in. "Yep. Got it all planned out."

Jackson held the smile until he couldn't see Kevin's face anymore and then he let it go, his skin crawling anew. He hated snakes and hated small spaces, and here he was facing both, all because he'd gone and got curious.

"Not smart, Jackson," he muttered to himself, lowering himself hand over hand. "Not smart at all."

He made it past the point where he'd assumed the ledge was without a single warning rattle going off. Maybe it had been an echo after all.

"You still sitting pretty down there, Mimi?" he called softly.

Her "You came back" was a breathy expulsion of air.

"Told you I would."

"Yes, you did."

"I always keep my word."

"I'll remember that."

"Good." He lowered himself a few feet more. "Let me know when I'm just above your head."

A minute later, he felt a tap on his boot. "Stop."

"I want you to light another sulfur for me, honey." She did. Putting his weight in the loop he'd set in the rope, he ordered, "Now hold it up high."

The faint light revealed two big rattlers too close for comfort and the others a few feet away.

"Is that high enough?"

He drew his revolver from its holster. "That's just perfect."

He pulled back the hammer. "For the next couple seconds, I'd suggest not moving."

Her eyes grew huge. "What are you doing?"

He took aim at the snake on the other side of her. "I'm

going to take out a few of these creatures. It's going to be loud. Real loud."

"You could shoot me instead!"

That brought a chuckle. "I've missed a time or two in my life, but I don't feel like today's going to be one of those times."

"Oh, my heavens!"

"Pray all you want, but whatever you do, don't drop that sulfur and don't you jump."

He fired. She screamed. The rattler's head exploded. Mimi screamed again. A second snake struck. He blew its head off right before it bit. Its tail whipped in a death spasm, filling the well with an unholy rattle. The rope jerked, tossing him to the right.

"Hold, God damn it!" he hollered up the well.

A second later, through the ringing in his ears he heard Kevin echo, "Hold, God damn it!"

The rope lurched once more and steadied. Snakes slithered in a panic, bodies slipping over bodies as they bit and fought, looking for the enemy. As if death wasn't all around, Jackson smiled at Mimi. "See, honey? Easy as pie."

Mimi looked at him blankly and then motioned to her ears. "I can't hear you."

She didn't need to hear to know what it meant when he held out his hand. She placed hers in it with the quiet dignity he'd noticed before. Her hand was dainty and feminine, without a callus, but there were a few bumps he bet were blisters.

"Ready to go?" he mouthed, drawing her to her feet.

Watching the snakes nervously, she nodded.

"Put your arms—arm—around my neck."

She hesitated. The snakes were taking advantage of the

hesitation to fill the empty space around them. It was only a matter of seconds before they attacked.

"Hurry, honey."

"Will it hold both of us?"

"I don't see why not." If he discounted their combined weight, and the roughness of the wall rubbing against it, they were clear. And if he ignored the possibility of a snake sitting on a ledge halfway up ready to take a bite, they might make it out of here. Shaping the words clearly, he ordered, "Now, put your foot on mine and let's leave these snakes to their fun."

Her foot topped his and her good arm went around his neck. She smelled of honeysuckle, of all things. Not giving her a chance to change her mind, he locked his arm around her waist and called, "Go, Tony."

The order was repeated. The rope lurched. They swung. Snakes struck. He felt their fangs hit his thick boots before they fell harmlessly back. Jackson used his free leg to bounce them off the wall. The rope slid a little faster. Time limped as they were hauled up, leaving him nothing to do but hope. Hope the rope wasn't being too chewed up by the wall. Hope that damn snake halfway up had only been an echo. Just the thought of those fangs sinking into Mimi's soft flesh made him sick. She'd never survive. He wrapped his arms around her, tucking his shoulders in, shielding her as best he could. If God was paying attention, there wouldn't be a snake.

A minute later, he knew God wasn't paying attention. The biggest snake he'd ever seen was perched eye level a foot from his face on a ledge too small for its thick coils. A deeper shadow amidst the shadow. And it didn't look happy. Slowly, it pulled into a tight coil.

"Damn!"

"What is it?" Mimi asked, stretching up.

"Grab the rope above my head with your good arm, and for God's sake, don't let go."

She did as he said, and the move brought her face even with his. In spite of the danger, he couldn't help but notice she had very kissable lips. Keeping his eyes on the snake, he yelled, "Fast, Kevin. Tell Tony, fast."

"But you said slow."

The snake coiled tighter, head poised, tail shaking so fast the rattle sounded like a steady roar. And they were sitting ducks.

"Go!"

The rope lurched as they were yanked up level with the snake and then just stopped. Shit! Jackson saw the rattler's intent a second before it struck. Kicking off the wall, he spun them so his back whipped toward the snake.

In that second, that split second in which time slowed to a morbid crawl and his focus narrowed to the dirt-scuffed cheeks of the soft woman with the pouting red lips and pure sass attitude, Jackson realized he didn't want to go out with his boots on and a heroic devil-take-the-hindmost smile. No, he decided as Mimi's eyes widened and her full lips parted in a gasp as she looked over his shoulder. He didn't want that at all. Not when he could finagle a reality sweeter than his unfulfilled dreams. Mimi's eyes flashed to his. Blue. Her eyes were a deep summer sky blue.

Nice.

The snake struck. It was hard to sort the first impact from the second. Jackson didn't even try. Accepting his fate, he leaned in and stole his last kiss.

Three

It seemed like they flew over the wall, bound together by the strength of her savior's arm, by the desire to live, by the hope of a miracle. Mimi felt every thump as the stone hit Jackson's back just as she felt the jerk of his body when the snake struck with that horrible rattle. The expulsion of his breath hit her soul. Leather dragged over rock in a hiss as evil as the snake's. Sunlight flashed and disappeared as they spun. He was bit. They were doomed. And then . . .

They hit the ground with another jarring thump that drove the breath from her body. Jackson didn't move after that, and she was afraid to. So they lay there, not moving and not talking. Which was so odd because the man hadn't shut up since she'd met him. But he was silent now. Everything was. Morbidly and completely silent, as if even nature was afraid to take the next breath for fear of what it might reveal. Only the sun showed life, burning through the back of her blouse like heaven on the brink of hell. Because it was all going to go bad in a minute when the shock wore off. She knew that. Jackson was strong, but no one was that strong. And there was always a price to pay for heroics. All she had to do was wait for it. She hated waiting.

She couldn't even feel the ache in her arm for the ache in her soul. She was very afraid Jackson was dead. That was completely unacceptable. She'd sworn the day she'd escaped from Mac's den of inequity that she was only going to be responsible for good things happening, from there on out. She wiggled free of the rope, leaving it where it flopped around her legs.

Apparently, that promise had had a life span of a year, because here was Jackson—this man she didn't even know—who'd refused to let her give up. Who'd braved snakes and a muddy pit in the ground to save her. Who was about to die, and she hadn't even thanked him. But she had managed to sass him. To make light of his efforts. Because she hated looking weak. *Dang.*

"Mimi! Mimi!" Screams of her name shattered the silence. The children. How could she have forgotten the children? Bracing her good arm beneath her, she pushed up, jostling her injury. Pain from her elbow swarmed over her. Her vision blurred.

"Mimi?"

Blinking rapidly, she quickly mustered a smile. Taking a breath that felt as shaky as her smile, she soothed Kevin's concern. "I'm right here."

Kevin skidded to a halt. "We thought we'd lost you."

"I promised you I wouldn't leave you."

There was a moment when she felt the weight of his fear heavier than his gaze. Then he nodded. "I know."

But he didn't believe her. Yet.

"Is the pretty man all right?" Melinda Sue asked, plopping down beside her.

Tony put his hand on the child's shoulder, stopping her from throwing herself into Mimi's arms. His solemn gaze raked over her. "Are you all right?"

"I think so, except for my elbow, but I'm not sure about Mr. Jackson."

"His name is Montgomery, and he doesn't look all right," Kevin said, taking another step forward.

"He's bleeding from his head," Tony chimed in, as if she couldn't see that herself.

"I think he hit his head coming over the wall." She tugged at the rope at Jackson's waist. One-handed, she was helpless. "Tony, help me untie this knot."

He immediately did. Tony never hesitated to help. He was too responsible by far. She'd give anything to see him misbehave. Just once.

"It's not letting go."

No, it wasn't. "Just leave it." With her good shoulder she pushed her hair off her face. She had to think. She had responsibilities. "Kevin, you go back and hold that mare."

It was a measure of Kevin's upset that he behaved rather than argued. Sometimes she despaired of them seeing her as the mother she was supposed to be. Maybe it was because she didn't feel so much older than them. Maybe it was because of how they'd met. Or maybe it was because she just wasn't that motherly.

She sighed in relief as the horse was secured. If the man didn't live, they would need the horse. It was a horrible, practical thought in the middle of chaos, but she couldn't let it go. She couldn't let him go. She couldn't do anything but keep moving forward. Her course had been set all those

months past when she'd decided she was making the life
she wanted rather than the one she'd been given.

Habit had her reaching to push her hair out of her face.
Pain in her elbow made her regret it. Moaning again, she
leaned her head against her shoulder and rode out the reality. They were in such trouble. *Darn. Darn. Darn.*

"Are you hurted?"

There was no point in flat-out lying to the child. "A little."

The softest of kisses touched her shoulder. Melinda Sue
was a big believer in kissing things better. Mimi wished she
could muster a smile to go with her words. "Thank you,
Mellie."

She decided to leave the rope for now. Shifting her
weight, Mimi knelt beside Jackson, shifting again as her
skirts pulled at her legs. She was going to have to turn him
over to take off his jacket to see how badly he was bitten.
Her initial impression that he wasn't a huge man took a
tumble as she pushed on his shoulder. It was going to take
more strength than she had to turn him over. He was all
substance. She gave his shoulder a quick poke. "You would
have to be all muscle."

He didn't answer. Naturally.

"He's still bleeding."

"I can see that, Mellie."

Melinda Sue stuck her thumb in her mouth. "On his
head."

"I know." It wasn't the bleeding from the head wound
that was fretting her, though. It was the snakebite she
couldn't see. "We need to get him out of this coat. I think a
snake bit him."

Tony squatted down and started tugging at the corner of
the leather duster, only to discover what she already had.

"It's stuck." Standing, he gave the hem another yank. It didn't pop free. "He's too heavy."

"We don't have much time," Kevin offered from where he stood. "The book says you have to hurry before the poison spreads."

Kevin was a big fan of frivolous Western novels. He devoured them like others devoured candy. He was so in love with the tales of high adventure, he wasn't picky about whether he had the money to afford his habit or not. If he wanted a book, he just took it. Theft was a terrible habit for a child to have. She wondered if the benefit they were getting from it in this case justified the sin. She hoped so.

"How long does that take?"

He frowned, his green eyes narrowing. "A few pages."

"That's not an answer," Tony scoffed.

"Is too," Melinda Sue shot back. In Melinda Sue's eyes, Kevin could do no wrong. Mimi expected it was because the boy had a spirit of adventure that made him her perfect cohort in crime.

The man began to shiver in barely perceptible tremors.

"Did those stories say how many snakebites it took to kill a man?" Mimi asked, fighting the creeping dread.

"They say rattler's venom is so strong, one bite can take down the biggest of men."

He didn't have to report it with such relish. Gathering her courage, Mimi took charge. "Kevin, keep a hold of that mare."

No matter what happened, they were going to need her. She checked the knot in the dirty rope wrapped around the man. It was tight. Her insides felt just as tight. *And maybe*, she thought as she took the rope with an equally grimy hand, *just as dirty.* No matter how many miles she put between herself and the "mistake," the bad luck clung to her. She'd been such a fool.

"Is he dead?"

She looked up at Kevin. The horror and fascination in his voice ran rampant in his expression. She'd never understand men, no matter what age they were.

"No." Yanking the annoying tangle of her skirts out from under her knees, she settled back down, telling herself that was better. It wasn't.

Kevin sighed. "Oh."

"Sheesh, Kevin. Don't sound so disappointed," Tony muttered.

"Tony," Mimi cut in before a fight could start, "help me turn him over."

Kevin huffed. "I'm strong, I can—"

"You can hold tight to that horse." Mimi snapped. "We can't afford to lose it."

"But—"

As Tony knelt beside her again, she cut a glare at Kevin. "There will be no 'buts,' young man. You'll do as I say."

Tony grabbed the man's shoulder. Once again, she instinctively reached out with her left hand. Once again, she regretted it. Three sets of eyes snapped her way when she gasped. She quickly switched arms. It still wasn't easy. The man was all dead weight.

Tony wasn't faring any better. His hand slipped. Catching himself before he toppled, he muttered, "He's not making it easy."

She had a feeling Jackson wasn't in the habit of making anything easy. She kept tugging. "We just need to turn him on his side, get his arms free, and then we can see."

"What?"

"If he was bitten." She knew he had been, she'd felt it, but part of her just kept hoping she was wrong.

"Don't forget you've got to suck the venom out of the bite," Kevin said, still sounding entirely too excited about that event.

Dear God. Please don't need me to do that.

"Are you sure?" She looked at Kevin and then Tony.

The latter just shrugged and braced himself. "Kevin is the one with the knowing."

"I told you I read it in my book," Kevin grumbled.

She pushed harder. Unfortunately, so did Tony, which just had them working against each other. "Do you think everything you read is true?" She forced the question out between gritted teeth and switched to pulling.

"Why would they write it if it wasn't?"

Kevin had more sass than was healthy. Unfortunately, she didn't have the knowledge or confidence to successfully counter.

"I don't know."

"His head sure is bleeding a lot," Tony observed.

Kevin piped up. "Snakebite makes a man bleed more."

"Wonderful." She looked up at Tony. "On three, all right?"

"Turn him your way or my way?"

She was stronger. "Let's turn toward me. You push. I'll pull."

He nodded. Mimi took a breath and anchored her fingers in the man's coat. "One. Two. Three."

Even with the two of them trying to maneuver his body, he just kind of twisted and flopped the way a conscious person wouldn't. And they were severely handicapped by her damaged arm. Just when she was about to start cursing, Jackson rolled onto his back. He didn't even grunt.

"Is he deaded?" Melinda Sue called with the same morbid fascination as Kevin.

"No. And you stay right over there, young lady."

Mimi might as well have been talking to herself, because two seconds later the scuffed toes of Melinda Sue's shoes showed up in her peripheral vision.

"He's still pretty."

"Men aren't pretty," Kevin scoffed.

But this one was. In a purely masculine way. The sun, usually so cruel to others by ruthlessly highlighting imperfections, seemed to kiss the planes and edges of his profile, increasing even more the impression of an unholy angel. If one discounted the trickle of blood wandering over the cut on his cheekbone. Mimi couldn't stop herself. She touched it with her thumb. The blood smeared across the dirt on his skin. A hint of beard abraded her flesh. Just an hour ago he'd been riding his horse on the way to somewhere. Maybe home. Maybe to a woman. Probably anticipating a warm greeting and a hot meal. And now he was here, in her front yard, snakebitten, dirty, bleeding, relying on her skills to make him better. She tugged off his right sleeve and then pushed him over so Tony could tug off the other.

Tony looked up at her when he was done. "What do we do now?"

"We need to get him into the house out of this dirt."

So she could get a knife, suck out the venom. Her stomach heaved just at the thought.

Tony grabbed an arm. She went for the other. Melinda Sue hopped up. "He can sleep in my bed."

Melinda Sue's bed was a small makeshift mattress in the room she shared with Mimi. "That's very kind of you."

Melinda Sue frowned. "Mama said only good people are kind."

"Well, that leaves you out," Kevin snapped.

Melinda Sue's rosebud mouth immediately went into a pout, giving her the look of a cherub with her curls and round cheeks. She really was adorable. "That's not fair. I was only bad once."

"Yes, you were," Tony responded soothingly.

He didn't look at anybody when he said it, though, because it was quite a whopper. If the circumstances had been anything but what they were, Mimi would talk to him again about the need for honesty, even when you were trying to be kind. But Mimi didn't have that kind of time right now. The man was dying.

She looked up at Kevin, the closest thing to an authority they had on the realities of Western life. "Is there anything else in those books you read about what one can do for snakebites?"

Kevin shook his head with discouraging enthusiasm and trotted out his only piece of advice again. "You've got to suck the poison out."

"How exactly am I supposed to do that?"

"You cut an X over the bite and then suck." His cheeks sucked in as he demonstrated. Her stomach did another flip-flop as he motioned her on. "You're supposed to do it as soon as possible after the bite."

Of course she was. He could have said that earlier. It'd already been five, maybe ten minutes. Was it too late? "Kevin, go get a clean knife from the kitchen. Tony, help me roll him back over."

Kevin dashed to the house while Tony grabbed the man's arm. She grabbed the other. Her fingers slipped.

Now that she was hurrying, her one good hand was all thumbs.

It wasn't two seconds before Melinda Sue announced, "He's stuck."

So he was. Right there in the dirt in front of her. And he was depending on her to save him. Her resolve quavered at the thought of sucking blood and poison out of a wound she first had to inflict.

Get a hold of yourself, Mimi Banfield.

To Melinda Sue she said, "Hush." To Tony she said, "On three. Just like before."

The procedure went smoother than she'd anticipated, which just worried her because when anything went well there was always a price to pay. Kevin arrived back just as they had the man balanced on one shoulder. As he started to slip, Kevin dropped the knife in the dirt and added his muscle to the mix. The man rolled over and planted face-first in the dust. She was very glad he wasn't awake for this.

"You did it!" Melinda Sue cheered happily. Kevin let out a whoop. Tony just looked at her with those old eyes of his before turning the man's face to the side.

Mimi eyed the knife in the dirt and sighed before picking it up. They'd be lucky if he didn't get an infection. She started cutting the man's faded blue shirt away. "How soon do we need to do this 'sucking' thing, Kevin? Did the book mention specifics?"

Like when it would be too late?

Kevin frowned. "Just soon."

Then there wouldn't be time to rewash the knife. Wonderful. Just wonderful. Pushing the shirt aside, she exposed the wound. Two evenly spaced puncture marks were surrounded by rapidly swelling, purpling flesh. She blinked. Only two? She touched the angry flesh, recalling the jerks of his body against hers as the snake or snakes had struck, once, twice, wincing with each memory. She'd been so sure he'd been bitten more than once, but had only one snake gotten through his clothing? And had that one only achieved a glancing bite? Optimism skimmed her horror. If so, Jackson might have a chance. She sucked in a bracing breath. He hadn't failed her. She wouldn't fail him.

Pressing the knife edge against the skin, she prayed in a disjointed gasp of desperation. *Please. Don't let it be too late. Don't let me cut too deeply. Don't let him die.*

The dent got deeper, but the skin didn't split. Her stomach turned. She gagged. Beside her Tony followed suit.

"I can do it," Kevin offered.

There was no way Mimi was going to let an eight-year-old do what she, a grown woman, should be able to handle. Except she'd never done anything like this before. The closest she'd come was cutting up the meat from the butcher. However, the skill was applicable. She owed this man her life. She couldn't repay him with cowardice. She wouldn't.

"No. I'll do it."

Taking a deep breath and sucking her lower lip between her teeth, she pressed down harder, sliding the knife across the wound as she did. Blood welled. So did her gorge. She wasn't cut out for this. The debilitating thought crossed her mind. Just as quickly, she pushed it away. What she hadn't been cut out for was the life of penance her mother had set out for her. She didn't know what she was meant for, but she knew she wanted more than a life on her knees apologizing for her existence. Her mother had made a poor choice in the man she'd loved. He'd courted her, promised her the moon, seduced her, impregnated her, and then abandoned her to a life of ill repute. Mimi didn't understand how as an illegitimate child it was her responsibility to atone for her mother's sin. She was finished with even trying. Especially after she'd found herself trotting down the same path, repeating her mother's story in some warped continuance of an unfinished destiny, even taking it a step further by ending up the wife of a brothel owner.

She shook her head. But she'd broken free of the pattern her mother had set. And she'd taken Kevin, Tony, and Melinda Sue along with her. She'd told herself there was no need for them to pay for the accident of their births, either. Or maybe she'd just wanted to be a hero more than a martyr. Whatever the truth that drove her, they were where they were, doing what had to be done. She made the second cut across the wound, this time more competently. Sometimes, that was just how life was.

Besides, who knew and who even cared what force brought the children and her together? They were a family now. She was their mother. Whatever they needed to learn, they'd learn together. They might trip, they might fall, but they'd get up together. And she'd give them the best future she could. Without guilt. Without making them feel like they needed to apologize for their existence to anyone, least of all to society. She looked at the ugly wound she'd just made—at the welling blood. She had to suck poison out of that mess. Her stomach heaved harder. Not for the first time she thought she didn't have the fortitude for frontier living.

"I can do it." Tony offered this time.

She mentally sighed. Carefree might be harder to deliver for Tony. He seemed to naturally carry the responsibility of the world on his shoulders, but if she could temper that, he'd be a fine man. A happy man.

"I can do it, but you need to take care of Melinda Sue. She's too young to see this."

As if on cue, Melinda Sue gasped again. "He's dead-ing?"

The child was too perceptive by far.

Tony took Melinda Sue's hand. "Mimi will make it better."

"What can I do?" Kevin asked, not sounding the least bit skeptical that she would work miracles. While Mimi was nothing but skepticism. She'd thought her upbringing had been hard. It was only since coming out West that she'd realized how fortunate she'd actually been.

She got in a better position. "Just stay here and try to remember everything you've read about treating snake-bite."

He looked as worried as she felt. "All right."

There was nothing to do then but lower her mouth to the wound. As she did, a bitter copper taste filled her mouth. She imagined she could taste the poison threaded through the life. She spat it out as fast as she took it, shuddering internally, but sucking and spitting as quickly as she could until the flow of blood became a trickle and she could no longer taste the difference between life and death. Wiping her mouth on her sleeve, she sat back on her heels and looked up at Kevin. "Now what do I do?"

Kevin just shrugged and bit his lip. "I don't know. Wait?"

Lord, she hated waiting. "All right."

"I think we should check his head," Tony called from the porch.

As always, Tony was the voice of reason. The wound on the man's head *was* still bleeding, but she had no idea if the amount was too much or normal. She parted his hair gin-gerly, revealing the wound just above his temple. The gash was about two inches long. The edges looked clean. The bleeding was sluggish. He probably needed stitches, but she didn't even know if she had anything appropriate with which to stitch. She knew enough that regular thread wouldn't do it. Sitting back, cradling her elbow in her hand, she sucked her lower lip between her teeth. Her head began to pick up the throb in her elbow. She wasn't qualified to make any of these decisions, but she had to lead them somewhere. "I think that wound just needs to be dressed."

Tony and Kevin nodded. Not one to be left out, Melinda Sue joined in. "Are we going to leave him here?"

"No." She wasn't going to leave him in the dirt. She just wasn't sure what the alternative was. Until the mare nickered. Then she got an idea. They might not have the muscle to move him, but the horse did.

"If he up and dies, it'd be a lot easier if he started stinking out here," Kevin offered with infallible logic.

"Kevin," Tony growled.

Kevin had the grace to look ashamed, but he didn't back down. "Well, it would."

Tony bristled and balled up his fists. Standing and stepping free of the rope, Mimi interrupted before a fight could break out.

"This man risked his life to save me." Holding her arm, she caught Kevin's gaze. "In this family, we don't pay people back by leaving them to die."

Kevin looked away. She could see his mouth work, before he muttered, "I don't know enough to keep him alive."

Her heart broke. She sometimes forgot how young they were. "Oh, honey, I don't, either, and it's a shame, but we're not just going to hand him over to death."

"What are we going to do, then?" Tony asked.

That, she had an answer for. "We're going to fight."

"How?"

One step at a time. She looked at the rope still tied around him. "First, Kevin's going to fetch that horse, and then we'll see what we can do about using her to get him into the house."

Getting Jackson onto the porch wasn't nearly as difficult as treating his wounds. They'd managed to get the man up onto the porch by strapping him to the side of the saddle, where he'd hung like a sack of grain, feet dragging and head lolling. The mare had balked at the steps, but with a bit of tempting in the form of some honey-dipped greens, she'd lunged up onto the porch, dragging the man with her. If it hadn't been for Kevin's quickness it would have been all over, but he'd jumped up the steps and waved his arms. The mare had lunged to the side. Mimi barely managed to keep him from being crushed by waving the greens in the mare's face. Hard to believe the thought of food could calm all that panic, but one whiff of the honey and she'd stomped her hoof, snatched the greens out of Mimi's hand, and then proceeded to chew. Mimi hadn't wasted a second sawing through the ropes. She felt she took her first breath in ages when Jackson plopped down onto the worn wood. After that it was only a matter of rolling him onto a blanket and dragging him into the house, where he now rested, smack-dab in the middle of the living room. A living, breathing challenge of an expectation for her to meet, overcome. Or fail. She smoothed her tattered skirts. She was done with failing.

"What do we do now?" Tony asked, his words laced with the effort it'd taken to get the man into the house.

She didn't know. She wasn't a doctor, and Rivers Bend, the nearest town, didn't have one. She'd have to go all the way to Cattle Crossing to find a doctor, and that was a three-hour ride, assuming she didn't fall off Jackson's fancy horse and break her neck. By then, it could be too late. She sighed and looked at Jackson again. His shiny blond hair was matted to his head, the waves as flat as his color. His thick lashes were almost invisible against the dirt caking his tanned skin. His clothes smelled of mold dust and an underlying something that wasn't unpleasant. She might have called him pretty except for the square set of his jaw and the fact that, even unconscious, he radiated this energy that demanded attention. There was something just so . . . touchable about the man. She bet the ladies loved him.

"Too bad you're stuck with me, pretty man."

And stuck he was. She was nineteen, a woman grown, but she didn't have a clue as to how to treat the sick or wounded. Rolling up her right sleeve, she studied Jackson's long, lean form, the way his chest rose and fell with shallow breaths. He could be dying from the snakebite, the head wound, or something in the mess of dirt caking his body. Or he could just be sleeping. It all looked the same to her.

"What do we do?" Tony asked again.

She awkwardly rolled up her left sleeve, tugging at the edge when it caught on the button, biting her lip against the pain. "We boil some water." No matter what happened, his wounds needed to be cleaned.

"I can do that."

"I know." The button gave, and with the release went some of her nervousness. If she did nothing, he'd die. If she did something, he still might die, but she would have tried.

"What do I do?" Kevin asked as Tony dashed across the small room to the slightly rusted potbellied stove and grabbed the cold coffeepot off the top.

Replacing the pot with his hand, Tony announced, "Fire's out."

Darn it.

"Start a new one."

"We don't have any wood."

Why did bad days only have to get worse? Her "Of course not" was a resigned sigh.

"I'm sorry," Kevin whispered. "I meant to get the wood, but . . ."

He'd gotten distracted. Because he was a child. "I didn't mean for you to hear that. It was just my frustration talking."

His shoulders hunched. "But it was my job."

"Which you can do now."

Melinda Sue stomped her foot. "I want a job, too."

"You can help Kevin fetch wood for the fire."

Kevin pouted and jerked his chin toward the makeshift pallet. "I want to help with him."

He was clearly taken with the man. "I need hot water to clean his wounds. If we don't, infection will get him. Getting that wood could save his life."

Kevin straightened. "How much?"

Quick to mimic, Melinda Sue pulled straight right along with him. "How much?"

"As much as you can find without wandering too far away."

"Don't get too many big pieces of wood. And make sure it's not green," Tony warned. "We need it to catch fast."

"And hurry." The two children shot out of the room. Mimi retrieved her scissors.

They had laid him on the bed on the floor on his stomach so she could have access to the wound on his back. The sharp scissors snipped through the soft cotton as if it were butter. The material slid to the side with every snip, revealing tanned skin stretched tightly over smooth muscles and interposed with old puckered scars. A warrior's body. A warrior who'd sacrificed for her. She hesitated. She was so over her head.

Tony glanced at her face, frowned, and bit his lip before offering, "I can go look for a doctor."

"There isn't one. And that butcher they call a doctor in town would just kill him."

"Does it matter, if he's going to die anyway?"

"He's not going to die."

"Just because you say it doesn't make it so."

She started cutting again. "I said I was going to get you out of Mac's place, didn't I?"

"Yes."

The scissors snagged at the shoulder seam. This would be easier if she could use two hands. "You doubted me there."

"I did."

Re-angling the scissors, she muttered, "You were wrong."

"I don't think I'm wrong here."

He had to be wrong. Putting more pressure on the scissors, she sawed at the seam. It finally parted. Her arm ached. Her heart ached. When were things going to get easier? "He's going to live, Tony."

"How do you know?"

"Instinct."

Instinct had become her new war cry. Every time she set out to do something she didn't think she could do she latched on to that faint little hope that maybe it was possible, labeled it instinct, and plunged forward. As a philosophy, it'd worked up until now.

Pushing the shirt aside, a little of her belief faltered. The snakebite was looking ugly. All dark and swollen and putrid. As if maybe Jackson was already dead and the bite was just waiting for the rest of his body to catch up.

"That doesn't look good," Tony said.

No, it didn't. "I'm going to put hot cloths on it. See if I can draw more of the poison out." It was what her mother had done with infection. Maybe it would work for poison. Who knew?

As if he heard her doubt, Tony asked, "Is it going to work?"

"How the heck am I supposed to know that?"

Tony's head snapped up and his face went white. Every muscle in his body tensed. It wasn't hard to figure out why. He depended on her to keep him safe from Mac. They all did. If she grew angry and abandoned them, they would likely starve. Or end up back in another whorehouse, this time as prostitutes rather than children of prostitutes. She pushed her hair off her face with her good hand. She was their mother now. It was her job to give them confidence. She couldn't afford these moments of panic. "I'm sorry."

Tony didn't say anything for a moment, but then he, too, apologized. It came out gruff and awkward. Like her, he didn't know what to believe. The glue that held them together was their fear of Mac finding them. Mac stole from everyone with impunity. No one stole from him. That she had was something he would never let go.

She placed her hand over Tony's briefly. "We're going to have to make this work, Tony. And to do that we're going to have to keep this man Jackson alive."

"Why? Why is it so important he lives?"

She looked at the arsenal of weapons they'd removed from Jackson's horse and person stacked by the fireplace.

The collection dwarfed the too-small mantel above the huge fireplace. "Because I think he might just be the one who could get Mac out of our lives permanently."

Tony looked down at the man, then back at her. His concerns were clear in his expression. "Mac is a big man."

She had to agree that Jackson didn't look that tough in his current condition, splatted on the floor, bruised and bleeding, but at the brothel she'd seen many a smaller man win a fight despite a size disadvantage. "But this one's tough."

"Mac is mean."

Mimi touched her cheek, remembering his first lesson on meanness. "I know."

The memory of the explosion of pain when Mac had slapped her hadn't diminished much in the last two years. Neither had the sense of betrayal. She'd been a fool to see the power of a bully as the power of a man, but she wasn't one now. Now she was a woman with responsibilities. A leader. "I can handle this, Tony, so why don't you go check on Kevin and Mellie? You know how easily they get distracted."

"You might need me," he said, despite his clenched fists and that haunted look that he always got when the specter of Mac loomed too large. He was such a good boy who'd been hurt too much.

"I'll call if I do."

"But . . ."

"Without that wood," she pointed out inexorably, "Jackson will die."

Tony got to his feet and hesitated. "Do you really think he can help us?"

She smiled as she spread the lie. "I really do."

Mimi kept that smile until the door closed softly behind

Tony. Only then did she let out a slow, deliberate breath. Being the adult was hard. Being responsible was hard. Moving forward when all she wanted to do was curl into a ball and give up was harder still. She hadn't been raised with high expectations. Truth be told, she'd been raised to fail.

"But I'm not failing you," she told Jackson.

There was no sign he heard. Shifting around until she was comfortable, Mimi placed her hand on Jackson's shoulder above the wound. The heat emanating from his skin was as alarming as the strength beneath her palm was soothing. He was a man in his prime. Stubborn. Leaning forward, she brushed her lips against his ear. "You're going to live, Jackson Montgomery. No choice about it. You're going to live. Because if you don't, I'm coming down to hell to fetch you back."

Four

Jackson knew three things before he even opened his eyes. He hurt like a bear, he was as cold as hell, and he was being watched. He lay perfectly still, controlling his breathing while he gathered as many facts as he could. A twitch of his fingers revealed the coarse fabric of what was probably a blanket, and beneath that, something harder still. It wasn't much of a jump to assume he was lying on the floor, and from the sensation of leaning while lying flat, he had to be in Bentley's half-assed house, which left only the question of who was watching him.

Tensing his back sent pain ripping down his spine. That fast, he remembered everything that had happened: the dank scent of the well, the softness of a kiss, and the piercing horror of fangs sinking into his flesh. Just as fast he pushed that last memory away, controlling his breathing while his heart raced. Fuck, he hated snakes.

Lying there, he pulled up the second memory. It was

much sweeter to focus on a blue-eyed angel with siren tendencies. The woman was a fighter. In many ways she reminded him of his mother. Inherent grace and calm were traits his mother had had. In others, Mimi was uniquely herself. Sassy. Strong. Composed. She was a very intriguing mix. Pain throbbed outward from his spine. He bit back a moan and cracked his eye open. He needed a distraction. There wasn't a siren in sight, but there was a blond-haired cherub. Melinda Sue was sitting cross-legged by his right knee. The drape of her petticoat revealed a tear at the knee in her woven hose. From the darker dangling threads, it was clear it wasn't the first time they'd suffered a tear. Sitting there with a plate in her lap, she looked far too innocent to be involved in anything that would snag a stocking, but he knew better. The girl had more zest than was healthy. As did her sister, Mimi. Melinda Sue grabbed up her knife and fork and sawed at the hunk of potato on her plate. It was a sad state of affairs that his mouth started watering at the sight of that potato. The potato rolled off the plate. She caught it in her skirt with a curse no cherub should utter.

He cleared his throat. Melinda Sue dropped the potato back on the plate and gave him a big smile. "You're awake."

It took everything he had to hold back a groan as he nodded and slid his arm behind his head. "I am, and your sister is going to wash your mouth out with soap."

She frowned at him, clearly not happy with his statement. Stabbing the potato with her fork, she muttered, "Mimi says you're not supposed to move."

"Mimi's not lying on the hard floor." He winced at the harsh rasp of his voice.

"We couldn't get you to the bed." Waving the chunk of

potato, she went on as if she was making sense. "The horse didn't like the room and you're too heavy."

That was as clear as mud. "You brought my horse into the house?"

She nodded, pigtails bouncing. "There was no other way to get you up the porch. You're too heavy," she repeated again, as if his size was a crime.

"I see." The images that filled his mind might explain a few of his bruises. One thing was for sure: they certainly had been inventive. "Where's my horse now?"

"Kevin tied her to the tree out front. I picked her grass."

Lady was going to need more food than the grass a child could pick. "Thank you."

The potato waved again. He got the feeling she liked the emphasis it gave her. For sure, he couldn't take his eyes off it. As if on cue, his stomach rumbled.

"Mimi says you almost deaded."

He rubbed a tender spot on the back of his head. When had he hit it? Coming out of the well or when they'd hauled him in with the horse? "It sure feels like it."

"Does your head hurt?"

He squinted at her. "A little."

"Does your back hurt?"

He shifted and groaned. Like the very devil. "Only when I move."

She took a bite of the potato. "Mimi said you weren't supposed to move."

Apparently Mimi's word was next to God's. "So you said."

He watched her chew. His stomach gnawed at his backbone with the same rhythm. How long had he been out?

"Are you hungry?"

He nodded. She looked at the potato and then at him. "This is our last potato."

She took a slightly more aggressive bite, eating it like an apple on a stick. Apparently, she wasn't sharing.

"Aren't you supposed to use the knife, too?"

Melinda wrinkled her nose. "That's hard."

"You're not going to get better if you don't practice."

She sighed. "I'm not supposed to waste food."

Maybe he was still fuzzy headed, but he couldn't make sense of that. "How is practicing wasting?"

The look she gave him was pure pity. "It keeps rolling off the plate and you're not allowed to eat dirty food."

Another Mimi edict, he was sure.

Melinda Sue cocked her head to the side and eyed her potato. "Tony does, though. He says he's not starving for a bit of dirt."

He had a recollection of dark hair, thin arms, and too-old eyes. "Tony's your older brother?"

She nodded.

"He sounds like a sensible person."

She nodded again. The potato wobbled. He caught his breath.

"Mimi says he's the most sensible person she's ever met. Kevin says he's sensible, too, but I don't think he is."

"You don't?"

She scooted forward, revealing a hole in the sole of her ankle-high shoe as she slid up onto her knees. Leaning forward, she offered him a bite. "He gets mad too fast."

A better man wouldn't have taken a bite. He'd never strived to be better. And damn, a potato had never tasted so good. He savored the treat. He couldn't be that close to death if he was hungry. "Thank you. Kevin's the one with the hair always falling in his eyes?"

She nodded. "He gets in lots of troubles."

Jackson just bet he did. That one had attitude.

Melinda Sue frowned at the remnant of potato on the fork before glaring at him accusingly. "You took a big bite."

"I'm sorry, but you baked a good potato."

She cocked her head, debated, and then sighed the truth. "Mimi cooked it."

"Well, thank you both." Jackson gingerly tested his other arm to see if he could move it. He could, but he was stiff as hell. His back hurt as if he'd been dragged through a knothole backward and there was an evil leprechaun in his head banging on a drum. For this much misery, he hoped he was going to live.

"Where's Mimi now?"

The potato waved toward the window. "She and Tony went hunting."

A woman and a boy out in the woods, greenhorns the both of them, trying to do a man's work. Jackson just shook his head. "And Kevin?"

"Kevin's supposed to be digging a privy."

"But?"

She sighed dramatically and polished off the potato. "He's probably frogging. He likes to find frogs."

"Frogs are good eating."

Melinda Sue looked at him like he'd just sprouted a second head. Eyes rounded in horror, she gasped, "You can't eat frogs!"

"Why not?"

"'Cause what if they're a prince?"

"A prince?"

She nodded. "I kiss them."

Shit. He suppressed a shudder. "For heaven's sake, why?"

"Mimi said to."

He highly doubted that. He might not know Mimi well, but he damned well knew she wasn't the frog-kissing type. "I see."

Melinda Sue warmed to her story. "Just like the book, I'm going to find my prince and he's going to take me away."

It was an odd thing for so young a child to say. "To where?"

Again he got treated to that pitying look, as if he'd just come up short on brains. "To Princeland."

"And what will you do in Princeland?"

Her whole face lit up like a sunrise and her arms spread wide, embracing the idea. "I'm going to dance and chase butterflies and eat apple pie forever and ever."

Apple pie forever was a worthy goal. "What about your prince? Is he going to be there, too?"

"If he's good."

So her paradise had conditions. "What if he turns ornery?"

She shrugged. "Then I'll kiss him again and he'll go back to being a frog."

"And you'll stay in Princeland."

"Yup."

"You've got it all figured out."

She nodded. Her left pigtail was coming loose. It dipped, giving her a lopsided charm. "Mimi says a woman always needs a plan."

Mimi was apparently an enchanting siren with a plan who tempted with the sweetest of kisses. Yet another reason to get off the floor. He tested rolling to his side. It was—surprisingly—difficult.

Easing back, he concentrated on breathing steadily as his head threatened to explode from the inside out.

As he lay there he realized he had another problem. He had to pee. Badly. A quick check under the blanket and a sigh of relief. He was still wearing his pants. He didn't think he could manage the contortions it would have taken to get dressed before finding the privy, but he damn sure wasn't wetting himself. Gritting his teeth, he strove for an even tone. "Well, Melinda Sue, I've got to see what Kevin's doing out there with that privy."

Melinda Sue shook her head vehemently and scooped a bit of potato off the fork.

The last of the last potato disappeared with a lick of her fingers. "Mimi says you're not supposed to move."

"Tough. I'm moving."

He pushed up to his knees. The room spun in a crazy off-balance arc. Shit. That is, if he didn't pass out first. Taking slow breaths, he waited it out. As he knelt there, his shoulder screamed, his head ached, and every single bruise along his back and legs tightened. Closing his eyes, he groaned beneath his breath. This was not going to be easy.

"Are you deading?"

The child was obsessed with death. "No. Just getting ready to find the privy."

Melinda Sue scrambled to her feet. Slitting his eyes, he saw her dress settle against her legs. The small sway set the spinning off again.

"I'll show you where it is."

There was entirely too much enthusiasm in her voice and too much bounce in her step for his liking as she skipped to the door. She was out it before he could even get straight, which was just as well, as it saved him the embarrassment of having her see a grown man on the verge of crying. Fuck, he hurt.

A second later, Melinda Sue popped back through the door. Sunlight spilled in with her, assaulting his eyes. The flinch hurt as much as the light.

"Are you coming?"

"Yup. But a lot slower than you," he muttered under his breath.

With grim determination he started shuffling—shuffling!—toward the door. The afternoon breeze slid across his bare chest in a clammy caress. The morbid thought that he was halfway to his grave intruded on his determination as he looked around. His shirt and coat weren't anywhere in sight. The blanket was on the floor. Right there at his feet. No way in hell was he bending down for it. "Do me a favor, Melinda Sue? Pass me that blanket."

She frowned from the doorway. "It's right there."

"I know. Could you hand it to me?" After eyeing him a second, she went over and picked it up and handed it to him. He awkwardly tossed it over his shoulder. As his breath hissed out, she bit her lip and peered around his hip at his back. "The snake bitted you. I saw your boo-boo."

Wonderful. "Thank you. How's it look?"

"Awful bad." She made a circle with her finger. "Like this with black all around."

Great. No wonder it hurt like a son of a bitch. He awkwardly inched the blanket over his shoulder. Without a word, Melinda Sue grabbed the corner and tugged it around to the front. He got it from her before she could pull it too tight. "Thank you."

She nodded solemnly and headed back out the door. He followed her a bit slower, wondering for the first couple steps if he was going to pitch face-first to the floor. By the fourth step the room wasn't spinning so crazily. Catching his balance on the back of a chair, he paused as knives stabbed at his brain. Rubbing his bandaged forehead, he promptly winced. Then groaned. More damage. Probing revealed a ridge beneath the bandage. He must have hit his head twice.

"Are you coming?" Melinda asked impatiently.

"Yup."

Just as soon as he figured out up from down. As Jackson stood there struggling for equilibrium, he noticed how primitive the room looked. The planks on the floor were rough and unsanded. There were huge gaps between the boards, allowing anything to come up between. Sunshine filtered through everything except the windows, which were broken and covered with shutters that blocked out all light. It was all backward, right down to the wilted bunch of flowers in a cup on the table. As cheery notes went, it failed abysmally. The place was a dump. Not a place for a princess cherub and her family.

The porch step creaked. He whipped around, instinct drowning caution. The reach for his gun was as reflexive as the repression of the agony. Grabbing Melinda Sue's arm, he tugged her behind him as he swore under his breath. Where was his gun?

"Hey!"

A shadow loomed through the door.

"Quiet."

"Just where do you think you're going?"

He relaxed instantly. He knew that voice. It'd haunted his dreams, pitching him between anger and intrigue without a care for what he wanted. He'd thought it an illusion, but now he knew. Mimi had kept him alive after the snakebite. The woman was full of surprises. She stood in the doorway, backlit by the sun, leaving nothing of her curves to the imagination. The woman had a body to make a man drool, but it wasn't her body that he wanted to see. He wanted to put a face with that voice, because the angel he remembered from the well could not be the same siren who'd poked and prodded him through hell for the last— Shit. He didn't even know how long he'd been unconscious.

"Well?" Mimi prompted.

He blinked through the lingering haze. Oh, yes. She'd asked him where he was going. "I'm going to help Kevin with the privy."

Her skirts rustled as she rushed into the room. "Oh, no, you're not."

His head came up as she approached. He might be sick. He might be hurting. He might be a far pace from his normal self, but it'd be a cold day in hell before he took orders from anyone.

He straightened. "I'm sorry you feel that strongly about it."

His determination didn't falter but his strength took a tumble. The room spun. Clutching the back of a chair, he took a deep breath and closed his eyes. The next instant, he felt an arm slide around his waist and a rather delicate, slightly bony shoulder poke into his side.

"Bravado will only get you so far," Mimi muttered.

He looked down at the top of her head. The part was straight and centered. Her braid was just as neat. "You thinking of holding me up?"

"Yes."

"I appreciate the thought, but if I go down, you're going to get squashed like a bug." And he was pretty sure he was going down.

She didn't move. "I'm not that little and you're not that big."

He couldn't help a twitch of his lips through the nausea. He remembered that about her. The woman had a lot of sass.

"I think you think you're a bit bigger than you really are."

"I'm big enough. Got you in the house, didn't I?"

He was careful not to lean on her. "With the help of my horse."

"How did you—" She huffed as realization dawned. "Melinda Sue has no sense of discretion."

"She's what? Three?"

"She's four."

"Not many four-year-olds are big on discretion."

"So I'm learning."

Learning? He felt the twitch that went through her shoulder. Interesting.

"Every child's different."

He just bet. But not usually as different as her family. There was a story here, and when his brain stopped clawing at his head, he'd figure it out.

Her shoulder pressed into his side and her palm pressed against his back. "What you need is to go back to bed."

"What I need is to help Kevin."

"Kevin probably isn't even there."

"Then I'll inspect his work."

"But—" There was a pause. She looked up and he had a clear view of her face. It was intriguing as always, with its compelling mix of feminine softness, strong angles, and complete composure, but her eyes were what he wanted to see, and it was her eyes that the dim light hid from him. As he watched, she blinked. Comprehension dawned with a blush and a slight hitch in her breath. "There's a chamber pot in the other room."

He shook his head and took a step, stumbling forward, taking her with him. Her hand caught the doorjamb a split second before his hand slammed into the jamb above it. "I'm not using a damn chamber pot."

Melinda Sue gasped and immediately hopped up from the bench upon which she'd sat herself. "I'll get the soap."

"Never mind the soap," Mimi snapped at Melinda Sue, before tightening her grip on his waist. "Well, I'm not fighting to get you up those dratted steps again."

He resisted her tug. "Who asked you to?"

"Your stubbornness is going to force me to force Lady again. Trust me, that's not pretty."

"Lady doesn't belong in the house."

"Well, heroes don't belong in the dirt," she snapped back.

Hero. The term grated his nerves. He didn't want to be a hero to this woman. Heroes were untouchable. "I'm not a damn hero."

"What are you, then?"

"I'm a man." He paused and then added significantly, "A man with a need to visit the privy."

Because everything was so out of control and he couldn't afford misunderstanding, he added, "Badly."

He had to give it to her. Even though color flooded her cheeks, she stuck to her guns. With more pressure at his waist she tried to maneuver him to the pallet.

"I know you're a man, and I understand your problem, but I don't think you understand how sick you are. You've been in and out of awareness since yesterday."

"I'm fine now."

"I'm not a doctor. I'm not even much of a nurse, but I know that's a load of horse hockey."

Not to be outdone, Melinda Sue added her two cents. "Yeah. Horse hockey."

The laugh caught him by surprise. The pain not so much. But it was manageable now that he was used to it and could predict it better. He touched the wound on his head through the bandage. "Did you stitch me up?"

"Yes."

"Ever done that before?"

"No. Did I do it right?"

The wound felt tender to the touch, the stitches even. "Feels like it."

"Good."

He looked down in time to catch her studying him, fine white teeth sunk into those full lips. Desire that he had no business feeling hit him like a punch in the gut. Along with understanding. She put up a good front, but if he looked closely, there was a tension at the corners of her eyes and mouth. He wanted to ease that stress with a brush of his fingers. His lips. Damn. "You really don't know what the hell you're doing, do you?"

"Not a clue." She shrugged. "It's all just one big experiment, mostly."

Wonderful. "Well, while you're experimenting, experiment with the notion that you don't tell me what to do, all right?"

That got him a raised brow. "I prefer to think of it as making sensible suggestions."

He untangled her arm from around his waist. "Uh-huh. I bet."

Folding her arms across her chest, she asked, "Do you think by sheer force of will you're going to be able to get back up the steps?"

"Yup."

She threw up her hands. "Heaven save me from fools and idiots!"

Gritting his teeth, he tottered through the door. "Wasn't saving you from snakes enough?"

"I'm finding I'm a woman of many needs."

"Wonderful." Sunlight hitting his eyes just sent the banshee screaming in his head again, which increased his nausea, which increased his light-headedness, which increased his dizziness.

"Is that a problem?"

"I haven't decided yet." Two more steps and he made it to the edge of the porch. Grabbing the rail kept him from pitching face-first down the steps. He took three slow breaths, fighting nausea. This was definitely going to be a sheer-force-of-will trip. He stood there a second, gathering his determination.

From the doorway Mimi fussed. "I'll come with you."

He turned. "The hell you will."

"Me, too," Melinda Sue chirped.

"You get back inside the house, Mellie."

Melinda Sue pouted and stamped her foot. "I can help catched him."

Mimi pointed. "Inside."

Melinda Sue stomped her way into the house, her pout leading the way. When a chair rattled against the floor, signaling her flop into silent protest, Mimi put her hands on her hips. "Now you have no one to catch you if you fall."

Falling was more likely than not. He started down the steps. One. Two. And a very shaky three. "Then I'll get my ass back up."

Her skeptical "uh-huh" sounded remarkably like his.

He cocked a brow at her as she followed him down the steps. "You realize that I won't always be this weak?"

She blew a strand of hair off her cheek. "You realize I'll always be this sensible?"

In the late-afternoon light, he could appreciate the fine porcelain texture of her skin, the soft brown of her hair tinted with just a touch of blond, the sweep of her brows, that damn kissable mouth, and those remarkably innocent blue eyes. And beneath all, that strength of character. When she tipped that chin up and arched her brows, it reminded him of the first time he'd seen Little Lady. All fire and fine stepping. Despite the pain, despite the nausea, despite the ignominy of being too dizzy to pull her close and taste the sass on her lips, he smiled. "'Sensible' isn't the word I'd use to describe you."

"I'm not surprised. You don't seem to have a strong acquaintance with the definition."

It wasn't the first time he'd been told that. "I'm doing this. Unescorted," he added, in case she didn't think he meant it.

"Fine." Another puff of air and then she folded her arms across her chest. "But if you go splat halfway there, I'm not dragging you back in. It's been a long day and I'm tired and I still have to make dinner, so suit yourself."

She spun on her heel and stomped up the steps. He appreciated the view. The woman did have a fine ass. When she reached the top of the steps, he asked, "What are we having?"

"Make it back and find out."

Staying on his feet had never been so tough. He'd been knocked on the head enough to know how that felt, but this was more than that. And he wondered, as he eased his way across the yard, was this how snakebite took a man? Did the poison just seep through your body in a slow, gradual pass into nothingness?

The outhouse was up ahead. Like everything else on Half-Assed Bentley's place, it didn't have a right angle so the door didn't shut quite right, but that wasn't a negative considering how badly it smelled. When he was done, he looked around. He didn't see any fresh-dug hole and he didn't see Kevin. The boy was playing hooky. He shook his head. Mimi needed to get on him for that. Young boys weren't fond of work, but work at a young age taught a body responsibility that carried over to manhood.

Leaving the privy was like taking a step off the ledge. He wasn't sure if his foot was going to land or if it was going to just collapse beneath him. But he made the first step. Granted, his knees were a little quivery, but he made it. He took another step. The mare whickered. He patted her flank as he passed, then reconsidered and just stood there a minute, leaning against her. Her scent was familiar. Stabilizing. They'd been through a lot together.

"Thanks for getting me out of the dirt, beautiful."

She tossed her head and snorted. He smiled and patted her again. "Yeah. I won't ask it of you again.

He noted a little pile of seeds on the ground, probably leftovers from the grass that Melinda Sue had brought the horse. Little Lady deserved more than that. He remembered Melinda Sue's comment about the potato being their last. Hell, they all deserved more than that, but even if it wasn't too late to plant crops, this wasn't the place to settle down. Its beauty was deceptive. The first big rains in the mountains would prove that. As much as Mimi and her family wanted to put down roots, they couldn't stay here. This land would kill them. He couldn't allow that.

He scratched behind the mare's ears. "I don't think they're going to want to hear the truth about this place, Lady."

The mare butted him with her head and whuffled his pocket, looking for her favorite treat. Patting her cheek, he sighed. "Sorry, honey. I'm just full of bad news today."

Five

⌐∞⌐

Jackson was about five steps away from collapsing, but Little Lady needed tending. While she'd been fed and watered, no one had bothered to unsaddle her. He ran his hand over her sun-warmed withers, leaning heavily against her, breathing in the familiar scents of horse and leather. It was almost like coming home. As if she felt the same, Little Lady leaned right back before reaching around and nipping his hip the way she always did when he dawdled over her care or food.

He pushed her head away. "Not now."

She tossed her head and snorted. Jackson sighed and looked to the house. Two temperamental women he didn't need.

"Don't be difficult now, honey. I know things haven't been what you're used to, but I'm here now."

Her response was a swish of her tail. He'd expected Mimi to at least have come out and checked on him, to make sure he hadn't fallen, but she hadn't. She'd just respected his wishes, giving him exactly what he'd demanded. Damn it.

Lady fussed again. Jackson couldn't blame her. The saddle had to be irritating. Jackson shook his head and grabbed the back of the saddle to steady himself as he worked forward. In truth, he didn't think Mimi owed him a thing. He would have dove down that well for anyone. That was just how he was, how his parents had raised him. But he rather enjoyed her fussing.

He looped the stirrup onto the saddle horn. "Mimi called my bluff, didn't she, Lady?"

Little Lady stomped her foot.

Jackson couldn't remember the last time a woman had called his bluff. Hell, he couldn't remember the last time a woman had walked away from him. Maybe he was too used to getting his way; maybe he was too spoiled. Maybe his mother was right. Maybe he was his own worst enemy when it came to settling down. Jackson shook his head. He didn't know. He glanced at the house again. And up until lately, he hadn't cared.

There was some movement behind the window. A shutter cracking open? A tingle of something positive blended with the pain. She was watching him. He braced himself against the mare's body, trying not to lean too obviously on her for support. "Make me look good, Lady. Our reputation is resting on the next three minutes."

The mare held steady, but even with her support, getting the leverage to yank the cinch strap free had him moaning out loud. This time when Lady nudged his thigh, it was with sympathy.

He rubbed her ears. "Have I told you today you're my best girl?"

She tossed her head. The bridle jangled right along with his nerves. He took another steadying breath. The six feet to Lady's head was another step-counting, breath-measuring exercise in endurance. Holding tight to the bridle's cheek piece, he stilled before testing the situation. The knot someone had tied in the reins blurred in and out of focus. He was sweating by the time he got it undone. Working his way back, he eased the stirrup down and started counting. On five he hefted the saddle up. Normally the saddle came off in a fluid motion. This time it awkwardly slid off Lady's back and tumbled to the ground. The only thing that saved his pride was at the last second, he was able to swing it sideways so it landed on the wood-chopping stump.

At least it was off the ground. That would have to do for now. He hunched there for a second as the pain washed over him. He couldn't control his breath, the pain, or his balance. The world was spinning again. If Mimi hadn't been watching, he'd have sat his ass down, but she was. He could feel it.

Forcing himself straight, he was glad distance disguised the raggedness of his breathing. He stood there long enough—Lady gave him a look. He waved away her scorn and muttered, "As if you haven't had a stallion prance a time or two to get your attention."

With all the nonchalance he could manage, which he hoped was a whole lot more than it felt like, he stroked his hand down the mare's back, ending with a pat on her flank. She started wandering off, nibbling on the grass beyond the tree. He sighed and shook his head and tied the rope around her neck before making a loop in the other end. One thing about Little Lady, she could be headstrong to the point she didn't take a ground tie too seriously. Like most women, she liked to push her limits.

Making sure she had plenty of length, he dropped the loop over the stump, effectively anchoring her to the area. There should be plenty of grass for her to eat. The water in the dented bucket by the stump seemed fresh. In the morning he'd have to come up with something else, but for right now that would have to do. As Lady settled into her dinner, he took another breath and released it slowly. Turning back, he caught another movement behind the window. Mimi had closed the shutter.

He smiled and dragged the blanket over his shoulders. And groaned. He hurt, from head to toe. His back especially, and then there was this lethargy he couldn't get rid of. It just kept creeping through his system, building momentum like a slow, oozing mudslide, consuming every bit of his resolve in its path.

The house was a long way away. His legs wanted to quit right where he stood. He honestly didn't know if he could haul his hurting ass across the yard, let alone up those uneven porch stairs, but God damn it, he hated losing a challenge. Even one he'd set up for himself.

A quick assessment cut to the bottom line. Either he lay down in the dirt here or he lay down in the house. It was completely up to him. Well, maybe not completely. His parents always said prayer as a last resort was an affront to the Lord, but the Reverend Brad said God was always open for a bit of conversation. The Rev might be the most unconventional preacher he'd met, but he was one of the most compassionate. A former gunfighter and bandit, he'd found his place in Cattle Crossing, preaching the good book, common sense, and personal responsibility and taking to wife the pretty but equally eccentric Evie Washington. If the good Lord could bring together two of the most outspoken, unconventional people in a blissfully happy conventional union, Jackson was willing to go with the Rev's definition. Glancing heavenward, he muttered, "I could use a bit of help here, Lord."

He wasn't sure anyone was listening as he took that first step, coming that close to digging a ditch in the yard with his face. Standing still, he swore, feeling everything at stake. A man's pride was a fragile thing. He'd been told that before, but he'd never been as keenly aware of it as now, when he took those fifteen shaky steps to the porch. Clammy sweat dripped down his face. The hinges on the offset door squeaked as it opened. Straightening the blanket around his shoulders, he bared his teeth in an easy smile that was wasted on the two boys looking back at him.

"Would you like some help?" Tony asked.

Mimi was a smart woman to send out the boys as a buffer.

"Mimi says supper is almost ready," Kevin added as if he needed more impetus to accept.

"I think I can make it, but I wouldn't turn away a helping hand."

Both boys came down to hover beside him. Tony was the one who put forth their concern. "Not fast enough. If you're not seated when supper hits the table, you do without."

"I saved her life."

Kevin shook his head. "That won't save our meal."

Our. Shit. He couldn't be responsible for two boys missing their supper.

He lifted up his arms. "Then we'd better get moving."

Each boy slipped an arm around his waist, Tony more hesitant than Kevin. Neither boy was particularly strong or tall, but there was something about having them on either side, willing to support him, that made a difference. Together, they made it to the top.

When they got in the house, Mimi was just setting a plate of eggs on the table. She glanced up. A smile hovered around the corners of her mouth as she took in his predicament. To her credit she didn't gloat. "Supper's ready."

Two sets of hands in the middle of his back propelled him forward. He caught himself on the edge of the table.

Melinda Sue piped up as he wavered. "Better sit. Supper is getting cold."

It was clearly a phrase she heard a lot.

"And you know how I feel about that," Mimi added.

The boys bolted for their chairs. Jackson made much more sedate progress to the empty barrel drawn up alongside Melinda Sue. As he took his seat, Mimi stood. When he went to stand also, she held up her hand. Her expression said *Stay down before you fall down*, but all she said was, "I'll fetch you some water to wash up with."

There wasn't anything to say but thank you. She was back with a water-filled bowl, a sliver of soap so small it wouldn't survive this use, and a towel. She had to have had it waiting. As he finished and handed her the towel, Jackson thought he saw a grudging respect in her eyes. It soothed the irritation inside him.

Placing the bowl back by the basin, she took her seat and scooped some egg onto his plate. "I hope you like partridge eggs."

"I love eggs." And he could have probably eaten everything on the plate and then the same amount again, but, looking around the table, he held up his hand before she could put on a second spoonful.

"Are you sure?"

He glanced pointedly at the children with their too-thin cheeks before saying, "My stomach's not that happy right now."

Her smile softened her expression. "Thank you."

"What are you thanking him for?" Kevin asked, shoveling food into his mouth.

"Nothing."

"Do you mind me asking how you came upon this place for sale?" Jackson asked.

Mimi's face lit up in what was probably the first heartfelt smile he'd seen her offer. "It was really fortunate. We were—"

"We were heading west!" Melinda Sue cut in.

Mimi smiled at the child indulgently. "Yes. We were."

"And you ended up here?"

"We just came over the ridge and saw the house." Mimi shrugged. "It looked so pretty with the sun sparkling on the stream."

He bet it did. "Did Bentley tell you that water gets pretty high come the rains?"

"We're a good way back from the stream."

They didn't know a thing about flash floods, that was clear. Before Jackson could break the news that they'd have to be a ways out of the hollow to be safe, Tony interrupted.

"We got here just in time!"

Jackson cocked an eyebrow at them. "Really?"

Mimi nodded. "Mr. Bentley had just finished meeting with another buyer. We were lucky to catch him here. He hasn't lived here steady since his wife died."

Shit. That was just like Bentley to add a heartbreak to a sale. Bentley had never been married. "But he took a deal from you instead?"

"Mimi had to bargain real hard," Kevin bragged.

Jackson just bet she did. Bentley always loved to run a good game. He wasn't particularly smooth, but if he could find a greenhorn eager to be convinced, he did well enough.

Off the beaten path as this place was, not many greenhorns wandered through. He must have been hopping in his boots when Mimi drove up. "So you bought it?"

Mimi nodded. "It took everything I had, but I had just enough."

"I bet."

"Nuh-uh," Melinda Sue cut in. "Mimi's still got the—"

Melinda Sue's "ow" coincided with a rattle of the table. A quick glance showed Melinda Sue rubbing her leg, Kevin glaring at her, and Tony looking entirely too innocent. Mimi's expression was carefully blank.

"I hope you kept a bit back for emergencies."

"I'm not a fool." The stern look she gave Melinda Sue, on top of the boys' reactions, set the hairs on the back of his neck to tingling. Something more was going on here.

He took a bite of egg and chewed slowly, making it last. The children, who had plowed through theirs, watched intently.

"So what are your plans?" he asked.

It was just morbid curiosity. No matter what Mimi's plans were, as long as they revolved around this place, they were at a dead end.

He stabbed another piece of egg. All eyes watched him bring the food to his mouth. Tony licked his lips. Kevin rubbed his fingers over his fork. Taking in their empty plates, Jackson put down his fork with a mental sigh.

"Is something wrong?" Mimi asked.

He shook his head and put a hand on his stomach. "I'm just not feeling that well."

It wasn't a lie. If his stomach could commit murder, he'd be a dead man. "You kids pass me your plates. No sense letting good food go to waste."

Mimi cut him another wary glance. "You need to eat."

"I'm sure my stomach will be talking to me tomorrow."

"And tonight?"

Holding the blanket put with one hand, he divided his portion among the children. It worked out to be a silver-dollar-size portion per kid. Damn. "Tonight, I'll get some sleep." And tomorrow he'd go hunting and put some meat on the table. The second portions disappeared just as fast as the first. This time when he looked at Mimi, she wouldn't meet his gaze. He could understand that. Deserved or not, shame was a heavy burden.

"So what are your plans for the place?" he asked again.

"I'm hoping to maybe get some greens in the ground. Maybe try some potatoes."

He shook his head. "It's a bit late in the season for potatoes, not to mention dry."

She finished the last bite of her eggs and placed her fork delicately across the top of her plate. He noted the unconscious reach for the nonexistent napkin. Wherever she came from, she'd been taught manners.

"I'm hoping it'll rain."

He sighed internally. Rain would only open up a whole other set of problems. "Do you even have starter spuds?"

She chewed her lip. It was surprisingly sexy watching her teeth massage the pink flesh.

"I'm working on it," she answered after a pause.

He caught the blanket before it could slip. "I see."

From the way four sets of eyes locked on him, he hadn't hidden his skepticism well. All different colors, different shapes, but united in the hope brimming within. Shit. He was too weary to dash hopes tonight. Tomorrow was early enough to tell them this place was a death trap and they were going to have to leave. He opted for a neutral response. It wasn't a lie. "It's not going to hurt to get some starter spuds."

Mimi eyed him warily. "That's what I thought."

Glancing out the window, he changed the subject. "I can see why you bought the place, though. It's a pretty piece of land."

Mimi relaxed and smiled, revealing those dimples. Damn, a man could get addicted to that smile.

"I couldn't believe we were lucky enough to get it." She looked around the dilapidated building with all its crooked angles and awkward gaps. "It's a dream come true."

Melinda Sue scooted over to lean against his shoulder and stuck her thumb in her mouth. "We're safe here."

He took a sip of water. It had the flat taste of being boiled. The pervasive weariness weighed on his shoulders like a ton of bricks.

He tried another stab at reason. "I'm not sure you know what you're getting into."

Mimi stood and collected the plates. "I'm sure we'll be fine. We just need to get enough foodstuffs together so that we don't starve this winter."

Least she had her wits about her to know that. "Yeah. That would be good."

She gathered up his plate and glanced at Melinda Sue. "Someone is ready for bed."

Jackson handed Mimi the little girl's plate. "Yup."

"Am not." Melinda Sue yawned.

Mimi rolled her eyes and then motioned with her chin. "I'll need to clean that wound and check those stitches after I get Melinda Sue settled."

"I'm fine."

She rolled her eyes again. "Has anyone ever told you you're annoyingly predictable in your stubbornness?"

He suppressed his grin. "I'll be fine."

The metal plates rattled as she placed them in the shallow basin. "Well, since you're my first patient, you'll understand my excess of caution and disbelief."

That got his attention. "I've been wondering, since you've never doctored anyone before, were you scared?"

Wiping her hands on her apron, she shrugged. "A little, but I've got to confess, it was exciting in a rather grim but challenging way."

And she'd enjoyed it. The lift in her voice and the light in her eyes left no doubt of that. Damn. Though why he was surprised, he didn't know. A woman who'd head across the country with three kids in tow was no shrinking violet. "Well, I'm glad I could keep you entertained."

A grin teased her mouth. "You did liven up my evening."

The humor caught him by surprise. She was always surprising him. The unpredictability kept him on his toes. It lent a little adventure to every conversation. "I've got nothing to say to that but thank you for the care."

Smoothing her apron. "It's about time you said that."

"I was a bit distracted before now." He took another sip of water to ease the rasp in his voice. "Where'd you come from?"

Kevin opened his mouth. Mimi shut it with a look.

Interesting. That was the second time one of them had been going to tell him something only to be silenced. There were some secrets here.

This time Mimi's smile wasn't genuine. "Back East."

Which could be anywhere.

Propping Melinda Sue back in her own seat, Jackson gritted his teeth, made sure the blanket was still secure, and pushed back from the table. He was stiff, sore, hungry, and tired. But he wasn't helpless. It took concentration to stand. Effort to not moan as tight muscles stretched. All the while he strove to appear normal. Mimi and the children watched every move. Just as he was congratulating himself on pulling it off, Mimi said, "Let me help you back to bed."

Damn. So much for his acting skills. "I can make it."

She folded her arms across her chest. "Are we back to that again?"

"I wasn't aware we'd ever left it."

"You're such a baby."

The hell he was. "No," he snapped, "I'm not. It would be a mistake to think so."

If he hadn't been watching her so carefully, he might have missed that subtle intake of breath, but he was watching. He had been since the moment he'd met her. Damn. Which only left one question. Was that fear or excitement? Common sense said fear. A perverse part of him wanted it to be excitement.

Her fingers tightened on her upper arms, creating pale half-moon indents. Just as quickly she relaxed. He made a note of the betraying gesture. Letting out a long breath and waving her hand, Mimi explained, "You were hurt saving me. Can't you just be a good patient and allow me to express my gratitude?"

He could lie and say yes, but the truth was he couldn't. He didn't want her pity or gratitude. He wanted her seeing him not as a patient but as a man. This woman he wanted to impress. This woman he wanted to hold, to cherish, to impress— Shit. What the hell was wrong with him? They were strangers. "No."

A small hand slipped into his. He'd been so caught up in Mimi, he hadn't even realized Melinda Sue had gotten out of her chair. Damn it. The woman was causing him to lose his edge.

"You have to do as you're told," she whispered, as if everyone couldn't overhear.

"Not always," he whispered back.

Her pigtails swayed as she nodded her head. "Uh-huh."

This clearly wasn't an argument he was going to win.

Mimi knelt in front of Melinda Sue and smoothed her blond hair off her face. "We're not fighting, baby. We're just deciding best how to get Mr. Montgomery to bed."

The boys hung to the side, uncertain how to handle this but ready to jump in if necessary. He appreciated their support.

Melinda Sue slipped her arm around his thigh, drawing his attention. "What are you doing, sprout?" he asked, catching the blanket before it could be pulled off.

She giggled at the name and attempted to lift him. "I'm helping."

"Why, thank you." Ruffling her hair, he held out his hand. "Why don't you lead the way?"

"All right."

It was hard to cooperate with her help and not topple. Sitting had stiffened him right up.

"Take him to my room, Melinda Sue," Mimi directed, hovering just off to the right. The look she gave him spoke loud and clear. *You're not fooling me.*

And put Mimi out of her own bed? Hardly. Not only would his father have him out behind the woodshed for such unchivalrous behavior, they were back to that whole problem of worrying about his slipping manhood. Jackson let Melinda Sue "help" as far as his pallet. There he put on the brakes. "I'm more comfortable on the floor."

Mimi was shaking her head before he finished. "I won't hear of it."

The hell she wouldn't. "Melinda Sue, plug your sister's ears. Things are about to get colorful."

The little girl chuckled and skipped over to Mimi.

Mimi pushed Melinda Sue's hands away. "Stop it, Mellie."

"But he said to—"

Frowning at him, she snapped, "Mr. Montgomery says a lot of things I don't listen to. No need for plugging my ears."

Jackson didn't even bother to hide his exasperation. "You'd be happier if you'd listen more."

"I think you're confusing listening with cooperating. I've heard you, but I simply don't agree. In our house, guests don't sleep on the floor."

Jackson studied her. The set of her jaws and shoulders said she wasn't budging. Well, neither was he. "I don't see where you're going to have a choice. Unless you're thinking of bringing my horse back in here?"

There was a pause. Those fingertips sank back into her upper arm. Her nails were ragged on the edges. She was too fine a woman to be handling a homestead alone.

"No, but—"

"Then, it's settled, but speaking of my horse . . ." He motioned the boys over. "I need you two to go take Little Lady—"

"Your horse?" Tony asked as if he couldn't believe his luck.

"Yeah, my horse. I put her out in the grass earlier, so her belly should be full. Bring her back into the barn. Give her fresh water."

"I'll do the water!" Kevin said. Jackson held up his hand before Kevin could dart off. "Rinse out the bucket first. Make sure there's no scum sitting in it. We don't want her taking sick. If there's any oats, give her some."

"There aren't any," Tony said, back to his usual solemnness, as if he didn't want Jackson to note his apparent love of horses.

Jackson nodded. "I figured." He added oats to his mental shopping list. "Then just get her settled down, give her some good pats. She might be nervous. One of you bring in my saddle."

Tony raised his hand. "I'll do it."

Jackson nodded again. "Thank you. Put it over an empty stall or something. Don't just throw it on the ground. Saddles get ruined that way. The bags you can bring to me here."

They stared at him.

"Did you understand all that?"

Tony hitched up his pants. "I did."

"So did I," Kevin jumped in, not to be undone.

"All right, then. Just take your time and do it right. The first rule over everything is a man takes care of his horse. Got that?"

They both nodded.

"Good." He really did need to lie down. "I'll be here waiting for a report when you're done."

The boys swaggered out, full of importance over their responsibility. He shook his head. Had he ever been that young? As the door closed behind them, he was keenly aware of Mimi's eyes on him. It couldn't be helped, though. He had to make good on his boast. The only problem was the remnant of his pallet was a long way down. A long way.

"Still want to be stubborn?" Mimi asked.

"It's called being gallant. And yes." Assuming he could get his stiff muscles to bend enough to kneel. Letting the blanket slide down his arm, he held out. "But if you want to help, you could make up the pallet. I'm pretty much at the 'lie down or fall down' end of my endurance."

She looked everywhere but at his naked chest as she took the blanket. For a moment, he felt a twinge of conscience. He didn't normally just bare his chest in front of women. Truth was, he hadn't been thinking. He just needed to lie down. She took his blanket. Unfortunately, she went in the wrong direction. Before he could question it, she disappeared into the bedroom. A minute later, she came back with a couple more well-worn blankets and a battered-looking pillow. Shoving the bundle into his arms, she ordered, "Hold these."

She was being very careful not to look at his naked chest. Because she was embarrassed or because she was intrigued? He didn't have an answer. Blushing, she grabbed the top blanket and spread it on the floor.

"Just out of curiosity, what happened to my shirt?"

The blush deepened.

"I had to cut it off. It was filthy so I washed it. I'll mend it when it dries."

Did she think he was criticizing? "Thank you."

"No problem."

Taking the pillow next, she tossed it to one end of the pallet. The next blanket she snapped out over the other with unnecessary force. She was annoyed. When she knelt to smooth it out and fold back the top, he admired the view. She was a very attractive woman.

"There. Your bed is made."

He held out his hand. "Thank you."

After a brief hesitation, she placed her palm in his. Her fingers curled gently around his. They felt small and dainty. Right. He shook his head at the fanciful thought. He must be running a fever. With a tug, he pulled her to her feet. Pain seared his back. Her face blurred out of focus. His skin grew clammy. Mimi came up against his chest with an awkward stumble.

Her gasp caressed his chest. Something warm and wet

trickled down his back. In the hazed reality of the moment, he understood he'd broken open his wound. "I suspect I'll be as right as rain once I get some sleep."

He desperately wanted to sleep. Or pass out. He didn't care which any longer, as long as he was flat on the floor when it happened.

"Right as rain might be stretching it," she muttered disgustedly, steadying him as he swayed.

"I'm not a lying man."

"Just a delusional one."

He probably wasn't supposed to hear that. His knees buckled. He sank, knowing he was giving her a full-on view of his weakness.

Some days it just didn't pay to get out of bed.

Six

He woke up with his stomach gnawing through to his backbone and a hard-on trying to drill a hole in the floor. The latter was Mimi's fault for sure. The woman seemed to have an insidious ability to sneak past his barriers. He might not have minded her intrusion so much if he could remember the details of a single one of those dreams, but all he had was a sense of passion and a vivid awareness of missing out on something good. Sighing, he rolled onto his back. He waited for the spinning to start. It didn't. He waited for the pain to rip through him. Instead, it throbbed with a bearable ache, centered in his back and his head rather than all-encompassing. Releasing his dread on a long sigh, he let himself focus on other things. Like how hard the floor was against his aching back.

It was early, so as quietly as he could, he got to his feet. Gritting his teeth against the pull on his wound and the pounding in his head, he took a step. A splinter lodged into his foot. Swearing under his breath, he searched for his things. His boots, bedroll, and saddlebags were piled over by the mantel. His weapons were nowhere in sight. Muscles protesting every inch of the way, he tiptoed to the mantel, shaking his head at the absurdity. He hadn't tiptoed around a woman's house since he was eighteen and too much booze and too much temptation had landed him in the Widow Myer's bed.

He would have liked a change of clothes, but the ones in the bag were as dirty as what he was wearing. He was going to have to do laundry. Picking up the bags, he frowned. They were too light by far. A quick search revealed only the clothes were gone. Which could only mean one thing: Mimi had taken them. No doubt to clean them.

He normally didn't like people touching his things, but he kind of liked the thought of Mimi's hands on his clothes, cleaning them, preparing them for him. Pulling out his high-top moccasins, he smiled and checked the second bag. His gold was there. So were his bullets. Whatever they were, these folks weren't thieves. He closed the saddlebags and slung them over his shoulder. Picking up his moccasins, he eased his way to the front door in search of his guns. He didn't feel naked without his shirt, but without his knives and guns? That was a whole other matter.

The front door squeaked slightly as he opened it. Making a shushing motion to the noisy hinge, he slipped out and closed it gently behind him. Bracing against the jamb for support, he pulled on his moccasins, laced them up, and straightened.

Standing on the porch, he took a deep breath and basked in the sunlight creeping in on the morning mist. Morning had always been his favorite time of day. He loved the quiet, the scent of damp earth, and the soft calls of newly awakened birds. There was so much promise in the morning. His mother had always said if they could harness that promise, life would be easier for everyone. He smiled as a bee buzzed around the clover. He'd spent a lot of mornings as a young boy trying to harness morning's power. He'd really wanted to make the world an easier place back then. Now, twenty-two years later, he'd gone in the opposite direction, carving a living out of making life harder for some of the state's worst criminals. It was odd how life took dreams and turned them around sometimes.

He took another deep breath and pushed away from the jamb. Nothing like a snakebite to make a man appreciate his life. After stopping at the privy—it really did need to be redug—he headed toward the barn. He figured Mimi had to have stashed his weapons somewhere out of Melinda Sue's reach. That child was pure mischief and curiosity. The barn was the most likely location.

The barn door creaked louder than the house door when he opened it. It stuck unexpectedly halfway, almost knocking out his teeth. That needed adjusting. Little Lady whickered as soon as he entered.

"I bet you're hungry, aren't you, honey?"

Standing up to the edge of the stall, she tossed her head. Her silky brown mane fell over her eyes as she tucked her chin and waffled at him. Smiling, he walked over and rubbed her forehead. It was their morning ritual except he didn't have a cube of sugar. Lady did like her sugar, but he'd run out a couple days back.

"When we get to town, I'll be getting you some sweets."

She bumped him with her head. He scratched her ears. "I promise."

This time she stomped her feet and nibbled at his coat. Lady didn't like to take no for an answer.

"Sorry. How about we go for a ride later?"

It might be his imagination, but Lady seemed to perk up.

The barn door creaked a short warning. He turned and saw a familiar silhouette. The fresh scent of morning swept over the stale scent of the closed-up barn.

"What are you doing?" Mimi asked.

"I was checking on Little Lady."

She handed him his shirt, laundered and mended, along with his hat. "I suppose you'll be wanting your guns soon?"

There was a lot of belligerence in that statement. He rubbed the shoulder near where the snake had struck, flexing at the stiffness before awkwardly putting on his shirt. "I'd really like them now."

She shrugged. A sunbeam expanding out from a knothole in the wall embraced her as she came deeper into the barn. The light highlighted the curve of her cheek and the creaminess of her skin, and he realized just how young she was. Her hair fell in a neat braid down her back. A long plaid shawl was draped around her shoulders, covering up most of the white nightgown beneath. The shawl's fringe swayed around her thighs. The nightgown brushed the dirty floor. On her feet she wore what had once been sturdy shoes but were now battered shadows of their former selves. She walked over to a long, wide ledge set high above the left of the door. When she bent to grab a wooden crate, the gown pulled tightly across her buttocks as if to disprove his notion of her as a child. She did have a fine figure.

Unaware of his attention, she dragged the crate over to beneath the shelf. A mouse scurried out as the box brushed the wall. Mimi screamed and jumped back.

Just as quickly, Jackson jumped forward, catching her as she stumbled on the uneven floor. She screamed again, whirling on him, fist raised.

Cupping her shoulders in his hands, he put an end to the attack. "Whoa, there!"

She blinked and that fear disappeared behind a mask of calm. He could still feel the fine shivery remnants of it under her skin. She slowly lowered her fist. The shawl had slipped from her shoulder, giving him a glimpse of her pulse pounding in the hollow of her throat and the delicate line of her collarbone. He eased his grip. She licked her lips.

"I'm sorry. It's just that—"

"You hate mice," he finished for her.

She nodded. Through the thin cotton of her gown, he could feel the curve of her shoulder and the heat of her skin. He pulled the shawl gently up. Taking her hand he put it over the edges. She clutched them reflexively as she cast an anxious glance around.

"Don't worry, that mouse is long gone."

She didn't look convinced.

"You were going for my guns?"

She nodded.

"Where are they?"

She pointed to the ledge. He let her go. The shelf that was too high for her was just a stretch for him.

"Be careful," she warned as he kicked the box aside and reached for the guns. "There might be spiders."

From the way she said that, it seemed spiders ranked more fearsome than mice. He smiled and felt along the long shelf. His hand landed on his rifle. "Thank you."

It was just as easy to locate his gun belt and knives. He pulled them down one at a time, dutifully inspecting them for spiders as he did. Fastening the gun belt around his waist first, he buckled it quickly, before tucking one knife into its sheath at the base of his spine. It settled there with the familiarity of an old friend. It took a bit more work to put the other into his bootstrap. The rifle he leaned up against the wall. Through it all, she just stood there watching him, arms folded across her chest, holding the shawl tightly. He couldn't tell if she was still sweating over the mouse or fretting because his weapons gave her second thoughts about who'd she'd invited into her home. Pulling his pant leg down over his boot, Jackson said, "I appreciate you putting them out of curious hands."

Her fingers clenched on the shawl. "I hope they're all right."

"Triggers can be sensitive, but the weapons themselves aren't that delicate."

Motioning to the knife in his boot, she asked, "Don't you worry that will slip and cut your leg?"

"The sheath protects me."

"What if it slips out?"

"There's a strap to hold it in."

"Oh."

"Only reason to leave a weapon loose is if you're expecting trouble."

Her head cocked to the side. "Were you expecting trouble when you rode in here?"

Jackson shrugged. "Bentley hasn't lived here for a long time. There was no knowing who took up residence."

She relaxed and shook her head. A hint of a smile colored her voice. "So you're saying you were curious."

He smiled. "Pretty much." Wincing with the motion, he adjusted the knife at his back. "What about you? Do you have a gun?"

"Nope."

No? He pulled his shirt down slowly. "Surely it occurred to you that trouble might come calling this far out?"

"Yes. Definitely."

"And yet you don't have a gun."

After a slight pause, she admitted, "I thought it prudent to learn to shoot first."

He blinked as he took the revolver out of the holster. "What the hell did you intend to do if trouble showed up in the meantime?"

She pulled the shawl tighter and shrugged. "Offer them supper and pray for the best."

"That's not much of a plan."

"No. It isn't."

Her agreement took the bluster out of his lecture. He holstered the revolver and took out the second.

"I want to thank you again before you leave."

The hitch in her breath pulled his gaze up. Her eyes were very blue in the morning sun. They shimmered with suppressed tears like wildflowers after a summer shower. She was upset. "Who said I was leaving?"

With a wave of her hand she indicated his stuff. "You're gathering up your belongings."

He checked over the gun. "That doesn't mean I'm leaving."

"What else could it mean?"

"Well, my sunny little siren, it means I'm hungry. So, I imagine, are you. That being the case, I figured I'd get my butt moving and get us some meat." Cocking an eyebrow at her, he mentioned, "Guns are good for other things besides self-defense."

Mimi swallowed convulsively, the way a person did when they'd been a long time without food and their mouth flooded with saliva. Her fingers grasped reflexively at the shawl. His respect for her went up when she protested, "You can't. You're hurt."

"For sure I'm dragging, but I've been worse." Not much, but it was a certainty if he didn't get in some food, none of them were going to survive. The image of Melinda Sue with that potato bothered him. Mimi cut him a glance that spoke eloquently of her doubt.

"If it weren't for the children, I'd debate the state of your health with you."

The revolver was fine. He holstered it. "If it weren't for you and the children, I'd let you."

Her "thank you" wavered with the weight of reality. She couldn't afford to demand he recuperate before he ventured forth. Once again, he wondered what had brought the family here. They clearly weren't cut out for this life.

If he were the prying type he would have asked, but there was time enough for explanations. "You're welcome."

It was just a few short steps to the saddlebags. Her gaze weighed on him with each one. Any second he expected her to blurt out an explanation or to ask for his help, but he opened the bags without interruption. Taking out the coin pouch, he pulled out some dollars, jingling them in his palm as he debated before adding a couple more. The family couldn't stay here, but they needed to eat between now and then. Mimi was still studying him as he stood. She didn't say a word as he took her hand and put the coins in it, but she tensed.

"While I'm hunting, I want you to take Little Lady and go into town—"

"I can't ride."

He almost rolled his eyes. Of course she couldn't. Another piece added to the puzzle that was this family. He folded her fingers over the coins. "Lead her, then, but go into town and get supplies."

"I can't take your money."

"Can you make corn bread?"

"Yes."

"Then take my money."

She tossed the coins in her hand until they jangled discordantly. Her stubbornness was beginning to irritate him. "Why?"

"My mouth is set for some venison stew with a large helping of corn bread and some fresh milk if you can find it."

"For that I don't need a horse."

She was being deliberately obtuse. "I said I wanted you to get supplies. Supplies are flour, potatoes, vegetables, cornmeal, sugar, and whatever spices it takes to make all of it taste delicious. And for the love of all that's holy, I want coffee. *Real* coffee."

She did that swallow thing again. He pressed his advantage. "Come on, now, wouldn't you like a hot, steaming cup of coffee in the morning? Maybe flavored with some cream and a spoon or two of sugar?"

The flutter of her lashes was another break in her composure. So was the lick of her lips. She wanted that coffee badly, so it was a shock when she took his hand like he had hers, turned it over, and gave him his money back. Pulling her shawl tighter around herself, she stepped back.

"We don't need your charity."

Damn, the woman was stubborn. He had no wish to humiliate her, but the truth needed facing, and he was too sore and too tired to fight over nonsense. He pointed toward the house. "I've seen those children's faces and they're more than a little lean."

She flinched but held her ground. "We'll be fine."

The hell they would. "I'm not saying you haven't done

the best that you could, but things are at the point where what matters are Kevin, Tony, and Melinda Sue."

Jackson didn't mention herself because he knew she'd balk, but she was just as high on his list. Her chin came up.

"We'll be fine. I've just got to find some work."

What the hell kind of work did she think she'd find out here? A young, beautiful woman with three kids and, apparently, no real skills? "You have to eat between now and then."

Her jaw set. "We're not a charity case."

Son of a bitch. Running his fingers through his hair, he strove for patience. "Look, I'm not trying to stomp all over your pride, but when times are hard, you take what's offered and pay those helping you back later."

For a long minute, she looked at him, her fingers white-knuckled on that shawl, pride warring with necessity. Was he getting through at all?

He thrust out his hand. "Damn it, woman. Take the damn money."

With just as abrupt a "thank you," she did. The coins landed in her palm with soft clinks. Slowly, she closed her fingers around them. "I'll pay you back."

"I expect you will."

Her chin came up again. He braced himself for another battle. "This doesn't mean I owe you anything . . . more."

He raised an eyebrow. "A lady usually waits until she's asked."

She didn't even blink before shooting back, "I'm circumventing the asking for the surety of understanding."

"Then drop your shield. We've got an understanding."

Instead of leaving, like he expected, she stood there looking him over from head to toe, as if he were a particularly odd sort of bug.

"I don't understand why you're doing this."

He picked up the rifle. "I told you, I'm hungry."

She shook her head and turned on her heel. "You are a very strange man, Mr. Montgomery."

Her scent drifted around him in a tantalizing reminder of the dreams he couldn't recall but in which he wanted to wallow. After grabbing the lariat he followed at a much slower pace. He was stiff and sore and weaker than he wanted to admit. The first two would ease with movement. The latter, only with food.

"I thought we'd settled on you calling me Jackson?" he called after her. That might just have been a smile on her lips as she stopped to let him catch up. He thought it was sweet she extended the courtesy, but pain or not, if he'd wanted to catch up with her, he would have caught up with her.

"I'm being churlish, aren't I?"

He hadn't expected her to admit it. "A touch, but a lot of people are testy in the morning."

Another wave of her hand. "It's not that. It's just . . ."

A breeze blew a strand of hair into her face. "You've discovered people can do a whole lot of bad under the guise of being nice," he finished for her.

She licked her lips. "Yes."

Like Bentley, though she didn't know enough yet to be braced for that blow. She flinched when he raised his hand. "Easy . . . ," he said. "I . . ." He lightly grazed the backs of his fingers down her soft cheek, drawing the hair away from her lips. It fell to the side in a soft wave. "I don't hit, Mimi."

Though someone in her past clearly had.

Her chin tipped higher. "I didn't imply that you did. I was just . . ."

Startled. Scared. Jackson placed his finger over her lips, silencing the explanation.

"I just wanted that understood between us." He tugged the shawl up over her shoulder and pinched the sides together. He could feel her pulse against the back of his finger. It was faster than normal. So was her breathing. "You're safe with me, Mimi."

Emotions chased across her face. Surprise. Suspicion. And lastly, maybe, acceptance? It was enough for now. He changed the subject.

"Do me a favor when you're in town. Buy more soap and whatever else you need for bathing."

Her eyes widened and she slapped his hand aside. "Are you inferring I stink?"

"Hardly. You smell as sweet as a summer day, but those boys are getting a bit gamey."

Her lips twitched in a smile. "They act like bathing is a cardinal sin. Every Saturday night I stop taking excuses and the battles begin. They've been eyeing that disappearing soap like a blessing."

"Cardinal sin" was a Catholic term. Another tidbit for the puzzle box. He released the shawl slowly. Truth be told, he didn't want to let her go. He liked her scent. Her smile. The sound of her voice. "Most boys do, but I've got a sensitive nose."

Despite the fact that she clearly couldn't tell whether he was serious or not, she smiled. She had a beautiful smile that took her face from serene to gamine. It was almost as seductive as her voice.

"Is that so?"

"Cross my heart."

Her hands twisted in the shawl before smoothing it. It was such a charmingly feminine gesture that it brought everything male in him to the fore. Funny how long treks in the wilderness could make a body forget how tempting innocence could be. How refreshing. Because that was what he saw when he looked at her. Sweet innocence tempered by confidence and an underlying current of unawakened passion. He tucked that stray strand of hair behind her ear. It was supposed to be a brief gesture, but his fingers lingered. She had very smooth skin. And no idea what to say. He took pity on her, filling the awkward silence. "If you throw in some kind of dessert with supper, I'll take over getting those boys to bathe."

Mimi's soft lips smoothed into a curve of pure charm. His breath caught. Another sign he might just be in trouble here.

She held out her hand. "You've got a deal."

Wrapping his fingers around hers, Jackson shook it gently, before answering wryly, "I kind of figured that."

She was the one to end the handshake. He liked to think she did so slower than normal. The imprint of her touch lasted long past the point the contact ended. The ensuing pause was fraught with emotion. From her to him and him to her.

The rumble of his stomach broke the silence.

Brushing her hand down her skirt she said, "Seems like it's time we both got on about our chores."

"I'm thinking you're right."

Picking up his rifle and slinging it over his shoulder, Jackson headed toward the woods. He made it ten feet before Mimi's whisper reached him.

"Be careful."

The warning snuggled right under his guard and into that soft spot in his heart he swore nobody would ever get to. Being vulnerable didn't set well with him. With another wave he acknowledged the concern and kept on walking. One thing was for sure: as soon as he was recovered and the family settled, he needed to get the hell out of here or he would succumb to temptation. Mimi was the exact kind of woman to turn a confirmed bachelor's head.

S trolling across the field, Jackson unbuttoned the top few buttons of the shirt he'd just buttoned. The day was warming fast. From all the signs it could turn into a scorcher. Glancing up at the sky, he gauged the time. A bit late to start, but with the river just down the way, there ought to be some sort of game around. Maybe not a deer, but there would be game. Jackson was just glad he wouldn't have to walk too far. A man didn't live long out here if he didn't know his limitations, and he was injured, weak, and already almost at the end of his endurance. And he still had to haul whatever he killed home.

A few feet inside the woods at the bend of the river, the hairs on the back of his neck lifted. Behind him came the unmistakable sound of something or someone else in the woods. He was being followed.

Ducking to the right behind a tree partially surrounded by a thick clump of bushes, he waited. The clomping came faster. One, two sets of footsteps. There was only one logical conclusion. Kevin and Tony had followed him. They definitely needed a lesson in stealth. With that much noise chasing away game they'd all starve to death. He smelled them before he saw them. They definitely needed to wash up. He waited until they passed, completely oblivious to his presence, before asking, "Where are you two going this early in the morning?"

He got a small measure of satisfaction as they jumped and spun around. He had to give Kevin credit for a quick recovery.

"We're going with you."

"To do what?"

The challenge threw Kevin, but Tony just settled into his position and stated, "Whatever you're doing."

"I thought I'd hunt down a few meals."

"Then we'll help."

The "no" was on his lips, only to be silenced by longing in both boys' eyes. He couldn't help but remember the first time his father had taken him hunting. He'd been about Kevin's age. He remembered the sense of adventure and the desire to be able to provide like a man. To do what his father did. The thrill of just doing manly things. He motioned the boys over.

"If you want to help, the first thing you need to do is slow down and walk quietly. Don't step on sticks."

"How do you see a stick under the leaves?" Tony asked in his serious way.

"Try to feel around with your toes."

As soon as they tried, he saw the problem. Their shoes were hard soled, whereas he had on moccasins that allowed him to sense the ground better. "Just do your best."

They nodded again, excitement radiating off them in waves. "One thing you need to understand if you come with me. It's serious business providing for your family. It's got to be done right. A man doesn't let women and children starve, so you need to do exactly as I say, no hesitation."

More enthusiastic nods. He had a feeling they'd promise him their next five meals to tag along. "We're likely only going to get one shot so it matters that our aim is true, but

it's equally important that we get the chance to take that
shot, which means you need to be quiet. Very quiet. Do you
understand?"

"Yes."

"Yes."

He nodded. "Good. Listen up, then. I'm not going to
repeat myself later."

He couldn't have asked for a more devoted audience as
he explained the plan to the boys. The wind changed direction and he got a whiff of them again, reminding him of the
promise he'd made Mimi. He'd have to deal with that later.
When he was satisfied both boys knew the plan, he jerked
his head toward the path. "Then let's go get us some breakfast."

Kevin jumped up so fast he tripped. Jackson caught his
arm. Tony was outwardly more cautious.

"Remember, stay behind me, stay close, and stay as
quiet as you possibly can." Lips pressed so hard together
they all but disappeared, Kevin nodded hard enough his
hair fell over his eyes. Clearly he was already feeling the
strain of silence. Jackson patted him on his shoulder. He
ruffled Tony's hair. The boy was too stoic by far. "Good
job."

Working steadily downwind of the deer path he'd noticed coming in, he settled behind some heavy brush,
propped his rifle, and sat down on his haunches. The boys
looked at him. He frowned as soon as they opened their
mouths. Snapping their mouths shut, they hunkered down,
too. Tony's stomach growled loudly. Tony clutched his
stomach and blanched. What the hell had the boy been
through that such a small infraction had him terrified?
Jackson leaned over and whispered, "I'm hungry, too."

Tony relaxed and managed a weak smile, which Kevin

echoed. Together they sat and waited. The boys did well at first, but about twenty minutes in he could feel them twitching in their skin. He empathized. The hardest part of hunting was the waiting, but if one waited, it paid off. A slight rustle of the leaves alerted him. Like right now. Holding a finger to his lips he pointed down the trail. A young buck walked down the trail, head up, ears twitching warily. The boys nodded.

Jackson carefully took aim. A few steps closer, a couple more head tosses, and Jackson pulled the trigger. The gun barked. The buck went down. The boys jumped and fell backward. A few birds squawked, and then the woods went silent.

Kevin and Tony followed him to the kill, jumping around all excited.

"Did you see that," Kevin cheered. "You got him with one shot. Just one shot."

Jackson hid his smile. "Bullets are expensive."

Their enthusiasm waned when they got to the carcass. The buck was still twitching, the last of its life fading from its eyes. Excitement dimmed at the reality of death. Overhead a crow cawed. Awkwardly slinging his rifle over his shoulder, Jackson put a hand on each boy's shoulder, squeezing lightly. "This, my friends, is the part of hunting where we pray."

"For what?" Kevin asked, not looking away from the deer. All excitement was gone from his tone.

"In gratitude for our bounty. Taking any life is no small thing."

When the prayer was done, this time it was Tony who asked, "Why?"

"My father told me everything has a right to live, and when you have to make a trade, their life for yours, you need to be respectful of their sacrifice."

Tony didn't look at the deer, but Kevin couldn't look away from it. Jackson placed his hand on the boy's shoulder again. What came out of Kevin's mouth wasn't what Jackson expected. "You had a pa?"

Did they think his mother found him under a leaf pile? "Everyone does."

It was Tony who answered. "We don't."

Damn. Beneath his hand, Kevin stiffened. He couldn't imagine not knowing who his father was. Jackson's father had been everything to him: his guide, his mentor, his disciplinarian, his friend. He still was. "I'm sorry, son. That was none of my business."

Kevin shrugged, still staring at the deer. "It doesn't matter."

But it clearly did. Again, Jackson had to wonder at what had brought the boys and Mimi together. They weren't blood, that was for sure.

"I didn't think hunting would be so sad," Kevin whispered. He motioned to the body. "He just wanted to get a drink and we killed him."

Jackson could remember that feeling after his first kill, too. "I know. And we just need to eat. It's life, son, and that's why you have to honor it even when you have to take it."

"I don't want to eat him," he declared emphatically.

Tony whispered, "I don't, either."

More crows cawed, the rustle of their wings disturbing the morning as they settled in the branches above. They weren't going to be squeamish about a meal.

"Life's hard, boys, full of many hard choices. Unless you killed this animal for sport, you need to set about dressing it and bringing it home for dinner. Otherwise, his death has no meaning."

"And so will Mimi's and Melinda Sue's," Kevin whispered, looking up. "They'll starve without food."

That answered the question if the boys understood the gravity of their situation. "Exactly." Jackson rested his rifle and the rope against a nearby tree. "If we as men don't provide, our women won't survive, and that we don't allow."

Kevin swallowed hard. "I don't want them to starve."

"Neither do I. That's why we make peace with the hard decisions."

Tony touched the deer's ear. "I read that the Indians believe that when you kill something and then eat it, its spirit goes into your heart. In some way it becomes part of you."

Kevin looked up, a shock of his red hair falling over his eyes. He wanted confirmation. Jackson was more than happy to give it to him.

"In general, the Indians believe that we're part of everything. That we don't live apart from anything."

"So he'll live on in us?" Kevin asked.

"Yup."

Kevin smiled. "I like that."

"So do I," Tony agreed.

Reaching around his back, Jackson took his knife from his belt. "Good. Then it's settled. We're bringing home venison for supper."

Kevin's eyes bugged at the sight of the blade. "What are you going to do with that?"

"We're going to skin it and then field dress the meat."

"And after that?" Tony asked.

"After that we'll butcher it, but right now you need to pay attention. The kill only starts the process. There are certain things that have to be done correctly after that or, instead of feeding the people you love, you'll poison them."

It was the first time Jackson had seen Tony truly rattled. Handing him the knife, Jackson assured him, "Don't worry. I'll teach you how to do it right."

Surprisingly, Jackson enjoyed the experience of passing on the knowledge that had been passed on to him. There was a timelessness in it. A comfort and strength. He took it slowly, showing them where to cut, which knot to tie, which tree limb to use. The process was peaceful in a way Jackson had never felt before, and he discovered, as he passed on the lessons taught to him, why his father always said the joy of knowledge only took life when shared.

Seven

———

Jackson hadn't counted on giving lessons when he'd bud-geted time for hunting; as a result, the sun was high in the sky by the time they were ready to head home. He was feeling every extra minute as he leaned back against a tree and waited for the boys to load the slabs of meat onto the deer skin, which they'd use as a sled to get it back to the house. They were flush with newfound confidence, compar-ing their butchering skills as they positioned the load. It was good to see them working together.

"That's enough, now," Jackson ordered before they could grab more meat. "Time to tie it up."

Tony glanced up from where he was packing in another chunk. "But there's a whole lot left."

Leaving as much as they were was wasteful, but he was about played out. The nausea had reared its ugly head an hour earlier, and weakness had come tripping in on its heels, leaving his knees with an unmanly shake. "It can't be helped. It's going to be hard enough hauling back what you've got there."

Kevin, ever the optimist, piped up. "We can do it."

The boy was all enthusiasm. Jackson shook his head and waved his hand. "Try it, then. Just grab a corner and tug."

He did. The hide barely moved. He looked surprised. Shoving his hair out of his eyes, he glared at the pile. "I can't."

Tony gave it a tug also, with a little more success, before standing back. "Wow. It doesn't look that heavy."

"Nope, which is why you can't run on assumptions. You've got to plan ahead. In this case, you've got the weight of the hide, the weight of the meat, and the roughness of the terrain to take into consideration. And you've got to balance that against how much muscle you have to do the job."

Kevin put his hands on his hips. "There's three of us."

Jackson blew out a breath. "I'm afraid it's just going to be you two. I'm feeling a bit puny."

That got Tony's attention, followed by an unflattering proclamation. "You look like those corpses propped up outside at the undertaker's."

Jackson's "thanks" was dry.

"Shut up, Tony," Kevin muttered as he gathered up the rope. "Come help me tie this up."

Tony and Kevin followed Jackson's instructions on how to wrap and tie the rope around the hide so they could get the meat safely home. After giving their knots a quick inspection, Jackson nodded in approval. "Now, that's a fair decent piece of work."

And it was. The boys had done well. They'd followed directions. They didn't have the wrist strength for some of it, but they'd pitched in and hadn't whined. He admired that, because it wasn't easy work and it was clearly nothing they'd ever done before. They'd have blisters for sure, but there was also an aura of satisfaction about as them as they washed up in the stream and prepared to drag the meat back to the house, a confidence that hadn't been there before. Jackson was proud of them.

"Ready?" he asked, drying his hands on the sides of his pants and gathering up his rifle.

Both boys nodded. Above, the flock of crows cawed in a raucous cacophony, clearly wanting a turn at the carcass.

"Then let's get out of here and let those crows get to feasting."

"I can't wait until we can feast," Tony declared, grabbing up one of the ends of the rope woven around the hide-wrapped meat.

Kevin grabbed the other and started pulling. "Me either. I'm starving!"

"Is Mimi a good cook?" Jackson asked, grunting as he lifted the bundle over a bush.

"Mimi's good at everything."

Cold, clammy sweat broke out on his brow as he heaved the bundle forward. "All the more reason to hurry."

On a cheer, the boys surged on. The bundle bounced over the ground. Or maybe that was just his vision wavering. For a moment, Jackson wasn't sure he wasn't going to pass out.

"Come on, Mr. Montgomery!" Tony called.

"Supper's waiting!" Kevin added, with a disgusting amount of enthusiasm.

Clenching his teeth, Jackson took a step forward. And then another, sheer grit keeping him moving. "Right behind you."

No one seemed to notice how weak the statement was.

* * *

The boys broke through the trees into the meadow, whooping and hollering. They were a quarter of the way to the house before Jackson cleared the trees. He was just in time to see Mimi burst out of the house, her hand shading her eyes against the noon sun. Jackson immediately got that peculiar punched-in-his-gut sensation that he always got upon seeing her. There was something just so . . . perfect about the woman. Something both soothing and exciting at the same time. The boys waved and hollered some more. She waved back and smiled. Even from here he could see how it lit up her face. Looking pretty as a picture in a light blue dress with a lace-trimmed scoop neck and her hair pulled back in a braid, she descended the porch steps, jerking to a stop at the bottom.

A second later the reason revealed itself in the form of Melinda Sue. She pushed past Mimi. Pigtails bouncing, petticoats flapping, she screamed his name. In her hurry, she tripped and tumbled to her hands and knees. Before Mimi could reach her, Melinda Sue was up and brushing herself off. Before Mimi could catch her, she was running again.

"Mr. Jackson. Mr. Jackson!"

The child was all energy, whereas Jackson had all he could do to keep placing one foot in front of the other. He wanted to vomit. Pass out. Eat. In that order.

"Mr. Jackson!" Melinda Sue yelled again when she got close enough to launch herself at him. He caught her in midleap and settled her on his hip, grunting at the pain. He didn't stop walking, though. If he did, he'd never get started again.

"Hey, sprout."

"How come you didn't take me?" Melinda Sue demanded, her angelic face contorted in a full pout. How on earth did that make her even cuter?

"Mellie," Mimi chided. "Don't be rude."

"It's all right," Jackson said in a tight voice. To Melinda Sue he explained, "You were sleeping."

Melinda Sue's frown deepened. "Next time waked me up!"

"Melinda Sue!" Mimi shook her head. The child was impossible. Every day was an exhausting struggle for control. There were days when she simply didn't feel up to the task.

Jackson just laughed and ruffled Melinda Sue's hair. "Sure thing."

Waving to the deer hide bundle wrapped up in rope, Mimi asked, "What's this?"

"We brought breakfast!" Kevin boasted, coming to a stop.

"We hunted us a deer!" Tony chimed in, dropping his end of rope.

"A deer?" Mimi blinked. They'd brought down a deer? Her two town-living boys had brought down a deer? "That's impressive."

Melinda Sue wiggled in Jackson's arms as he came up beside her. "I wanna see."

This close Mimi couldn't help but hear Jackson's groan. The lowered brim of his hat obscured his eyes, but he was pale. He was trying to act normal, but he was hurting.

"There's nothing to see yet," Tony countered.

Kevin smacked the bundle. Dust flew. "But there will be once Mimi starts cooking this up."

Mimi smiled at the boys' enthusiasm. "There will be, huh?"

They looked so happy. So joyful. Mimi couldn't remember when she'd seen the boys so carefree. So proud. And why wouldn't they be? They'd provided for their family. That was something men did. Something she wasn't even sure they'd seen before, growing up in the whorehouse as they had, but in their eight- and ten-year-old minds, they recognized the importance of it. Maybe because they'd seen through her struggles just how hard it was to provide.

"Yup."

"What if I burn it?"

Kevin's face fell. "You can't."

She nudged his shoulder, teasing him. "No, I can't because I'm hungrier than you are."

"Not possible."

"Oh, it's possible."

Beside her, Jackson stood quietly, a slight smile curving his lips, but his breathing was strained. As the boys wrestled with the bundle, she touched his forearm. His skin felt clammy. She whispered too low for the children to hear, "Are you going to make it to the house?"

He whispered back, "Yup. Or die trying."

That was not a reassuring response. "Please. Spare us that."

The left side of his mouth quirked up in a half grin. He cut her a glance. Even bloodshot, his eyes were beautiful. "Getting fond of me, are you?"

She steadied him when he wove on his feet. "Some, but there's also the onerous chore of burying you to consider if you just up and croak."

His laugh was little more than a rasp. He really might not make it to the house. "Heck, just dump me in the well with the snakes."

"The only thing I want to put in that well is a wagonful of dynamite."

"We think alike."

An ecstatic "whee!" spun her around.

The boys were dragging the meat up to the front door. "Melinda Sue, you get off that dirty hide!"

Melinda stuck her lip out and folded her arms across her small chest. "I wanna ride."

Of course she did. Tony scooped her off before Mimi could grab her. "I'll give you a piggyback ride later," he promised as she struggled.

"No."

Mimi held out her hands. "Give her to me."

Melinda Sue shook her head. "I want Mr. Jackson."

Before Mimi could stop her, Melinda Sue scrambled over into his arms. He had no choice but to hitch her over or let her fall. A flinch shook him from head to toe. If possible, he got even paler. Intercepting the glance he shot the boys, she understood. He didn't want them to see him like this. Stroking her fingers over his hand, she called the boys' names.

"As happy as I am to have breakfast, I thought we had an agreement that you'd tell me before you take off." She frowned at the boys, diverting their attention. "Mr. Montgomery took you hunting?"

The boys stopped smiling.

"You're in trouble," Melinda Sue gloated.

Mimi silenced her with a glance. "Hush, Melinda Sue."

Jackson frowned at the boys, who had the grace to look guilty. "You didn't tell your sister where you were heading?"

"No, they didn't. I had no idea where they were."

"I did," Melinda Sue crowed victoriously before realizing her mistake. Slapping her hands over her mouth, she stared at them, horrified. Mimi had to suppress a smile.

"Because you were supposed to tell her, brat," Tony growled.

Melinda Sue removed her hands long enough to throw them wide, almost smacking Jackson in the nose as she did. "I forgots."

"Careful."

Melinda Sue was oblivious to the strain in his voice. Mimi brushed her fingers over his hand again.

"It wasn't her job to tell me," Mimi corrected. "It was yours."

"You're not my mother," Tony snapped, grabbing up the rope.

The truth hurt. Before Mimi could snap back, Kevin waved to the bundle with the other rope end. "Stop fighting and look! We've got lots and lots and lots of meat. We're going to eat big today."

The distraction worked for everyone but Jackson. In a voice that brooked no opposition he demanded, "Tony, what did we talk about when hunting?"

"I don't remember," Tony muttered, looking away.

Mimi recognized the lie. From the arch of Jackson's brows, it was clear so did he.

"The first rule of a man is to always respect those around him." Looking pointedly at Mimi, he added, "That includes your sister."

The apology Tony offered was grudging, but Mimi accepted it.

"Thank you, Tony."

Obviously feeling too much attention was being squandered elsewhere, Melinda Sue braced her hands on Jackson's shoulder and pushed herself back so she could see into his face. "I wanted to go hunting."

Kevin was quick to counter. "You're too little."

"I am not!"

Jackson moved Melinda Sue to his right hip. He immediately swayed. Mimi switched her grip to the middle of his back. He glanced down as if to imply she was out of line. His pride, no doubt.

As if she cared about his pride. If he passed out, she'd have to drag him and they'd already been through that. He shifted his grip and winced again.

"Are you sure you're all right?"

It was a stupid question. The man was ready to drop. She didn't know why she'd asked it.

"Yes."

With a sigh, Mimi pried Melinda Sue out of his arms and set her down. The child immediately scampered over to harass the boys. Hands on hips, Mimi turned back to Jackson. "You, Mr. Montgomery, are a lousy liar." To the children she directed, "Finish getting that meat up to the house. I'll be there in a minute."

As soon as she turned back, he said, "The name's Jackson, and I'm working on the lying."

At least honesty fit with her image of him as an angel.

With a lift of his chin he indicated Melinda Sue. "Thank you for rescuing me. As cute as that girl is, I'm about done in."

He said the latter like it was some sort of secret. "Of course you are. Crazy man. Fresh from your sickbed and you're out hunting." She shook her head. "I should never have allowed it."

She suddenly had his full attention. His finger under her chin lifted her face to his in a purely masculine gesture she'd experienced before. Her ex-lover-partner-maybe-husband Mac had been fond of the practice.

"You don't *allow* me to do anything," Jackson stated in that deceptively easygoing drawl of his.

"Now," she pointed out helpfully, "when you're about to fall on your face, is probably not the best time to be going all manly."

"And yet I'm insisting we get this straight between us. I'm the man. You're the woman. Which means I give the orders." His finger rubbed delicately under her chin, sending little goose bumps chasing down her arms. "And I like it that way."

In the distance the boys chattered, the breeze blew, and birds sang, but she couldn't look away. A shiver rippled down her spine, blending with the goose bumps. Grabbing his wrist, she held on while her world rocked. She'd never had that reaction with Mac. It took her a moment to find her voice. When she did, it came out airy and high. Not at all the way she wanted. "Well, so do I. What does that have to do with you being about to collapse?"

"Not a goddamn thing."

Mimi didn't know what to do with that. She released his wrist. She'd been crazy to grab it in the first place. The man was always throwing her off balance, but at the same time there was something about him that held her steady. It was disconcerting. It was comforting. He held her just a second longer. A second that stretched timelessly in her mind. He smelled of sweat and blood but also, beneath that, something more elemental. His hand brushed down her arm comfortingly.

"So why are we standing here?" she asked.

"Because it feels good."

He was so full of horse hockey. A gorgeous, experienced man like Jackson didn't loiter over barely there touches. "Or maybe it's because you really don't think you can make it to the house after all."

"Oh, I can make it."

Hands on hips, she demanded, "Prove it."

With a wave, he motioned her onward. She could easily have outdistanced him, but instead she paced him, strolling along as if a snail's pace were entirely normal, walking close enough to catch him if he stumbled. And for those goose bumps to spring up every time his hand accidentally brushed hers.

By the time they got to the house, the boys had the pack open and the meat displayed at the foot of the stairs. "We've got steaks," Kevin crowed when they got close enough to see.

"Butterfly steaks," Tony clarified for Mimi. "Mr. Montgomery says they're the best ever, melt right in your mouth before your teeth even have time to chew!"

"Is that so?" Mimi asked.

"Got to be quick if you want your teeth to sink in," Jackson confirmed.

She shook her head, but she was smiling. "I'll be careful cooking them, then."

Jackson's stomach rumbled loudly. "I'd appreciate it."

"So I hear."

He shrugged the rifle off his shoulder. "Never made a secret of the fact I was hungry."

Melinda Sue tugged at Mimi's skirt. "I'm hungry, too."

"So are we," Tony chimed in.

So was she. "Well, then. I guess I'd better get the stove fired up."

Picking up her skirts, she headed up the steps, rifle tucked in the crook of her arm like she knew how to use it. "Come on up into the house. You can take a nap while I cook."

The sound Jackson made could have been a laugh or a curse. Or worse, a last gargle before he passed out. She'd

heard people made strange sounds before they fell unconscious. She turned. He hadn't budged. He stood there, legs
slightly splayed, hat pushed back, looking for all the world
like a disgruntled fallen angel.

"A nap, woman? What am I, four?"

From his expression and tone of voice, she concluded he
needed to find more adults to talk to. Directing children
about all day was taking a toll on his conversation skills.
"What you are is a sick man who has done too much too
soon and is going to set himself back."

"I'm not taking a God-gosh-darn nap."

She was relieved to see he used the handrail coming up
the steps.

"Of course not." She waited until he was in the house
before adding, "But a rest might be a good idea before
lunch."

Jackson didn't know how long he slept, but when he
awoke, he was surrounded by the delicious scent of stew
simmering. Taking a deep breath, savoring the aroma, he
took inventory of his condition. His injuries were making
themselves heard but nowhere near as loudly as his stomach. He was starving.

Pushing up on his elbows, he spotted Mimi standing
by the stove. She was still wearing the light blue dress from
that morning, the one that made her eyes such a vivid
blue. She still looked neat and tidy. He liked that about her.
That somehow, no matter how hectic things became, she
always appeared composed. The boys were nowhere in
sight. Melinda Sue was at the table, doing something with
a piece of charcoal and some birch bark. He tossed the
blanket back.

"Well, good afternoon," Mimi said over her shoulder.

"Good afternoon yourself." Frowning, he noticed the fading light.

"What time is it?"

"It's almost dusk."

Damn, he'd slept the whole day away. Shifting his weight off his bad shoulder, he breathed deeply. "Smells like you made it into town this afternoon."

She suddenly became engrossed in stirring the stew. "No."

"Why not?"

"There wasn't a need. I had some spices in the cupboard, and the boys found some potatoes and vegetables in the old garden."

That didn't explain why she was avoiding his gaze.

"Is there something you need to tell me?"

Her start would have been imperceptible if he hadn't been watching her. A man had to admire that much control.

"Not at all. I just didn't feel comfortable leaving with you so soon out of your sickbed." She shrugged with her back to him. "Just in case."

Another excuse.

"I'm fine."

She looked over her shoulder. "You've been saying that since the moment before you collapsed. You'll have to forgive me if I don't take you seriously."

"I know how I feel."

"And I know I don't trust your assessment."

Checkmate. "Where are the boys?"

"Outside. I was afraid they'd wake you up. Melinda Sue gave it a try, but you were dead to the world."

At the sound of her name, Melinda Sue looked up from her drawing. He waved. "Hey, sprout."

She waved and went back to what she was doing, humming a nursery song.

"She's making you a present," Mimi explained.

He was touched. He could hear the boys arguing outside. Something that would normally have brought him awake, yet he'd slept through lunch preparation, Melinda Sue, and the boys. She was right. It probably hadn't been a good idea for her to go into town.

"I'm usually a light sleeper."

"So I figured." She nodded to the left. "I put your guns in the cupboard for now."

"Thank you."

"It's going to be tricky around here with those guns. Melinda Sue is fascinated. So are the boys."

"They won't touch them."

Mimi banged the wooden spoon on the side of the pot. "I'm sure you'll tell them not to, but I don't know how safe that strategy is going to be."

She resented his guns? "This isn't some pretty Eastern town, Mimi. It's the West. Out here knowing how to defend yourself will save your life."

"It's important back East, too."

There was that tension again. And, once again, he wondered just what had sent the city slicker heading west with three children in tow. "Speaking of back East, just what was it that brought you out here?"

Mimi put the spoon down beside the pot, turned, and wiped her hands on her apron. Her cheeks were flushed from the heat of the stove. The strands of honey brown hair that had escaped her braid hung around her face. Her lips compressed into a tight line.

"Now is not the time to be discussing that."

Over at the table, Melinda Sue stopped humming. The

charcoal clattered to the floor. As it bounced, Melinda Sue whispered, "Because of the monsters."

Jackson perked up. "What monsters?"

Bracing herself against the counter, Mimi glared at him. "Hush, Melinda Sue."

And Melinda Sue, the intrepid child who feared nothing, paled and shut up. Interesting.

"Mind telling me when would be a good time?" Jackson asked, keeping his drawl level.

"Maybe never." Pushing her hair off her face, she snapped, "I don't go asking you about your business."

"I'm sure you'll get around to it."

Her hand dropped to her side and clenched into a fist. "And if I do, I'm sure you may or may not answer me."

"True enough."

"You're admitting it?"

He stood and brushed the dirt off his pants. "I don't lie."

But she did, though never smoothly or with any confidence. It was obviously a newly acquired skill. He felt grimy and dirty. The boys weren't the only ones who needed a bath. "Do you have any soap?"

She blinked at the change of topic. "I do."

"I need a bath."

She didn't disagree. "You also need a change of clothes. The ones from your bag are out hanging on the line."

Tension still shook her voice. They weren't done with the subject of monsters by a long shot, but for now, he'd let it go. "Thank you."

He made short work of folding up the blanket. At least it was easier to move now. Gathering all the bedding, he put it on a chair in the corner. As he did, he noticed another gap in the floor. Only a desperate person would consider this place a godsend. "How much time do we have before supper?"

She relaxed with the change of subject. "Probably another hour. There are some steaks on the table to tide you over."

"I'll grab some on the way out, but . . ."

She raised her brows.

"I still need the soap."

"I know."

"I'm sensing some reluctance."

With a sigh, she went into her bedroom. A minute later she came out with something wrapped in wax cloth. The soap, he presumed. She opened it carefully. Inside was a small beige oval. One sniff and he was back to thinking of hot, lazy summer days and endless possibilities. Honeysuckle.

"Is the reason you don't want to give it to me because it's your last or because you object to a man smelling like a flower?"

That got him a glimpse of her smile. "Would you believe me if I said the latter?"

"Nah. I know how partial women are to their luxuries."

"In this case, soap isn't a luxury." She handed it to him. "You do stink."

He didn't take it. "I'll make do with the laundry soap until we can get to town."

She pushed the soap into his hands. "You won't have any skin left. Just take it."

He did, inspired by the way she wrinkled her nose and stepped quickly back. He was probably reeking as bad as the boys.

"I'll replace it when we go into town tomorrow."

Her "thank you" was distinctly unenthusiastic. What the hell? Women loved shopping and town.

Jackson added that idiosyncrasy to his growing list of contradictions that were Mimi. Before he got to the door, she asked, "Could you see if you can get Kevin and Tony to at least splash some water on themselves?"

Grabbing his Stetson off the nail by the door, he settled it on his head. Giving the brim a tug, he asked, "Didn't I promise to?"

He found the boys arguing around the side of the house, sort of chopping wood. Sort of, because they were more in danger of chopping off their foot than they were of splitting a log. He could tell from the way they were swinging the axe that they had no experience with it. Didn't Easterners need a fire? Tony swung hard. Jackson held his breath. It hit the log with a thud. And stuck. The language that greeted that disaster would have gotten their mouths washed out with soap if his mother had heard it.

They looked up as he approached. Kevin immediately feigned confidence whereas Tony stepped back and waited. Both actions were signs of nervousness. The whole damned family was jumpy. "I see you got the wood in."

They nodded. "Mimi says it takes a lot of wood for cooking and heating. We thought we'd get started on it," Kevin offered, stepping in front of the stuck axe.

"Good plan."

Tony held his hands out. The palms were peppered with red marks and the beginning of blisters. "My hands aren't tough enough yet."

"They'll toughen up, but if you're interested, I could share a trick that would make it easier."

Ever eager, Kevin piped up. "I'm interested."

The more cautious Tony asked, "There's a trick?"

"Oh, yeah. There's always a trick."

Kevin stepped away from the chopping block. "Even for this?"

"Even for that."

Turning the log on its side and pinning it with his foot, Jackson loosened the axe head with some solid thunks on the handle.

"Usually," he said as he straightened the log and wrenched the axe free, "it's just a matter of applying the proper leverage."

"And muscle," Tony muttered as Jackson took a moment to manage the pain. That bit of showing off had cost him.

"And muscle," he agreed. "But you're not always going to be the biggest so sometimes you have to be the smartest."

While the boys chewed on that, he set up the wood. "If you've got enough muscle backing you, your axe is sharp, and it's not too stubborn a piece of wood, you can just try to drive the axe right on through."

More nods.

"But it doesn't matter how much heft you have, if your axe blade isn't sharp." He ran his finger over the edge. "And this is as dull as a butter knife. All you're going to do is lodge the blade."

"We've been swinging it forever."

They smelled like they'd been working hard.

"Do you know if there's a grinding wheel in the barn?" It was a faint hope that died as the boys shook their heads.

"Nope."

He sighed and set the axe aside. "We'll bring it with us when we go into town tomorrow and get it sharpened." He had a small whetstone that he used for his knife, but the axe edge was so dull and damaged, it would take a grinding wheel to fix it.

Tony and Kevin looked at him like he'd sprouted a second head.

"What?"

"We never go into town."

"Any particular reason for that?"

"Mimi doesn't like it there."

"Why?"

It wasn't an unreasonable question. Certainly not one that should have them clamming up and dodging his gaze.

He repeated the question. Kevin kept his gaze averted. Tony met his dead-on. When it came to Mimi, the boy had no caution.

"She has her reasons."

He bet she did. "Well, unless someone gives me a darned good reason that makes starving a better option than going to town, tomorrow, we're going to town."

He waited. Neither boy offered a reason.

"That's what I thought."

"You don't know everything," Tony muttered.

"I know we need a sharp axe, oats for Lady, and"—he made an exaggerated sniffing sound—"soap for you two."

The boys grimaced. He wasn't totally unsympathetic. He'd hated baths at their age. "And maybe, if we have enough money left over, we'll hit the mercantile and get a bit more of that penny candy."

That got some enthusiasm showing.

"But there's one hitch in our git-along. You boys can't go into town smelling like skunks."

Their faces fell.

"I'm heading down to the river. Y'all need to come with me. You've got to get washed up."

"We don't have any soap."

"Mimi spared me a bit."

As one they took a step back. "That smells like flowers."

Kevin belligerently folded his arms across his chest. "I'm not smelling like a flower."

"Me neither," Tony echoed.

"Well, right now you smell badly enough to put me off my meal, and trust me, boys, that's not happening. So follow me."

They stopped at the clothesline before heading to the river. It took more threats to get the boys fully undressed and headed to the water. He was prepared to throw them in, they smelled that badly, but they eventually opted to enter the water under their own steam. Kevin in a mad dash, Tony a lot slower. He didn't seem to know where to place his hands, trying to cover this part and that. No boy had ever been that shy in Jackson's experience, but as Tony got closer, understanding dawned. Someone had beaten the boy, badly. To the point they'd left scars all over his body. Shit.

Jackson drew him short with a hand on his shoulder. Tony's chin came up. "The man who beat you, is he still living?"

Tony just shrugged and stared straight ahead.

"Look at me, son."

He did finally, shame warring with anger in his expression. From the water, Kevin watched.

"I want an answer. Is whoever did that to you still alive?"

Tony's lips set in a thin line. His eyes took on that too-old expression. "I'm told I deserved it."

"No one deserves that."

Kevin came sloshing out of the water, fists balled.

"Leave him alone."

Jackson stopped him with a raise of his hand. "I'm not asking to shame you, son."

Tony bristled. "I'm not your son."

"No, you're not, because if you were, the man who hurt you would be dead."

"He needs to be dead," Kevin whispered, coming closer.

So he was still alive.

Tony ducked out from under Jackson's grip and grabbed the soap. "Shut up, Kevin."

As Tony and Kevin headed into the water, Jackson drawled with deliberate casualness, "If you ever want to settle that score, Tony, you let me know."

The boys looked at each other. Kevin ignored Tony's frown. "There are too many of them."

"Shut up!"

Jackson smiled and let the rage settle into purpose. "I wouldn't be going alone."

"You'd need an army," Kevin added, a touch of hope perking his voice.

Jackson thought of Clint, Cougar, the Reverend Brad, and Asa. Former bounty hunters, bandits, and lawmen. Cold-eyed men whose names struck terror into the hearts of those they hunted. He nodded. "I have one."

"They don't know me," Tony whispered, dipping down in the water. "Why would they help?"

"Because I'll ask them to." It was as simple as that.

Kevin's eyes got wider; Tony's lips drew tighter; but neither said a word. They finished bathing in tense silence. As they headed back up the path to the house, with Kevin leading and Jackson bringing up the rear, Tony stopped, clenched his fists, and looked back over his shoulder, not quite meeting Jackson's gaze.

"Did you mean what you said?"

"There's never a time that I don't."

A pause and then, "And your friends? They're good?"

"They're very good."

The boys exchanged a glance. Kevin was the one who spoke. "Good enough to kill someone?"

Both boys watched him intently. And why not? They clearly thought their lives hung on the answer. He tugged his hat down over his brow. "Without batting an eye."

With a nod Tony resumed walking. "I'll think on it."

Eight

～

Dark had fallen by the time the children finally fell asleep bundled up on the pallets on the floor in Mimi's room, all that energy finally exhausted by a hard day. And boredom. Mimi claimed she didn't have enough lamp oil to burn at night, leaving the children with nothing to do but sit quietly. They soon said they were tired. Jackson had a suspicion it was a trick to get some peace and quiet. If so, it was a success.

Sitting out on the next-to-the-top step of the porch, Jackson breathed deeply of the cool air. Fall was coming. There wouldn't be many more evenings like this. The house was quiet. The night was calm. The moon had yet to rise. A hoot owl in the distance punctuated the chirps of crickets. Jackson sat on the steps, sharpening his knife on the small whetstone he carried with him, letting the peace of it all wash over him.

The door slowly creaked open. Mimi's scent teased his

nostrils with the promise of summer and laughter and happy times.

"I always did like the scent of honeysuckle," he mentioned, not looking over his shoulder. He heard that little betraying intake of breath that indicated her surprise, and then he heard the smile in her response.

"Did you, now?"

Her skirts rustled as she sat down on the step just above him. Her utter femininity appealed to him on many levels. But where she was sitting? That would have to change. He didn't like her hiding from him. "Either I'm going to have to move up or you're going to have to come down."

"Oh? The great Jackson Montgomery doesn't want a woman sitting taller than him?"

He kept the knife moving in little circles over the stone. "A man's got to protect his reputation."

Her laugh was more of an expulsion of breath. "You're rather outrageous, aren't you?"

Not that he was admitting to. "Made you smile, didn't I?"

"That you did."

For a few minutes there was only the soothing rasp of metal over stone. With a sigh Mimi slid down a step, keeping a discreet distance between them, tucking her skirts around her as she settled. She was barefooted. She had very pretty ankles and cute toes.

"Are you sure we should be going to town tomorrow?"

It was the fourth time she'd broached that topic. It was also the most direct. "I'm sure." He tested the sharpness of the blade. Almost there. "Are you sure you don't want to tell me what makes you so nervous about going to town?"

She shrugged. "I've never liked towns much."

"Honey girl, you are as city as they come. You have no

sick training, no animal training, no farm training. Hell, you barely know how to cook."

It was the latter that got her back up. "I know how to cook just fine when I have all my spices."

"Well, now, that I'll have to see."

She bristled. "Bland food never killed anyone."

He set the knife and stone down. "Woman, it's clear as day, you're used to just walking down the street and picking up what you need."

"So? It's not a crime."

"No, it's not, but it makes one wonder what drove you out of your safe little city and into the big bad wilderness."

She pulled her shawl around her shoulders as the breeze kicked up. "Cities aren't as safe as you like to believe."

"I don't imagine they are, but they're what you know and you left, dragging three kids in tow. The way I look at it, it's got to be something pretty nasty to make you head out."

"It's not an exciting story, but since you saved my life, I'll tell you. But I'm not answering questions."

"Thank you."

"I fell in love with the wrong man. A bad man. Very powerful. At the time, I thought he was so sophisticated." She shrugged. "I had no money. He always had plenty. I didn't realize he made his money off a house of ill repute and other shady businesses until I was in deep. There was some trouble one night. I grabbed the children, some money and things, and left."

"Damn."

"It's a very old story."

"Most people would have left the kids."

She remembered that night. Melinda Sue getting caught playing with the beautiful "princess" necklace, Mac's fury.

He meant to kill the little girl. He had no use for the off-spring of the establishment's whores. If it hadn't been for Tony hitting Mac over the head with a vase, he would have succeeded. Knowing they had only until Mac woke up to get out of there, knowing they needed money, Mimi had grabbed the box out of the safe. It wasn't until that night, riding the train west, the kids sleeping around her, that she'd discovered the encrypted ledger. She never would have taken the box had she known what was in it, but there was no going back.

She shuddered, remembering Mac's fury when he'd reached for Melinda Sue. No. There was no going back. To Jackson, she simply said, "No, they wouldn't."

For a long moment, his gaze searched hers. Placing his hand over hers he nodded. "I'm guessing not."

He saw too much. She flashed him a smile that probably wouldn't fool the kids, let alone a grown man, and slid her hand out from under his.

"And now it's your turn. What brings you wandering through here? Dirty clothes, tired horse, no soap, and a whole pouch full of money."

"I could say I was good at robbing banks."

She rolled her eyes. He noticed she was real fond of do-ing that. "You could."

"I could say I'm good at killing."

She didn't roll her eyes at that. "You could."

"I could say a whole lot of things . . ."

"Or you could just tell me the truth."

"Why, when you're withholding yours?"

"Maybe there's a reason I'm withholding mine."

"Maybe I've got the same reason."

She looked him up and down. "I don't think so."

That piqued his interest. "What makes you say that?"

* * *

If Mimi had to guess anything about anyone, she'd guess that Jackson was used to being respected. It was there in the way he met the world with a direct gaze and squared shoulders. It was there in his easy humor and that devil-take-the-hindmost attitude. He carried his honor the way Mac carried his anger. As if it were the biggest part of him you could count on. Whereas Jackson was a man in every sense of the word, Mac was . . . Mac was just evil.

Mimi glanced at the knife in Jackson's lean hand. The blade glinted in the faint moonlight. He carried his weapons with the same ease. "Just instinct."

He cut her a glance. A strip of leather held his hair back at the nape of his neck, giving her a clear view of his profile with its strong jaw and bold nose. It also gave her a clear view of amusement crinkling the corner of his eye and cutting a shallow groove at the corner of his mouth.

"What else is your instinct telling you?"

She bought a little time by straightening the fringe of the shawl over her knees. This wasn't a conversation she wanted to indulge, because if she discussed him, sooner or later, he was going to want to discuss her. And that was a subject she couldn't broach. She had to be strong. Jackson was the hero type. An honorable man. The type Mac, with his twisted ways and cruel mind, would love to destroy. If Mac or his men ever found her, they'd kill Jackson. Likely in front of her. And laugh the whole time. A piece of fringe broke off in her hand. She closed her fist around it. Mac liked to see people suffer. What she needed to do, if she was as good as she'd promised God she'd be from here on out, was to send him on his way.

In response to her perusal, Jackson arched his brow. Her

heart did that particular ka-bump it did whenever he looked at her with that unnamed emotion that softened the masculine planes of his face. No, Jackson wasn't for her, but while there would come a day when she would send him on his way, it wasn't going to be tonight. Tonight she just wanted to feel that she wasn't alone. No matter how often she told herself she could handle things, that it was going to get easier, she just seemed to get in deeper. Small problems became big problems and big problems disasters, to the point that she was now in way over her head. She couldn't be a mother. She couldn't be a leader. She couldn't be a pioneer. If she needed proof of any of it, it was this last stand of a house she'd spent all their money on. The house that was falling down around them. The house with the snake-infested well.

Her stomach churned and bile filled her throat. A familiar taste filled her mouth. She knew the taste. Fear. Her new best friend. She didn't think Mac's people would find them way out here, but even if they could, there had to be an end to the running. And she'd hit hers. Rubbing her hands together, she tried again. "My instincts tell me there aren't going to be a lot more evenings like this."

Testing the knife edge on his finger, he looked over. "Changing the subject?"

She shrugged. "Why not?"

"Turns out a full belly is making me feel obliging." He set the knife and whetstone on the step. "So what would you like to talk about now?"

It was unadulterated curiosity that made her ask what she hadn't wanted to. "What do you do for a living?"

"Back to me, I see."

"Well, it's natural for me to be curious about the man who braved snakes to pull me out of the well."

"I've got news for you. If I'd known just how many snakes were in that well, I wouldn't have gone down."

But he had. The second time. "Why is that?"

"I hate snakes. There's a reason they represent everything evil in the Bible."

"You know about the Bible?"

His freshly washed hair caught a glint of the moonlight, framing his face in an illusion of pale light. It should have made him look womanly. Instead, it made him look . . . predatory. Like the manes of those lions she'd seen in picture books.

"Any particular reason I shouldn't?"

"I don't know. Maybe it's the guns, the hair, the knives." She spread her hands, wishing she could see his face clearly. "Just for some reason I never thought of you as a churchman."

"Most of the men in the Bible are warriors of some form or another. Moses. Job."

"Moses had a staff and Job the jawbone of an ass."

"Everyone has their battles to fight and nobody fights them unarmed."

She'd never thought of it that way. "That's true."

"Are you a churchgoer?"

"It's safe to say I spent a lot of time on my knees as a child." Apologizing for her existence. "I'm a bastard."

"And now?" Beyond that, he didn't react. Could he really not care?

"I'm not so willing to kneel anymore."

"Disillusioned on God?"

She shook her head. "No, I believe in God. It's the church's view of him with which I'm having a problem."

Surprisingly, he chuckled. "You ought to meet the Reverend Brad. He's got his own way of roping folk back into the fold."

"I don't think so."

"That's an awfully quick judgment."

"He's a reverend." She flicked the fringe. "They're all the same."

And she was tired of pretending otherwise.

He picked up the knife. "Funny, because I was thinking you two had a lot in common."

Branches rustled as a breeze blew up. Pulling her shawl closer about her, she watched the shadows dance. Every preacher she'd ever met, no matter what the denomination, was all about sin and consequence. She'd been told she was going to hell so many times for things over which she'd had no control, she'd quit listening.

"Now, what would make you think I would have anything in common with a reverend?"

Bracing his elbows on his knees, Jackson balanced the knife in his hand. "Because you, like him, are unique."

Her stupid heart did a flip-flop. Did he really think she was special? "Just how unique is he?"

"His pa was a preacher and about beat the religion out of him. He went outlaw. When he came to Cattle Crossing, he used the church as cover, but, well . . ." He flipped the knife. "Man's calling is a man's calling."

"What happened when everyone found out?"

"He tried to step down, but the town folk picked up some weapons and convinced him to stay."

"That sounds like quite a colorful story."

"The Rev's a colorful man and his wife is just as interesting. A good woman, but opinionated."

"She would have to be to have married such a man."

"She really didn't have much choice. Both she and the Rev had a shotgun at their backs."

Damn him. Now she was intrigued. "You're not going to leave it there, are you?"

That might just have been a slight smile on his lips. He flipped the knife rhythmically.

"Well, it seems Evie, the Rev's wife, is an artist and a bit of a rebel."

"What did she do?"

"I'll put this as delicately as possible. She did a portrait of the Rev without his knowledge and with all his parts . . . exposed."

"She painted him nude?"

"Buck naked." He flipped the knife higher. She caught her breath as it came down. He caught it deftly, casting her a glance and a smile when she gasped.

"Rumor is, the painting wasn't that flattering, her being an innocent and all. When her father found it and the Rev saw it, there was a lot of yelling. But for totally different reasons."

She covered her laugh with the shawl. "And he was an outlaw?"

"A quite successful one."

"But he's your reverend."

"You've got to understand Cattle Crossing. We don't get many preachers through and never the understanding kind like the Reverend Brad, so we don't take kindly to having him snatched out from under us."

"Even though he had a past."

He shrugged. The blade flashed. "Everybody who comes out here has a past."

The question just popped out. "Do you?"

"I was born here. My past is an open book." The knife clunked softly as he placed it on the step. Cotton whispered against cotton as he reached out. "What's your excuse, Mimi? What secrets are you hiding?"

Lean away. Lean away.

But she didn't. She stayed put, breath catching as his fingertips grazed her temple. Leaning in as a shivery tingle went down her spine, bounced back up, before spreading to her breasts. She kept her gaze straight ahead through sheer force of will. "I'm not hiding anything."

His thumb brushed her cheek. "I think you're lying."

Tingles kept prickling along her skin. Her breath kept catching on little notes and, in her mind, a tiny little whisper was beginning. *More.*

It whispered even louder when his hand dropped away.

She knew what it was, this feeling that was sneaking up on her. Her mother had warned her about it. Since as early as she could remember, her mother had told her all the ways that men would steal her innocence and her morals and leave her in an abyss, among devil's spawn. This was lust.

Except this didn't feel evil. This felt good and right. Clenching her fingers in her lap, she turned and faced him. It was hard to make out much of his face in the light, but his hair caught every pale shimmer, and again she had the impression of an archangel come to visit.

"Do you have a woman, Mr. Montgomery?"

"Now, honey girl, if you're asking about my women, don't you think we've gotten to the point where we can call each other by our first names?"

How to explain that it didn't seem proper to use his given name when considering a big step like propositioning him. "You haven't answered my question."

"No, I don't have a woman. And I'm going to insist you call me Jackson. Mr. Montgomery is my father's name."

"Your father's still alive?"

"Yup, and doing well."

"And your mother?"

There was a moment, and then, "She passed some years back."

Sympathy gave her an excuse to touch him. His thigh muscles were hard under her palm. Solid. Like him. "I'm sorry. You must miss her."

"I do. Pa was miserable for years, but, lately, he's been keeping busy courting a woman he met last fall."

She blinked. "At his age?"

His teeth flashed white when he laughed. He put the whetstone back in its pouch. He was leaving. "Honey, what makes you think there's an age when a man *stops* being a man?"

"I just assumed . . ." There was no good way to end that statement. No good way to keep her hand on his thigh. No good way to keep him here, just for a little longer.

"Well, you'd be wrong." Gathering up his possessions, he stood. "Right now, he's heading out to California to bring her back home."

"Do you have to go in right now?"

"Are you looking for some company?"

Was she? "Yes. Please. Just for a little while."

He sat back down. A little closer than before. "All right."

Closing her eyes, she let the still of the evening surround her with its calm. And, for the first time in a year, she relaxed. Touching his hand, she whispered, "Thank you."

"You're welcome."

"Didn't your mother ever warn you it was dangerous to sit out in the moonlight with a strange man?" Jackson asked a few minutes later.

Oh, dear heavens, had she. Mimi sighed and tilted her head back so she could see his face. "Constantly."

His brows went up, and again she was reminded of the endless dichotomy he presented, sinner yet savior. That push-pull combination that sucked her in. She had a feeling that even if he hadn't climbed down into that well after her, she would be in trouble with Jackson Montgomery.

"And yet here you are in the moonlight with me."

"Technically, the moon isn't fully up yet."

His chuckle wafted over her, digging in a little deeper, tugging a little harder against her reserve, freeing her just that little bit more from the rigid shell in which she'd encased her dreams.

"Clearly you haven't been courting much if you think that little detail makes a difference."

Imitating his confidence, she raised her eyebrows right back at him. It was a shame he probably couldn't see it, seated as she was in the shadow of the pillar. "Oh?"

His arm came around her shoulders. "No moonlight means no witnesses."

She figured that was where he was going. She leaned into his side. "Thank goodness you're an honorable man."

"And you think honor is enough to keep you safe?"

"I think, if it's not, nothing ever will be."

"Damn, woman, using a man's honor against him is just plain mean."

"I prefer to think of it as being honest."

"And that's what you want? My hands honestly tied?"

She smiled at the way he phrased that. And at the way his drawl reached out through the gloom and surrounded her in a sweet embrace that likely only existed in her mind but was sweet nonetheless. She cradled her elbow, remembering the dark, dank well. And that moment she'd seen his smile. And the sudden feeling that she could breathe. He'd made her feel safe. As the realization sank in, she realized she was still feeling safe. And maybe just a little brave. This time her sass didn't come from . . . fear. It came from inside. From her. It was a unique feeling. Freeing.

"I think, for now, it's a good idea."

"That's an interesting way to phrase things."

"It could be that you're an interesting man."

"Or?"

"I could just be so tired I don't know what's coming out of my mouth."

His chuckle was a soft prelude to his other arm coming around her. She should have expected it. After all, she'd led him on. When he tugged and scooted over, her hands balled into fists.

His hand covered her fist. "It's a hug, Mimi. Not a battle. No need for fists."

Then why did she feel more vulnerable than she ever had before in her life? "I didn't ask for a hug."

"I know."

But she was getting one anyway and it felt very, very good. Too good. So good, she couldn't stop her cheek from finding his shoulder. Nor the sigh from escaping her chest.

"It's been a long haul for you, hasn't it?" he asked.

She nodded and tried to glance back toward the house to make sure the children weren't watching, only to run into the barrier of his shoulder and the comfort of his hand against her cheek. It felt good.

"But the children and I are good now," she whispered. "We've got our home."

"Uh-huh."

"It was sheer luck we stumbled onto this place." She glanced around at the tromped-down yard. The shambles of what was the garden. "It does need some work."

"Yeah. About that."

She sighed again. "But it's going to have to wait. Repairs cost money and anything over a penny is a fortune just now."

"You're that strapped?"

"I wasn't lying when I said it just about took everything I had to buy this place."

Jackson sighed. It figured Half-Assed Bentley would unload the place on the one buyer Jackson couldn't just leave to their fate.

"But we've got our start now," she went on, oblivious to the position into which she was forcing him. "I've got something set back to help tide us over with hunting and fishing until we can get a garden in next spring."

"How much is a bit?"

She stiffened.

"Don't get your tail in a twist. I'm not after your money."

"I guess that was silly, considering that roll you shoved in my face earlier."

"I didn't shove."

"Enthusiastically presented, then. How's that?"

He could settle for that. "Better."

What he couldn't settle for was her moving away from him. He liked the soft press of her breasts against his chest. The trusting way she leaned against him. Hell, he liked being responsible for the relaxation taking over her muscles. Which was a warning sign for sure. Just as sure as he knew that, he knew he was going to ignore it. Because in this moment there was peace. That kind of peace he'd seen on Cougar's and Clint's—his best friends'—faces after they'd found their women. The kind that'd settled the Rev down. He'd never quite understood it, never wanted it, but he had a feeling if he could stand outside himself and look down at himself right now, he'd see the same contented expression on his face.

He shook his head.

"What?" Mimi asked, searching his expression.

"Nothing."

"You've got that odd expression on your face."

"Odd beats ugly."

She huffed. "You know darned well you're a very handsome man."

He leaned back, pulling his shadow away from her face. "How handsome?"

"You know."

The soft glimmer of her smile was the perfect complement to the peaceful nook they'd carved out of the evening. He couldn't pull his eyes away from her lips. "Well, when a man's out courting in the moonlight, he's hoping to rise a bit above 'You know.'"

He felt the little jump she hid behind her smile. Jackson was beginning to believe there was a lot Mimi hid. For a lot of reasons, all of which he wanted to discover.

"No retort?"

"Did you want one?"

Oddly enough, he did. "A good battle of wits fires the blood."

Her lips, those delectable, kissable lips, pursed. "Do you need help with that?"

Her eyes were luminous. The irises darker than normal, shadowed with mystery only the moon could cast, drawing him in.

"Nope. Not at all."

Her gaze flicked down to his mouth. Her breath drew in on a soft gasp. Her lips parted. His cock hardened. Hell no, he didn't need help getting it up. But he did need her and the energy arcing between them. He did need that connection that promised more. More heat. More passion. More pleasure. Sliding his finger across her neck, he cradled her nape in his palm. Her neck was delicate. Her lips plump and delectable. He had to taste her. To know whether she was as sweet as he imagined.

With a press of his thumb, he nudged her chin. Her head fell back naturally. He supported her gladly. It just took a new angle, a new approach, and her breath was his. Her mouth was his. Her kiss was his.

She kissed like a dream he'd once had back before he knew the world held evil. Like forbidden fruit. Like heaven imagined.

"Open your mouth."

She made him wait while her lashes fluttered against his cheek in a tantalizing prelude, but then her fingers wrapped around his forearm, anchoring herself, anchoring them, and her lips parted and all that delicious heat was his. His to savor, his to plunder. His.

The thought kept echoing in his mind as he cradled her closer. *Sweet. So sweet.*

His.

"Jackson . . ."

The plea into his mouth in a siren's song, luring him deeper into the swell of desire. His control unraveled in a growl of need. He tipped her back, pinning her with his thigh, pressing her against the stairs, ignoring the pain in his shoulder as he strove to get closer, to get more.

"Sweet. So sweet."

"Yes."

Her tongue teased his. Tempted him. Matched him, stroke for stroke. Caress for caress. Drawing him deeper. Passion imbued with innocence. She went to his head like whiskey. Smooth with a lingering burn. Addictive. Satisfying. He needed her closer.

"Closer, honey. Come closer."

She felt so good against him, the softness of her breasts, the curve of her hip. He wanted all of her. He twisted to get closer.

Pain shot down his back, bringing him to his senses. They were out in the open; any of the kids could come out any second. He pulled back. She blinked up at him uncomprehendingly. He'd never seen anything as sexy as Mimi dazed with passion. Smoothing his thumb over her lips, he eased her back to reality.

"I'm sorry. This isn't the time or place."

"For what?"

He eased her up. "Us."

"There is no us."

"Yet." When a man found a woman who called to the deepest part of him, he didn't let her go. Not before he discovered all there could be, which, looking at her now, might take a while.

She sat up and tugged at her dress, fussing with the buttons and patting down the skirt. "Oh, for Pete's sake, you're too old to believe a kiss leads to forever."

"No arguing with that."

She didn't look him in the eyes as she pushed her hair out of her face. "It's getting late."

Too late if she was planning to run.

"And we have the trip to town tomorrow," he agreed.

Standing, he held out his hand and helped her to her feet. "I plan on heading out early."

She stiffened immediately. "Ugh."

What did the woman have against town?

"Relax. It's just a trip to town. What could go wrong?"

Nine

❧

"I think living alone out there in the woods has warped your mind, honey."

Mimi looked at the blowsy redhead unimaginatively nicknamed Red sitting in the spartan kitchen of Cattle Crossing's brand-spanking-new house of ill repute and sighed inwardly. "Believe it or not, I've had that same thought."

At least twice before the sun had even come up. And not just because of that foolishness with Jackson last night. She hated going to town for the simple reason that a woman alone with a questionable past and three children in tow stood out. She didn't need to stand out. Especially here in Cattle Crossing, which was bigger and therefore had more traffic. Rivers Bend, which was small and off the beaten path, was risky enough, but it hadn't had what Jackson needed so they'd traveled the extra hour and landed at Cattle Crossing. And as soon as Mimi spotted the bustling saloon, she realized it didn't have what she needed, either. Women with a vested interest in attracting a variety of men for their livelihood.

"For sure, you need to think it again if you suppose we've got money for fancy dresses," the other woman at the table, who'd identified herself as Sunny, snapped as she dumped an amazing amount of sugar into her coffee.

This wasn't going well. Mimi gave her skirts a sharp tug down and winced when she heard the slight rip. Her clothes were getting threadbare and no amount of barter was going to fix that. But barter could help the children. They needed clothes. They needed food. And come the fall, they'd need schooling. She wanted them to blend with their peers, not sit as outcasts. That meant she needed money, and the only skill she had to sell was with a needle and thread. The only asset they had was what was in the box she'd stolen, but she couldn't touch that. Even if she could find someone with the knowledge to understand its contents, she couldn't sell it without alerting Mac to where she was.

A shudder went through her at that possibility. Mac's face as she'd last seen it filled her mind's eye, cold and hard, his gone-to-soft jowls quivering as he'd held her down, choking her, the image of his fist drawn back and then the world collapsing into that awful black. No, she wasn't touching the box anytime soon. That was their future, the only security they had, and, like all treasures, it had the power to save or destroy. Besides, she wasn't familiar enough with how one sold off treasure to bring it into the open without exposing herself and the children to predators.

"I don't design dresses."

Her attempt at creating anticipation fell flat. With a huff, Red leaned back in her chair and pulled her wrapper closed.

"Honey, it's nine o'clock on Saturday morning. I've been up all night. The ranch hands and workers will be rolling in at sunset. I've got a lot to do before I can finally sleep. I don't have time for nonsense."

"Especially as tonight is our busiest night," the blonde barked, as if losing patience with a lackwit.

As if Mimi didn't know she was running out of time. She'd been lucky to catch these two still up. "I apologize. I'd have been here earlier, but I swear it's easier to herd cats than it is to get three children out the door."

Red looked out the door to where Melinda Sue and Tony were just visible, sitting on the back stoop tossing a ball back and forth with Kevin. Curiosity lit her tired face as she looked back. "You're a bit young to have such a large family."

"Any fool can tell they're not kin," Sunny huffed.

"Make no mistake, we're family."

Sunny waved vaguely with her hand. "For whatever that gets you."

No one would ever understand what those children gave her.

"Best you hold up on that sweetening, Sunny," Red cautioned as the blonde reached for another spoonful of sugar. "You know Nina's been complaining about our mercantile account."

Sunny huffed. "I've got to have some pleasure."

"Your pleasure isn't what fills her purse."

Mimi sighed. She needed to get control of this. If they got distracted by an argument she'd never get the sale. "I wasn't talking about fancy dresses."

Red just looked at her. "Well, then, I'm not really sure what you are talking about."

Mimi studied the women more closely. Red's hair was

still vibrant, but gray was appearing at her temples. Sunny had crow's-feet starting at the corners of her eyes. Neither one was young. And there had been talk at the mercantile that a couple of new girls had been brought in. Young girls. Fresh meat. Competition. Red and Sunny had to be nervous. Dropping her former idea of persuasion, Mimi went straight for the kill.

"I heard a couple of younger women came into town last week."

"Younger just means hungry, not good." Sunny bit out her words with a pointed look at what encompassed Mimi's own lack of years.

The one area Mimi did not have insecurity was her talent. She could make a feed sack look good. And based on what these women were wearing, just a modicum of her skills would increase their profits. "It would be a mistake to hold my age against me."

"Says you."

"Yes, Miss Sunny. Says me."

Red took a sip of coffee and looked Mimi over from head to toe. Her frumpy robe gaped open, revealing some very impressive cleavage. An image popped into Mimi's head of a flowing undergarment. Lace with patches of strategically placed color.

"I'm a seamstress. A very talented seamstress with a very good eye for . . ." How best to say this? "Enhancing a woman's intimate bounty."

Sunny snorted. "Bounty?"

Red set her cup down. "No fancy dress is going to take a man's eyes off youth and beauty."

"Mine will." Her mother had supported them as a seamstress. As far back as Mimi could remember, she'd been stitching clothes. Starting with shortening hems and moving on to more complicated things. Tweaking dresses when the balance was off, gradually daring to create her own designs. With surprising success. Before she'd met and fallen in love with Mac, she'd planned on opening her own shop. After she'd met Mac, she'd discovered her innate talent for designing custom-made intimate apparel. Living in a whorehouse had turned out to be a truly life-expanding experience.

"Did you bring any samples?"

"No." She crossed her fingers as she lied. "I expect them any day, but I promise you a visual fantasy that will bring men from miles around."

"And after they get here, Miss Seamstress?"

"My name is Mimi."

"And after they get here, Mimi?"

"Then you bring to the table the one thing that you've got over those young girls—all those years of experience in pleasuring a man."

"Shit," Sunny muttered. "Doesn't take much to pleasure men."

Mimi eyed Sunny. "I may not look it, but I wasn't born yesterday."

"But I'm willing to bet that you weren't a working girl, either," Red countered.

"No, but I am the woman who can transform you into the walking fantasy men will crave." With a tilt of her head, she added, *"Over and over."*

Red eyed her up and down. "That's a lot of big talk for a lady whose skirts are threadbare."

It was too much to hope they hadn't noticed that.

"And drab," Sunny added.

Or that. "I have three children." She shrugged. "My money goes to them."

"Fair enough." Red motioned her on. "Tell me what kind of fantasy you see me as."

"A very sultry woman of mystery and heat to be fought over."

Red tried to look disgruntled, but Mimi could see she was pleased. "Burt won't be happy about his place getting busted up."

She dismissed that with a wave of her own. "He can charge your suitors for the expense."

"Suitors?"

"There's no sense in creating a half-assed fantasy."

She'd used the profanity deliberately. She wanted them comfortable with her.

"Amen to that."

"What about me?" Sunny demanded. "What kind of fantasy am I?"

Mimi studied Sunny, her inner eye seeing her strategically draped in hide-and-seek layers of icy blue. "An unattainable goddess to be wooed."

There was a long pause, then Red drawled, "Fire and ice?"

Mimi felt a spurt of hope. "Yes."

Sunny poked Red's arm. "Hear that, Red? I'll be a goddess?"

"Absolutely."

Red stood. She was an impressive woman, tall and big boned. Her peignoir was six inches too short, taking away from her assets rather than emphasizing them. "You know if you don't come through I'm going to kick your skinny ass from here to the next territory, right?"

Mimi dismissed the threat with a flick of her fingers. "Of course."

If she failed, she'd deserve to have her butt kicked.

"Go get dressed, Sunny," Red ordered.

"What for?" The other woman pouted.

Red rolled her eyes. "So we can get to the mercantile to pick out material before Clemit's wife nags him into going to church."

"Land's sake," Sunny huffed. "Sometimes I wish Clint McKinnley hadn't kicked the last shopkeeper's teeth down his throat for slapping his boy. A lack of scruples can make a woman's life easier."

Red's chair scraped across the floor. "Well, this one has a few, so let's get moving."

The women headed for the back stairs, Sunny's robe dragging on the rough plank floor. Mimi's confidence fluttered as they climbed the stairs. What if they got seduced by their beds and didn't come back down?

As soon as Mimi had the thought, the weight of all she was attempting settled upon her. Of what she'd become. She used to be so proper before she'd met Mac and given up everything for the security of the life he'd dangled in front of her like a lure. Everything Red had accused her of being. And now here she was standing in the middle of a whorehouse kitchen in her Sunday best, hoping to deprive a man of his religious salvation so she could go shopping this morning with two soiled doves. Rubbing her hands down the sides of her dress, she smiled.

Things were looking up.

"Mr. Montgomery! Mr. Montgomery! Come quick! Come quick!"

"Looks like someone wants your attention," Cougar said from where he leaned hipshot against the railing outside the small, traditional whitewashed church.

"And in a damn hurry, too," Reverend Brad said in his distinctly nonreverend way.

Jackson turned around, watching the boy run toward him. What the hell was wrong now? "That would be Tony."

"And the two coming up fast behind him?"

Jackson sighed. "Kevin and Melinda Sue."

"Any particular reason they would be calling your name like you're the second coming?" Cougar pushed away from the railing. He was an impressive figure. Taller than average, with broad shoulders, dark skin announcing his Indian ancestry, and a wild air that was only enhanced by the buckskins and moccasins he wore. As he straightened to his full height, his long black hair fell over his shoulders, casting his dark eyes in darker shadows.

"Probably the same reason you're letting your hair go long again." The Rev pushed his black hat back and squinted against the morning sun. He was not as tall as Cougar, but he wore the same wildness, which the white clerical collar around his neck couldn't disguise. "It's got to be a woman."

Cougar smiled. "Mara likes my hair."

Jackson snorted and narrowed his eyes. The hairs on the back of his neck tickled as he saw Tony's expression. "She's the one who asked you to cut it."

"And the one who asked me to grow it again." He jerked his chin, indicating the children. "So, what's her name?"

Jackson stepped down into the street. "Mimi Banfield."

Behind him he heard Brad mutter, "I knew it had to be a woman." Just as clearly he could imagine Cougar's sardonic grin as he said, "It was bound to happen sometime."

Tony was running so fast puffs of dust kicked up from his feet.

"Nothing's happening," Jackson countered. Even to his ears his words lacked conviction.

"Uh-huh."

"Mr. Montgomery!" Tony gasped, coming up alongside him and grabbing his shirtsleeve.

Jackson put his hand on Tony's. "Catch your breath, son, and tell me what's wrong."

"You've got to come."

Before he could ask why, Cougar and the Rev circled round. Tony stiffened, took a step back from the Rev, realized that only brought him closer to Cougar, and froze. His complexion blanched. Jackson couldn't blame him. Cougar was a big man with a sharply angular face that compelled with the ferocity of his namesake. The golden brown of his eyes only added to the appearance of a predator waiting to strike. The only other man Jackson knew who could match him for that predator-on-the-prowl impression was Cougar's cousin Clint.

"Where to?" Cougar asked in his succinct manner.

"Shit, you're scaring him, Cougar."

"Maybe he should be scared."

Tony stepped to the side. Cougar caught his arm. Tony gasped. That was all it took for Kevin. He launched himself at Cougar.

"Leave my brother alone!"

Melinda Sue went for Cougar's hand, grabbing hold and biting down with the ferocity of a badger, the fiercest of utterances coming from her throat.

"The hell now."

Cougar grabbed Melinda Sue by the back of her dress, lifting her off the ground.

"Bastard!" Tony snarled.

Jackson grabbed Tony before he could join the attack. Cougar switched his hold on the growling Melinda Sue, shifting her to his hip and catching her hand when she went for his eyes. He blocked Kevin's kick with his thigh. "Now, son, Mara would have a fit if you took to unmanning me."

Tony spit out a word so foul, even the Rev blinked. His ragged nails dug at Jackson's grip. His body shook with rage, as he clawed his way toward Melinda Sue. "If you hurt her, I'll kill you."

Cougar and the Rev stilled. Over Tony's head, their gazes met Jackson's.

Jackson slowly let Tony go. "It's too early in the day for murder, son."

The boy stood there, fists balled and feet braced. "Then make him let her go."

"Make him, Jackson," Kevin echoed.

"Yeah, makes him!" Melinda Sue joined in, swinging a tiny fist.

"There isn't a soul around that can make me do anything," Cougar drawled.

"Let her go, Cougar."

"It would break Jenna's heart to see this," the Rev said with a shake of his head.

"Mara's, too."

"I don't hurt little girls, boy." Cougar set Melinda Sue on her feet. She ran to Jackson's side and clung to his leg, her thumb stuck in her mouth, looking again so impossibly cherubic Jackson's heart caught.

"Tony, Kevin, and Melinda Sue, these are my friends." With a wave of his hand he indicated the men. "This here's Cougar McKinnley, and that's the Reverend Brad."

Tony took in Brad's blond hair, black hat, good looks,

and gun strapped to his hips. "You don't look like a preacher."

The Rev pushed his hat back and smiled. "So I've been told."

"Gentlemen," Jackson continued, "this is Mimi's family."

"Mimi!" Tony gasped, spinning around and grabbing Jackson's arm as he remembered. "You've got to come. They're going to kill her!"

The scene when they got to the mercantile was utter chaos. Two women wrestled in the corner of an aisle, while another yelled encouragement to someone he couldn't see. Clemit was in another corner with his hands held up, looking as if he couldn't decide if he wanted to wade in or run.

"Come on, get in there!" a redheaded woman shouted.

Cougar looked over at Jackson. "Is yours winning or losing?"

The women bumped into a display table. The barrel teetered and tipped. Flour exploded everywhere.

"Oh, hell no!" Clemit hollered.

"I'm not sure yet."

"That doesn't bode well."

"Well, whoever she is, this is going to cost you a pretty penny," Brad observed.

"You're right about that," Clemit growled, overhearing.

"Shut up, Clemit."

The place was a mess. So were the women. As far as Jackson could tell, Mimi was holding her own.

"You going to break it up?" the Rev asked.

"Not yet." It was just too fascinating, watching his

prim-and-proper siren lose her decorum so much she was brawling.

"She's got a hell of a right," Cougar noticed.

"Definitely wife material," the Rev observed.

"Hold on." Jackson held up his hand. "No one said anything about a wife."

Even Clemit gave him a pitying look. "No man pays for damages for someone he's not involved with."

"I'm setting a new tradition."

The Rev caught a stray projectile. It was a jar of jelly. "Just keep in mind there's been a string of engagements lately. Evie says the church is almost booked up for the summer."

"There's always fall," Cougar offered too helpfully.

"And you could always shut up."

Clemit groaned as the pickle barrel tipped. The scent of vinegar filled the interior. "This is really going to cost you."

Jackson covered Melinda Sue's ears. "Damn."

Insults flew as fast as objects. "Ignorant" and "fat" were the ones he caught best. And then, "Oh, my God! You're too stupid to breathe!"

"That one's mine."

"She's not much bigger than Mara," Cougar observed, arms folded across his chest.

No, she wasn't. Mimi landed another solid punch.

"Someone ought to tell her that so she stays out of trouble."

Oh, hell no. "I like her just as she is."

And surprisingly he did.

"Yup." The Rev set the jar down on the counter. "He's a goner."

Cougar nodded. Jackson elbowed him in the ribs.

The blonde grabbed a knife from the sheath on her calf.

The Rev grabbed Melinda Sue from Jackson. "Time to break this up."

Jackson leapt over the counter. Cougar was right behind him. Wrapping his arm around Mimi's waist, he hauled her back. Cougar snagged the other woman by the back of her dress and held her off the ground. Both were still swinging.

"Damn," the redhead said. "Just when this was getting interesting. Might just have been the first time Sunny lost a fight."

Removing the knife from Sunny's hand, Cougar ordered her to settle down.

The knife clattered to the floor.

Jackson heard the Rev order the kids outside. Mimi twisted in his grip. "You need to settle down, too."

She tried to head butt him. "The heck I will."

"The heck you won't."

Across the aisle, Sunny twisted around and went for Cougar's face with her sharp, red nails. A simple "I wouldn't" stopped her cold. Jackson wasn't surprised. When Cougar pulled out that low growl, people listened.

Pushing her hair back from her face, Sunny got a gander at who held her and suddenly melted in his arms. "Well, hello."

Mimi snorted in disgust. "Oh, for the love of Pete."

Jackson couldn't help but laugh.

The redhead summed it all up. "Lord have mercy, Sunny. You don't have a lick of sense."

Cougar shook his head. "Listen to your friend."

"You can't blame a girl, Red." Sunny ran a finger down his arm. "A fine man like this doesn't come into this town too often."

"I come in often enough."

"He just doesn't stop over at the saloon," Jackson elaborated.

Red snorted. "Don't you ever pay attention to anything, Sunny? That there's one of the McKinnley men."

Sunny looked up at Cougar and smiled enticingly. "McKinnley, huh?"

"Don't," Cougar warned.

Sunny slid her hand seductively up his forearm, his biceps, his shoulder. Cougar dropped her on her ass.

Red shook her head. "He told you not to do it."

Sunny rubbed her butt. "A woman's got to try."

"How many times have I told you to know who you're dealing with before you make a move?"

"I suppose you know who he is?"

"Let me introduce you. That angelic-looking fella holding Mimi is Jackson Montgomery." She waved toward Brad. "You know the Rev."

The Rev helped her up. "Morning, Sunny."

"Morning."

"In case you still don't understand," Red continued, "that one there is Cougar McKinnley."

Sunny blanched.

"They all ride together, and I'm guessing little Miss Mimi is under their protection."

Sunny swallowed hard. "I didn't mean anything. She called me fat—"

"I did not!"

"For the record," Jackson interjected calmly, "it wouldn't matter to me what she called you. If you'd hurt her, I'd take it personally."

Mimi turned to glare at him. "I don't need your protection."

There was a red spot on her cheek. It would likely bruise. "Tough."

"I was holding my own."

"Didn't look that way to me," Red offered, grabbing a peppermint stick out of a toppled jar.

"And to think I wanted to help you," Mimi grumped.

"You didn't want to help anything. You were just making a business deal."

"A business deal?" Jackson loosened his hold and looked around at the disaster of the mercantile. "I hope it was going to be a lucrative one."

"I'm not paying for it." Mimi pointed at Sunny. "She pulled a knife on me."

The Rev nodded to Sunny. "Any reason for that?"

"She called me fat."

Mimi slammed her hands on her hips. "For the last time, doubting your stated measurements is not a declaration of fat."

"Hold on," Cougar interrupted. "Why were you wanting her measurements?"

He took the words right out of Jackson's mouth.

"We have a business deal."

"*Had* a business deal."

"She's still got it with me," Red said around her peppermint stick. "If the woman can sew anything like she fights, she ought to make me a pretty penny."

"You're going into business with—" Jackson stopped and changed his wording. "These ladies?"

Cougar folded his arms and leaned back against the counter. "Looks like your woman's going to give the Rev's a run for her money in unconventionality."

"I'm not his woman."

"She's not my woman."

They said it at the same time. No one looked convinced.

From the doorway came a cheery revelation. "I saw them kiss."

"Go back outside, Melinda Sue."

"But I did."

The Rev grabbed four peppermint sticks and carried them to the door. "How about we have some candy while the adults talk."

Melinda Sue's eyes grew big. When he went outside, she followed right behind him.

As soon as they were out the door, Cougar observed, "I notice no one called her a liar."

Mimi stepped back and waved away the challenge. "What is it with men thinking a kiss is a claim?"

"Do you go around kissing a lot of people?" Cougar asked.

"No, I don't, so I'll thank you to keep that expression off your face."

Jackson knew from the crook of his brow that Cougar was amused. "And just how do you plan to make that happen?"

Mimi pointed to Jackson. "Apparently, that's his job."

Cougar chuckled. "I like her, Jackson."

"Glad to hear it."

"It's all wonderful that you're happy, but what about me?" Sunny whined. She spread her skirts wide, revealing the flour stains and the tears. "My dress is ruined!"

Mimi shot right back, fists balled, "So is mine."

Sunny frowned. "Mine was more expensive."

"Mine was more needed. What's your point?"

Jackson caught her hand just in case she decided to

throw that punch she had brewing. "I've got a feeling you two could argue this all day."

Red wandered over to the other corner of the store where the fabric was displayed. The only corner of the store that was intact. She opened a chest and pulled out a bolt of bright red fabric. "Seems to me you're arguing about something that's easily fixed."

"Nothing's getting fixed," Clemit cut in, "until I get paid for all this damage." He looked directly at Jackson.

"I'll cover it."

"Then I'll go get the broom." He did just that.

The Rev came back in the building. "So now that things have settled down, do you want to introduce me to your friend, Jackson?"

"Mimi, this is the Reverend Brad. Rev, this is Mimi Banfield."

The Rev tipped his hat as if the woman looking at him wasn't just a pair of eyeballs caked in flour.

"Nice to make your acquaintance." He held out his hand.

Mimi reluctantly gave him hers.

The Rev looked around the destroyed store. "Now that tempers have calmed, what will it take to get you fine ladies out of the mercantile before Clemit bursts a blood vessel?"

Mimi's jaw set. "I need Sunny's measurements."

"I told you—"

Mimi threw up her hands. Flour flew everywhere. Jackson sneezed. Cougar laughed and the Rev stepped clear of the dust.

"What is wrong with you? Why can't you understand it doesn't matter what your measurements are? When I'm done creating your lingerie, you're going to look gorgeous and nobody's going to be able to take their eyes off you, so what do you care what the numbers say? All you need to anticipate is the magic I'm going to create with the beauty that you have."

"I suppose . . ."

"Goddess, remember?"

While Mimi glared at Sunny, Cougar looked at Jackson. Jackson looked at the Rev. They all looked at Mimi, but Red was the one to sum it up.

"And that, gentlemen, is a woman who can turn this town on its ear."

Ten

It hadn't been her plan to meet anyone in Cattle Crossing with a swollen eye, a torn dress, and caked in so much flour that she poofed with every step. It certainly hadn't been her plan to meet some of Jackson's closest friends in such a state. And it was absolutely the thing of nightmares to be sitting naked in a bathtub filled with fragrant bubbles in the upstairs of Clint McKinnley's comfortable house while those friends' wives sat around pelting her with questions.

But she was, and it was all Jackson's fault that she was now subjected to a very enthusiastic, well-meaning inquisition. If he'd just been satisfied with the wagon available in Rivers Bend, she wouldn't be sitting here right now wishing a hole would open in the floor and swallow her up.

"So Jackson just wandered up to your house one day and saved you from a well full of snakes?"

She thought the speaker was Mara, Cougar's wife. It

was hard to imagine this petite, vivacious woman with brown eyes, cinnamon red hair, and delicate frame with the ferocious-looking Cougar, but there was no doubt that she was adored by her big husband. And that she adored him back. It did, however, boggle the mind. And not because Mimi didn't really believe in love. But because she couldn't imagine a love that big.

"Yes."

Mara sighed and put her hand on her very pregnant stomach. "That's so romantic."

Mimi discreetly piled bubbles up around her chest. "Actually, it was completely terrifying."

"I'm sorry, that was insensitive. Pregnancy makes me emotional. Were you hurt?"

"My arm and my pride took a heck of a beating. Jackson took the worst of it. If that snake had gotten all its fangs into him instead of a glancing bite, he'd be dead."

"But it didn't and now you're here. Together."

It did sound romantic when Mara said it that way.

"Busting up the local mercantile," Evie, the Rev's wife, added dryly.

Mimi groaned. "I might never live that down."

"Live it down?" Mara gasped. "Heck, I'm hoping you'll top it."

The door opened, and a tall, statuesque, blond woman limped into the room. Mimi smiled. There was something inherently welcoming about Jenna McKinnley. She just radiated kindness. The complete opposite of Evie. Whereas Jenna was sweet and calm, Evie was all quick wit, optimism, and restless perception. Mimi could see how she fit so well with the Rev. Just as she could see why Clint would love Jenna.

Setting the tray of tea down on the table, Jenna shook

her head at Mara. "I thought we agreed to ease into these conversations. You're going to scare Mimi away before we have a chance to convince her that Jackson's worth her time."

They were matchmaking?

"She'd be easier to convince if the man didn't insist on sporting all that curly hair," Mara grumbled.

Jenna smoothed her hand over her neatly coiled hair. "I would love to have his hair. Mine's as straight as a stick."

Pouring tea into the four cups, she handed one to Mara.

Mara rolled her eyes. "That's the problem. It looks like it belongs on a woman."

"Oh, please," Evie interjected as Jenna set a cup in front of her. "No amount of hair could disguise that man's masculinity."

For some reason, Mimi felt compelled to defend Jackson. "His hair suits him."

Evie clapped her hands. "Oh, good. Someone on my side!"

Mimi blinked. "We have sides?"

"We certainly do." Taking the tongs from the tray, Evie added a sugar cube to her tea. "I've been trying to convince that man to sit for a portrait forever, but every time I broach the subject, he threatens to see the barber."

"Why can't you paint him with short hair?"

Evie was shaking her head before she finished the question. "That won't work at all. I want to capture that whole dichotomy of beautiful wavy hair and utter masculinity. It's very unique."

Yes, it was, and so was he, but being unique didn't obligate him to sit for a portrait. "But Jackson doesn't want his portrait done."

"Evie doesn't accept that," Mara explained.

"That's because it's ridiculous." Evie set her cup and saucer smartly on the table. "His portrait would be fabulous."

Jenna hid a smile and placed her cup on the small table, too. "Evie doesn't understand that not everyone wants to be immortalized."

Evie huffed. "I repeat. Because that's ridiculous."

"Is it time to change the subject yet?" Mara asked, scooting back in her chair, trying to get comfortable. With a grunt, she leaned back and propped her cup on her belly.

Jenna pulled the wooden tray over. In the middle sat a cloth-covered plate. "Absolutely."

"So, Mimi, what was your first thought when you saw Jackson in that well?"

"Mara," Jenna chided. "Mimi might not want to discuss her relationship with Jackson."

"She doesn't have to answer if she doesn't want to."

"Mara's got a point," Evie countered. "So, do you feel like sharing, Mimi?"

Surprisingly, she did.

"When Jackson came down into that well and lit that match, I thought for a second that God had sent one of his archangels to my rescue. But then . . ." She sighed dramatically. "Jackson opened his mouth."

Evie snorted and grabbed a napkin. Mara and Jenna laughed right along with her.

When she caught her breath, Jenna wiped her mouth. "That was a good one."

"Speaking of good . . ." Evie peeked under the napkin on the tray.

"What?" Mara asked, struggling to get out of her chair. "What else did she bring?"

"Hush." Still smiling, Jenna waved them quiet. "I baked

a cake today, but if you don't lower your voice, Clint will be up here and we'll have to fight for that cake."

Everyone clustered around the tray. All except Mimi. She was trapped amidst her rapidly disappearing bubbles in the slippery tub.

"There's cake?" It'd been years since she'd had cake. "What kind?"

Mara listed to the side and stretched for the napkin. With the tip of her finger she managed to get a peek. "It's her mocha walnut chocolate torte."

A collective moan went around the room.

"But there's only one piece."

Another moan followed the first. But this one was of disappointment.

Jenna shrugged. "Clint and Cougar got into the kitchen when I was putting Bri down for her nap. It's a big piece, though." Mara stretched a little farther, clearly angling for a taste. Jenna slapped her hand. "And it's for Mimi."

Mara eyed Mimi assessingly. "You wouldn't want to deprive a pregnant woman of cake, would you?"

Such generosity would likely gain her a place with these women, and Mimi might've considered it, but just then Jenna lifted the napkin off the cake and she had a glimpse of the prize she'd be surrendering. The thick slice that sat on that pure white plate sported not one but four glorious layers of chocolate decadence.

"Not a prayer."

Mara's beautiful brown eyes creased at the corners with laughter before she attempted the most pathetically sad expression in human history. "But I'm pregnant. The deprivation could send me into premature labor."

"I'll chance it."

Evie harrumphed. "You've been moaning for a week

that you're overdue and ready to burst. As a matter of fact, rumor has it that you were considering seducing your husband just to bring on labor."

Mara didn't look at all guilty. "Seducing a man is only a sin if one isn't married."

"True, but I'm pretty sure trying to talk Mimi out of that piece of cake is."

Mara switched tactics. "Would you take a bribe?"

"No."

"Well, darn."

Jenna picked up the big kettle off the fire and limped to the foot of the tub to add more water. Mimi immediately felt guilty. Even though Jenna had explained the limp was from an old injury, she still felt uncomfortable. Jenna waved away her concern.

"If it makes you all feel better, imagine how much Clint is going to moan when he finds that slice missing. Word is, he's been hiding the cake from Gray. Piece by piece, though, it's been disappearing."

"And now it's gone." Evie chortled.

The ladies chuckled.

Warmth swirled around Mimi's toes. It was heavenly. She'd never been so pampered. And despite her nervousness, she'd never been so amused. She'd also never been so uncomfortable. Friends weren't something that she'd been encouraged to have growing up. This kind of camaraderie was new. And scary. And tempting. Why did everything forbidden always have to be so tempting?

Jenna huffed. "It's the competition they enjoy." She brought the slice over and handed it to Mimi along with a fork. "Don't take any of us too seriously, Mimi. We're just very happy that Jackson's finally found someone."

Steam swirled as Mimi reached for the plate. The scent of chocolate wafted up to tease her senses. Saliva flooded her mouth and her stomach rumbled. Any hope she had that no one would notice died with Mara's next comment. "Don't worry, we all react that way to Jenna's cooking. She has a restaurant in town and is becoming quite famous for her baked goods."

It was Jenna's turn to blush. "It's nothing."

Mimi took the first bite. She might not have had cake for years, but her taste buds remembered what it was supposed to taste like, and this far surpassed the most fantastic of memories. As all that buttery frosting and chocolate melted on her tongue in a perfect symphony of flavor, she had to disagree. "This is fabulous."

"Worth being the center of gossip in Cattle Crossing for the next few months?" Mara asked hopefully. "Pregnancy has so stunted my fun."

"Oh, yes."

Jenna limped back to her chair. As she sat down, she asked, "Did you really brawl with a prostitute?"

"I was merely getting her measurements."

"For what?" Mara asked. "A casket?"

The cake was wonderful. The laughter even more so.

"I'm a seamstress."

"Who deals in black eyes," Evie boasted. "I heard Sunny won't be able to work for at least a week."

Mara grinned. "I'm really going to like you."

"At last, someone who'll be more notorious than me," Evie added.

"And me," Mara interjected.

"And me," Jenna echoed before going on to say, "Which is just another sign."

Their assumption that she and Jackson were a couple made Mimi feel like a fraud. "There's nothing between Jackson and me."

Jenna raised her eyebrows. "Melinda Sue says you've kissed."

Melinda Sue had a big mouth. "Do all of *you* marry the men you kiss?"

Everyone but Jenna said "no," which had everyone in turn looking inquiringly at her. Jenna immediately blushed and rubbed her thigh. As Mimi was beginning to notice, being the center of attention made Jenna uncomfortable.

Everyone spoke at once.

"Are you saying your first husband never kissed you?"

"Clint's the only man you've ever kissed?"

"Oh, Jenna." Mara waddled over and hugged her. "I'm so sorry."

Jenna was clearly having none of it. "Why are you sorry?" she asked serenely. "It thrills me to the soles of my feet that I can give my husband that. I adore that man."

"Does he adore you?" The question just popped out. Not that a woman loving a man was an unusual thing in Mimi's world, but a man loving a woman back to the point she melted at the thought of him—Mimi had never seen anything close to it.

Jenna's smile was a breath-catching combination of confidence and bliss. "With every breath he takes."

She wanted to be loved like that, Mimi realized. She wanted to smile like that. To know from the top of her head to the soles of her feet that she was adored. For who she was, as she was, because only that kind of love could put that expression on a woman's face. "I'm glad."

"Damn it." Mara dabbed at her eyes. "Now I'm going to

cry again. I swear, if this baby doesn't come soon, I'm going to be a mental disaster."

"What does Doc say about the delivery?" Evie asked.

"What does Doc know?"

"Apparently a heck of a lot more than you're sharing."

Mara cupped her belly protectively. "I'm going to be fine and so is the baby." She glared at all three women. "And if any of you say one word to Cougar that hints the opposite, I'm going to shoot holes in all your drawers every time you hang them on the line."

The next bite of cake caught in Mimi's throat on a choke of laughter. She could picture that.

"Now, Mara. You know we're just concerned. You had such a rough time before—"

The atmosphere changed. Humor fled to be replaced by concern. Mara held up her hand.

"Please, don't say it. You'll jinx me and I refuse to be jinxed." Mara rubbed her belly. "I will give Cougar a child this time."

Jenna squeezed her hand. "Don't do this to yourself. Don't make it all-or-nothing in your head. All Cougar wants is you."

Mara shook her head. "Every man wants a son."

"Your man wants you."

Mara bit her lip as her face crumpled. Turning into Jenna's shoulder, she whispered, "But I want his child."

The pain contained in that utterance filled the room, bonding them together in an instant of common struggle. Mimi's heart wrenched.

"Oh, Mara," Jenna whispered.

Mimi turned her face away. She shouldn't be here. Be part of this. It wasn't her place. Passing Evie the cake, grab-

bing the jar of shampoo, Mimi sank down. Submerging
under the water provided her with at least an illusion of
distance. Above her their voices rumbled, carrying on the
conversation with that intimate camaraderie that lured even
as it intimidated. She didn't know how to belong here. Anywhere. She was the outsider. The one who watched from
afar and wove daydreams of how it could be. She was never
the center of attention. At least not the happy kind.

She stayed under longer than she needed, holding the jar
inelegantly above her because she hadn't thought out anything beyond getting away from that discomfort. Eventually, she had no choice but to surface. As she feared, when
she did, they were all staring at her. Water dripped into her
eyes. She blinked it away.

"I'm sorry." The foolish apology just popped out, gar-
nering more attention and more awkwardness.

Jenna sighed and took the jar from her hand. "No, we're
the ones who're sorry. You don't know us, and all we've
done is bully you and bombard you since Jackson brought
you through the door."

"And cry tears all over you," Mara added wryly.

"It's all right, but I think you should have the cake."

"We'll all share."

"Sit up," Jenna ordered, moving behind her.

"Oh," Mimi said over her right shoulder, "I can do it."

"It" being washing her hair, but she might as well have
been talking to herself. Cool cream plopped on her head.

"Hush. I'm apologizing."

By washing her hair? "Um, thank you."

Jenna was thorough and efficient. Mimi dug her nails
into her palms, counting to one hundred to avoid jumping
from the warm water. The tub was too small, the room too
crowded. Her emotions too raw. Her defenses, like the bub-

bles that were disappearing with a silent disregard for her preferences.

"Jenna?" Evie observed.

"What?"

"You're making Mimi uncomfortable."

"Oh."

What was Mimi supposed to say now? Holding the washcloth to her chest, she confessed. "I've been bathing myself for a long time."

Jenna stepped back, her limp giving her steps an awkward-sounding rhythm that further jangled Mimi's nerves.

"I'm sorry."

Evie gathered the stack of towels and set them by the tub. "I bet you've done it in privacy, too."

What could she say except the truth? "Yes."

"Darn it, Evie!" Mara cursed, struggling to get out of the chair. "Couldn't you have had this revelation before I sat down again?"

"Apparently not." Evie held out her hands. "Come on, Moby-Dick. I'll help you up."

"Don't think I don't know you're calling me a whale. I read that darn book."

"And did you enjoy it?"

Mara huffed. "I'm saving that for the book discussion. But safe to say, I think Ahab needed a kick in the butt."

"Mara always brings an interesting perspective to book club," Jenna whispered to Mimi as she put the cork back on the shampoo.

"Has she read *The Whale*, Jenna?" Mara asked over her shoulder as Evie half encouraged, half pushed her out the door.

Jenna raised her eyebrows. Mimi shook her head.

"Nope."

"She should. I bet she'd want to kick Ahab in the butt, too."
Mimi couldn't help a smile at the way Mara delivered
that decree.

"You just want someone to argue on your side for once
when we discuss motivation," Evie teased.

"Just for that, I'm taking this cake with me, by the way."
They continued to bicker as they left the room.

"You'll have to forgive Mara for her enthusiasm," Jenna
apologized as their voices faded. "The doctor has put her
on bed rest because of complications. On top of that, she
has to stay here in town with Evie just in case something
goes wrong again."

Again? "I didn't take offense."

"Good. Being separated from Cougar and being forced
to be still are the two worst things in the world for her, and
she's having to deal with both at the same time." Jenna bit
her lip and rubbed her thigh. "It wears on her."

"I understand. I'm not myself, either." That was an un-
derstatement.

This got her a long, considering look. "I can understand
that." With a last rub of her thigh, Jenna headed for the
door. She paused when she reached it, one hand on the jamb.
Mimi braced herself for whatever was coming. "I know the
water's getting cold and you want nothing more than to
rinse that shampoo out of your hair. I also know this is none
of my business, but Jackson saved my life once and Clint's
more than that. His happiness means a lot to me. So, if you
really do just think of him as 'a man you once kissed,'
please don't lead him on."

As if she'd even know how. "Jackson's a grown man."

Jenna drew herself to her full height. Her fingers
drummed on the wood. "Who's smitten with you."

Mimi didn't know what to do with that information. Should she believe it? Run from it? Her life was so complicated right now that Jackson caring for her was just one more thing to juggle when she already felt she had too many balls in the air. She couldn't even muster anger. But she wanted to muster something. Anything. She was just so darned tired.

"I'll keep that in mind."

Jenna hesitated a second longer, as if there was more she wanted to say, but with a last tap on the jamb, she settled for, "Thank you."

The door closed behind her with a soft click, leaving Mimi alone with her thoughts. And her fears.

The saloon was deserted this time of day.

"Looks like we've got our pick of tables," Brad said.

"The one in the back corner looks good."

"You read my mind. Far enough from the stench of the spittoon yet still affording a premium view of the occupants and the door."

As they passed the bar, Jackson snagged a bottle of whiskey off the counter and motioned to the bartender for four glasses.

"You ever miss that fancy life of yours?"

"Not for a minute."

"You're happy being a preacher?"

"I always was a preacher. I just used different methods of persuasion. That had to change."

"Bullets do have a way of limiting the congregation."

Brad's lips tilted in a half smile. "Exactly."

Jackson pulled out a chair. "Are Cougar and Clint coming?"

"Right after they finish up at the bank." Brad shook his head. "Still can't get over how respectable those two have gotten."

"Isn't that a little like the pot calling the kettle black?" Jackson asked. "It wasn't too long ago that you were the richest bounty out there."

"My motto has always been if you're going to sin, sin big."

"And now you're the Reverend Brad Swanson."

Brad smiled, revealing even white teeth and the charm that had allowed him to escape capture all those years as an outlaw. "And now I'm the Rev. Which only proves God does work in mysterious ways."

Jackson pulled the cork from the bottle. "Who drinks."

Brad chuckled and nodded. "Who drinks."

"A lot."

Sunlight flashed as the swinging doors opened, brightening the gloomy interior. Two men entered the saloon, their silhouettes unmistakable in similarity in height and breadth of shoulder. Jackson set the other two glasses out before filling all four. As Cougar and Clint reached the table he tipped his hat. "Afternoon, gentlemen."

"Afternoon."

"Howdy."

Clint sat kitty-corner to the Rev. Cougar grabbed a chair from the neighboring table, turned it around, and straddled it. "So what are we celebrating and who's paying?"

Pushing the glasses over, Clint announced, "I don't know what we're celebrating, but the drinks are on me today."

Cougar smiled. "In that case, I'll have two."

The first toast as always was silent, a glass raised in remembrance of those who'd passed. The second in friendship for those that remained. It was a long-standing tradition between them, the ritual as bonding as the emotion. It was a hard life out here, where friends tended to be few and enemies were plentiful. Good people, and good friends, were respected in death as well as in life.

"So, fess up. Where'd you find the woman?" Clint asked, taking a sip of his whiskey.

"Believe it or not, at the bottom of a well."

"Now, that has all the makings of an interesting story," Brad said, swirling the remaining whiskey in his glass.

It did. Jackson just wasn't sure yet how much of it he wanted to share. There was something different about Mimi. Something inexplicably appealing about her smile. Something addictive about her laugh. Something devastating about her tears. It wasn't that he was an unfeeling man on his worst days. It was just, with Mimi, everything was sharper. More intense. More . . . right.

"You going to spill it or make us guess?" Cougar asked.

The next table over, a gambler played solitaire to pass the time before the evening crowd piled in. The swinging doors opened one more time. A drunk stumbled in. His staggering gate perfectly matched the erratic timbre of Jackson's emotions. He finished his drink and poured another.

"Like that, is it?" Cougar asked, holding out his glass. Jackson topped it off.

"When I crossed the ridge, I noticed smoke coming from Half-Assed Bentley's place. I rode over to check it out."

"And?"

"The children were frantic. Mimi had fallen down the well, and it was filled with rattlers. When I got there, they were about to drop a lamp down."

"It's a wonder they didn't burn her alive."

"It wasn't lit, but yeah."

"Was she hurt?"

"Her arm."

"And you?"

"Nothing I won't recover from."

"Uh-huh." Brad leaned back in his chair. "Kevin was impressed with how you took on all those snakes. About a hundred, to hear him tell it."

Jackson rolled his shoulder. "Kevin has an active imagination."

"What were a woman and kids doing out there in the first place?"

"Bentley sold it to them."

Clint frowned. "I'm going to have to have a talk with Bentley. He had to know selling that place to a woman and children was murder."

Jackson forced his fingers to relax on the glass. "You'll have to get in line."

With a nod Clint acknowledged his right.

Cougar motioned to the bartender for another bottle before observing, "From what I've seen, Mimi's a scrapper."

"And that's bad?"

"Hell no." Cougar nodded thanks to the bartender for the bottle. He poured himself a drink. "It'd take a scrapper to keep pace with you."

"Maybe I don't want anybody to pace me."

Brad tossed back a shot. "Well, you sure don't want anybody you have to drag along."

Maybe not. Maybe so. Truth be told, he hadn't given much thought to what kind of partner he'd want in life. He'd just gotten to the realization that he was tired of drifting. "Honestly, I don't know what I want."

"If that's the case, you got no business playing with a woman who's responsible for three children."

He took a sip of whiskey. Rolling it through his mouth consideringly before swallowing. "I know that."

Cougar studied him through narrowed eyes. "But you're not going to leave her alone."

Jackson spun the glass in a slow circle, weighing his conscience against his desires. "Probably not."

"Damn, Jackson."

"I know."

"Jen and I can take in the kids," Clint offered.

"She'd never leave them." And he wasn't sure he'd want her to.

"She's young for that much responsibility," Brad said.

"She's young for everything."

Brad shook his head. "She's not too young for you, if that's what you're trying to imply, but I definitely get the impression that she's in over her head."

"Me, too. And she's running from something."

"Or someone." That was from Clint.

Jackson looked up. Clint was the spitting image of his cousin Cougar. If you looked closely, his face was a little softer in the angles. But that was the only place where they differed. Both the McKinnleys were tough as nails. "What makes you say that?"

"I didn't think much of it, but a week ago a couple men came through asking questions about a woman with kids. Claimed they were trying to catch up with a wagon train."

"You didn't believe them?"

Clint shrugged. "They didn't look like family men."

"Are they still around?"

"They moved on a few days ago."

"Did they leave an address or way to be reached?"

Clint reached into his pocket and pulled out a piece of paper. He handed it to Jackson. "You might take a drink before opening it."

Jackson didn't want to drink. He wanted the truth. The paper crinkled as he unfolded it. A sketch in black unfolded along with type. A familiar layout to a man in his line of work. He looked up at Clint. "She's wanted?"

"From the size of the reward, I'd say pretty badly."

Shit.

Jackson smoothed the flyer out on the table. It wasn't the best likeness, but the artist had nailed the eyes and the mouth. That kissable come-hither mouth. "A five-thousand-dollar reward for theft? What did she do, rob the pope?"

"Whatever she did, she pissed somebody off."

Brad held out his hand. "May I?" He read quietly. "I recognize the name of who's distributing the reward."

"And?"

"I wouldn't hand a rattlesnake over to him, but that's not the worst of your problems."

"Spill it, Rev."

Brad tapped the paper. "She's not only wanted by this man, she's also married to him."

Eleven

It was funny how two days could shake up a person's life and make mincemeat of all their plans. Standing on Evie's whitewashed front porch, a bag chock-full of donated clothing and other items from Jenna and Mara at her feet, Mimi waited for Jackson to bring the new buckboard around.

The spontaneous visit was over. The Rev and Evie had been generous hosts, but they were going home. From the side yard, she could hear the children's laughter as they played a game of tag. The sun was shining and a cooling breeze was blowing. She should be happy, but the last forty-eight hours weighed on her spirit like lead. It'd been two days since the fight with Sunny. Two days in which she'd bounced between enjoyment and dread.

It was nobody's fault but her own that she couldn't land on a single emotion. She'd put up the walls over the years and hidden behind them, never understanding that she had been building not a shelter but a prison. But she understood it now. She understood a lot of things now. She used to tell herself she didn't have enough experience living with other people to get along with them and that was why she preferred her own company. But the reality she'd discovered was that what she was lacking wasn't experience so much as trust. She simply didn't trust anyone.

She worried when Jenna invited the children over that she was stealing their love. She worried every time Jackson left the room that he wasn't going to come back. She worried if she let herself relax and enjoy her new friends, she wouldn't have the strength to do what needed to be done.

I won't let him hurt you anymore.

Most of all, she worried that she didn't have what it took to fulfill the promise she'd made the children in regard to Mac's threats.

Her whole life had been about worrying and keeping control. Growing up a bastard, a societal outcast, a repentant sacrifice to her mother's religion, she'd had no choice. That need for control was so ingrained in her that it'd become a form of arrogance. She could see that now. She'd become so self-reliant that she couldn't even trust herself. Not to do the right thing, anyway.

When she'd told herself she'd learned enough about deceit and treachery during her time with Mac to create a safe place for those kids, to give them everything their parents hadn't, she'd been deluding herself and ended up taking them along for the ride. But the die was cast. There was nothing left to do but push forward.

Before she'd come to Cattle Crossing, she probably could've kept deceiving herself that she was capable of all she'd set out to do. That she had everything under control. But now that she'd experienced having the burden she'd put on her shoulders lifted briefly by Jackson's friends, she didn't know how to go back.

And then there was Jackson. The man who'd called her his siren, who'd kissed her lips, captured her imagination, saved her life. Jackson, who was supposedly smitten with her. Jackson, who'd stopped seeking out her company. Jackson, who'd inexplicably become a polite, perfectly well-behaved stranger.

The front door squeaked open. Evie stepped through, looking as fresh as a summer day in her yellow dress trimmed with white. "Jackson will be here any minute now with the wagon. Are you sure you have everything?"

Mimi forced a smile. "I'm sure."

"I wish you'd let me wrap that material up in oilcloth to protect it. It's a big investment you're making."

"I'm more worried about the oil ruining the material than any rain. Besides, it's only got a three-hour journey. We should be all right."

With minimal fanfare, the flatbed and mule rounded the corner. Little Lady was tied to the back. From the way she was prancing, it seemed she wasn't too pleased at being regulated to second place.

Mimi forced another smile. "Here he is."

"Hold on, then. I've got something for you."

"You've done enough."

"Just a minute."

Evie went back inside the house and came out with another satchel. "I hope you don't mind, but I collected some clothes for the children, too."

"I bought some material."

"I know you did, but sewing takes time. And you need every spare minute to get that first order delivered."

The fact that Evie was right or that Mimi was grateful

didn't diminish the sting of charity. She waved her hand at the bags. "I'm sure there are others in town more deserving."

Evie sighed. "I was afraid you were going to feel that way."

"Then why did you do it?"

"Because you need help." She dropped the satchel at Mimi's feet. "And because I like you."

It would be foolish to reject the gift. "I like you, too. And thank you."

Evie gave her a quick hug. "And stop being so darn standoffish and invite me out to visit soon."

Hugging her back, Mimi promised, "I will."

The creaking grew louder as the flatbed drew closer. Jackson sat in the front seat, his hat pulled low over his eyes, his hair pulled back at the base of his neck. His mouth was set in a straight line. If his expression left her in any doubt of his mood, the stiff set of his shoulders dispelled it. He was annoyed. As he had been for the last two days. She had no idea why.

Calling the children, Mimi forced another smile. "As soon as we get settled, I'll arrange for you to come out."

It was a lie, but by the time Evie figured that out, Mimi would be gone. That was the other thing that this visit had taught her. Staying in one place was not an option. People got too curious. Asked too many questions. Gossiped too much. With the money from the lingerie sale she could buy train tickets. It wouldn't get them far, but it would be a start on disappearing.

"Good." Evie smiled and waved to Jackson. "Hey there, Jackson."

Jackson gave Evie a smile that sparked a kernel of pure jealousy in Mimi's heart. She missed his warm smiles.

"Hello yourself."

Jackson pulled the wagon up. "Whoa there."

The mule, acting like this was all happening far too early in the day, plodded to a stop. Lady, on the contrary, danced in irritated impatience at the back. The kids came running around the corner. Melinda Sue, looking adorable in a new pink dress with ruffles and matching ribbons in her hair, skipped up to the mule. Kevin, never one to be left out of anything, was right behind her.

"Don't get too close, Mellie," Mimi warned, hurrying down the steps.

As usual, by the time she got the warning out it was too late for caution. Melinda Sue was already within chomping range. The mule cocked an ear at the excited child and then stood placidly and let her scratch his nose. When she stopped scratching, he dipped his head down for more.

"I'm going to name him Samantha," Melinda Sue announced.

"You can't name a boy Samantha," Kevin scoffed, scratching behind the mule's ear.

Melinda Sue stuck out her lip. "Can too."

"All the other mules will make fun of him. Samantha's a girl's name."

Evie chuckled and shook her head at the exchange, taking it in stride. Mimi wanted to have the same nonchalance as Evie and the same carefree attitude as the children, but that wasn't possible. She was their parent now. They were her responsibility.

"I don't think we need to be fighting about the mule's name right now." Catching Melinda Sue's hand, she drew her away from the mule. "We need to get the wagon loaded so we can go home."

Melinda Sue dug in her heels. "But—"

Jackson cut the protest short. "Go get your things, Melinda Sue."

As always, when Jackson spoke, Melinda Sue listened. Mimi wished she could bottle that tone he had that made resistance disappear. Flouncing up the steps, Melinda Sue disappeared into the house. She came back carrying her doll and her parasol. Behind her came Tony lugging her satchel.

"Where's my stuff?" Kevin asked.

"Inside," Tony retorted, "where you left it."

Kevin said something Mimi was glad she couldn't hear before he went in after it.

Jackson hopped down off the wagon. As was his habit lately, all he spared Mimi was a glance. Evie, watching the interaction, frowned. With a shake of her head, Mimi deflected the silent inquiry.

"Hand me the bags, son," Jackson said. With that easy grace with which he did everything, Jackson tossed them up onto the loaded wagon, before fetching Mimi's. The glance he cut her as he passed was as inscrutable as his behavior.

Tony looked at the pile. "We sure are going home with a lot more than we came with."

"It's going to take you days to unpack, that's for sure," Evie agreed, clearly trying to ease the tension.

Jackson grunted an agreement as he heaved Mimi's heavy bag onto the wagon. "We're losing daylight here. Do you have everything?" he asked Mimi.

"I've got what matters."

Jackson's head snapped around. Mimi didn't bother to elaborate. She could play this game as well as he did.

"Then climb on up here and let's get going."

Kevin climbed in first and settled himself on the bag of oats.

"You're next, sprout," Jackson said, holding out his arms.

Giggling, Melinda Sue jumped. Jackson caught her and swung her up into the buckboard. Watching her, Mimi wondered if she'd ever been that young. There were days when she just felt ninety. After Tony scrambled up, there was nothing left for Mimi to do but take the hand that Jackson held out.

"Thank you." As he helped her into the wagon with the touch of a stranger, she couldn't help but remember that night on the stoop and how his fingers had learned the texture of her skin, his lips the shape of her mouth, his kiss the taste of her soul. Biting the inside of her cheek, she kept the tears at bay.

"Don't forget to plant that basil as soon as you get home. It'll die if the roots dry out," Evie said, shading her eyes from the sun.

"I won't."

"And, Jackson?" Evie added.

"Yeah?"

"Try not to be any bigger of a horse's butt than you have to be. Not everyone can see the world the way you do."

It wasn't until much later that Mimi had a chance to confront Jackson. First there was the trip home to endure. Then there was the wagon to unpack. After that, supper had to be made, the animals needed to be tended. And finally, the children to be bathed and the usual arguments about going to bed to be had.

But at last, when the moon was high, Mimi was able to turn down the oil lamp to a soft glow, tiptoe out of her bedroom, and step out onto the porch. Jackson was there, as she knew he would be. Sitting on the same step as before. Sharpening his knife as before. Everything was as it had been before, except for his attitude. She had the crazy notion that he thought by doing it over, he could erase what was.

Standing at the top of the stairs, Mimi folded her arms across her chest. "When are you leaving?"

Not by a twitch did he reveal any surprise at the question, but she was learning to read him, and the rotation of the knife over the whetstone was just a little bit slower. A little more controlled.

"What makes you think I'm leaving?"

"Well, if the last few days have been your way of making me want you around, I've got to tell you, you're failing abysmally."

"Is that so?"

"Yes, and I'm sick of it."

She could tell from the angle of his hat that he was looking at her, but the details of his expression were lost in shadow. "So am I."

Digging her fingernails into her arms, she held on to her even tone by sheer force of will. "You could have fooled me."

He set the whetstone beside him. Just as deliberately he placed the knife across it. "I've been wrestling with some questions for the last couple days."

"I noticed, but I'm not going to be treated like this anymore."

"Just out of curiosity, how exactly do you intend to prevent it?"

"That new shovel needs to be broken in."

The sound he made might've been a chuckle. It also could've been exasperation.

She shook her head. "I don't understand you anymore."

"But you're not blaming me."

She did recognize sarcasm. "No. I know my flaws."

She expected him to say something. Anything. The silly part of her even hoped he'd say she didn't have any. Look at her the way Clint looked at Jenna. The way the Rev looked at Evie. The way Cougar looked at Mara.

Instead, he patted the stair beside him. "Come here."

She sighed internally and dropped her hands. "I don't want to."

"That wasn't a request."

He used that steel-wrapped-in-velvet drawl. It was amazingly effective. She plunked down on the steps beside him. Not because she was intimidated but because she couldn't stop hoping.

He didn't say anything immediately. Just sat there a few scant inches away. So close she could smell him. He always smelled so good. Like man and leather and heaven. Her own personal archangel, who'd lost his taste for saving her.

"When were you going to tell me you were married?" he asked.

Her heart sank. Of all the questions she didn't want to answer, that was number one. She licked her lips. "What makes you think I am?"

The glance he cut her out of the corners of his eyes sliced clean through her bluff. "Are you?"

She tried a different angle. "Why does it matter?"

"I don't pursue married women. And why haven't you answered my question?"

Because it was complicated. And she had too much to lose.

"So?" he prodded. "When were you going to tell me you were married?"

He sat all outwardly calm, but beneath the surface she could see the tension coiled within him, waiting to explode. "I don't know. Hopefully never?"

He was so close. All she had to do was move her hand an inch and she could be touching him. She wanted to touch him to remind him of how good it felt the last time they were out here. The kisses. The passion. What stopped her was the knowledge that he might not kiss her back.

He wasn't buying her prevarication. He shifted to face her, his gaze as sharp as his tone. "You don't know? How could you not know? At some point, it was going to become relevant."

His skepticism cut to the bone. "Do you want to know the truth?"

A muscle in his jaw bunched. "There's no point in adding any more lies to the mix."

No, there wasn't. The answer came out on a sigh. "The truth is, I hadn't thought of it at all. One minute I'm down a well preparing to die, worried about how the children are going to survive without me, thinking, 'Oh, my God, what have I done?' And then when I'm just about to give up, there you are, looking like some angel descended from heaven. When you kissed me as we flew out of that well, you expected me to remember a man who I may or may not be married to?"

"Hold it right there." His hand came under her chin, turning her face to his, holding her immobile. She couldn't even tell if it was fear or desire that made her heart race. It probably didn't even matter. "Say that last part again."

"How do you expect me to remember anything when you're whispering sweet things in my ear? I've never met a man like you."

A faint glimmer revealed his smile. "That part you can repeat later. I want to hear about this man who may or may not be your husband. Are you married or not?"

"I don't know."

"Again, how do you not know?"

"My mother said this man approached her in regard to courting me. Older. Established. He was quite a catch for someone like me."

"Explain 'someone like me.'"

"I was born out of wedlock."

"I see." His thumb rubbed ever so lightly under her chin.

She doubted he did. Things were different for men. They had options not available to women.

"Continue."

She shrugged. "He started courting me. I was flattered. At first Mother insisted on chaperoning, but then he asked for permission to take me to dinner. Alone." This was so embarrassing. She struggled to catch her breath. Swallowing hard, she fought for her voice. His thumb caressed the tight muscles of her throat. Her voice came out thready. No amount of clearing strengthened it.

"I was very excited. I'd never eaten in a restaurant before. I practiced my manners for hours before he came. I didn't want to embarrass him."

"Mimi . . ."

She hated the pity she heard in his voice. She didn't want his pity. Anger gave her back the strength she'd lost.

"Dinner was delicious. I had wine. I didn't really like it, but I liked how sophisticated I felt with that glass in my hand."

"Christ. How old were you?"

"Fourteen." And dumb. So dumb.

"How old are you now?"

"Nineteen."

"How old was he?"

"Forty-two."

"Damn."

She was betrayed by a tear, seeping past her pride, spilling down her cheek. She didn't need his pity. With a lift of her chin, she dared him to say something.

It wasn't the tear that got to Jackson. No, he could handle a woman crying. It was the pride with which she bore the breach in her defenses. The shame she suppressed for something over which she'd had no control. Shit, she'd been only fourteen. What chance did a fourteen-year-old have against a grown man? Jackson sighed and turned, pulling Mimi into his arms. She struggled. He didn't care. He was done being an ass.

"Don't."

The whisper cut at his heart.

There was no way in hell he was respecting that "Don't." Not when Mimi's pain stretched so palpably between them. Not when he knew how the story was going to end. Not when she needed him.

"Come here, honey."

"No."

He settled the dispute by picking her up and sitting her on his lap. She didn't relax. He didn't care. He had his arms around her. For now, he could be satisfied with that.

"Do you want to hear the rest?" she asked without any detectable inflection.

"Yes. I don't want any more secrets between us."

"It's pretty simple and you've probably already guessed it."

"Tell me anyway."

She licked her lips. "One glass of wine led to two. Maybe three. I don't know. The next morning I woke up in his bed. I was sore. There was blood on the sheets. And he had a piece of paper saying we were married."

Cold anger settled in his gut. "He raped you."

"A husband can't rape his wife. I know, I checked."

He wasn't surprised. Mimi might be young, but she was determined and resourceful. "Which brings us to how you don't know whether you're married or not."

Another sigh. "Last year he told me I was too old and he was getting married to someone else. When I asked how that was possible since I was his wife, he told me not to be a fool. There was no way a man of his station would have married someone like me."

"Did you kill him?" He already knew the answer.

"No."

Tangling his fingers in her hair, he tilted her head back. The faint moonlight highlighted the fragility of her features, the pain in her eyes. The shame. "Would you like me to kill him?"

There was the slightest of hesitations. "I don't want you anywhere near him. He's a very dangerous man."

"So am I."

She didn't believe him. He couldn't blame her for that. Her husband had had years to convince her of his invulnerability, whereas she'd only known Jackson less than two weeks.

"He won't hurt you or the children again."

Her "thank you" was clearly a sop to his pride. He rolled his eyes.

"I just want to stay as far away from him as I can."

He thought of the flyer in his pocket. "I'm all for that."

Her fingers opened over his heart. "You need to stay

away from him, too. If he comes looking for us, promise me you'll stay away."

"Honey, I intend to be the first person to welcome him to town."

She leaned back. "Don't say that!"

"I can take care of myself, Mimi. I'm—"

She actually put her hand over his mouth.

"Not against Mac. He's big and ruthless and he knows so many people. He's like a snake in the grass. Always sneaking up when you least expect it."

Removing her hand, he kissed her palm before placing it over his shoulder. "I'm not afraid of Mac, Mimi."

Her nails dug into his neck. "You need to be."

"Why?"

"He'll come after me."

Those nails dug deeper. "You said he'd moved on. Selected another wife."

There was a pause.

He tipped her chin up. Her eyes were huge, shadowed by more than moonlight. "Why, Mimi?"

"I stole some things from him."

"What?"

"The kids. Some cash. A necklace. And a book."

At least now he knew why none of them looked alike. "Interesting collection."

"You don't sound shocked."

Sliding his fingers up her arm, he curled them around hers and eased her nails out of his skin. "I would have killed him. Seems to me like he got off lightly with some petty theft."

"He doesn't think so."

"Tough."

"He's an evil man. He has connections everywhere."

"Everywhere is a big place."

Her hands curled into fists against his neck. "I mean it. Governors, senators, policemen—he has a hold over all of them. It's all in the book. I think." She shook her head. "He was always consulting it. The names are encoded but not the deeds. Or the payments."

"You took it for leverage."

She shook her head. "I took the necklace to fund our escape. I didn't know the book was in there."

That must have been a shock. "Why didn't you throw it away?"

She shuddered. "Mac wouldn't be satisfied with that."

No, he wouldn't. "You could mail it back to him."

"He wouldn't trust that I didn't make a copy."

"Probably not."

Jackson was getting a pretty good image of Mac. And he had to agree with Mimi's assessment. Rich and powerful men who clawed their way to status over the bodies of their competitors tended to be ruthless in keeping those skeletons buried. Mac would have to be dealt with.

"So you've just been running?"

Her concession was a very heavy sigh. "Forever, it seems."

"It'd be easier without the children."

"I know."

But it'd never occurred to her to leave them behind, he knew. "Didn't their mothers complain?"

She shook her head. A blush stained her cheeks. "They were . . ." She waved her hand. "The children were discards. Kept around until the time they became useful. I was lonely when I got there. Bored. They were lonely, too. I started teaching the boys to read." She shrugged. "Things built from there. But the more I understood how things worked in that place, the more I realized the fate Melinda Sue had waiting for her. Already men were looking at her . . ." She shuddered again. The eyes she turned to his were filled with horror. "She's just a baby."

"Yes." A beautiful baby whose innocence could be sold for a hefty profit. He tipped her chin up again. "You're right. Mac is a bastard."

"I don't know what he planned for the boys, but I couldn't leave them."

"You did the right thing, and, Mimi?"

"What?"

"You won't be running anymore."

The comment was supposed to make her feel safe. He sighed when she hid her face in his neck. Her ensuing grunt could have meant anything. He doubted it was agreement. She was too scared to see things any other way. Resting his chin on the top of her head, he admitted, "You're not the only one who's been running."

"Excuse me?"

"You didn't notice I've been running around with my head up my ass the last couple days?"

"No."

"Liar."

She shrugged.

"I was trying to figure out how I was going to live with myself for taking another man's wife."

"I don't understand how you knew." Leaning back, she studied his expression with narrowed eyes. "Who told you . . . ?"

There was no shielding her from the truth. "There's a wanted poster out for you. Not the best picture but it's you."

The color drained from her face in a slow seep, ending in a hard swallow. "Mac?"

He nodded. "That'd be my guess."

"No wonder you've been acting so oddly. You were trying to figure out a way to get out of your promise."

"The hell I was." He shook his head at her blink, and lowering his voice, he elaborated. This needed to be clear between them. "What's mine stays mine." Another blink. "It was never a question of letting you go. I just had to learn to live with my conscience, seeing as you were another man's wife."

"I may be."

He tried to imagine her at fourteen. It was entirely too easy. As easy as it was to imagine Mac taking advantage of her. He'd met a lot of Macs over his career. "You're not."

"How can you be so sure?"

"Because men like your 'husband' don't make that kind of commitment when a lie will do."

"You don't—"

It was his turn to put his hand over her mouth. She blinked. Her lips moved against his palm in a soft tickle. He shook his head, cutting off her protest. Removing his hand he continued. "Think about it. If he had married you, when you got too old, the only way to remarry would be to divorce you or kill you. Divorce costs money. Time. Scandal. It'd be much easier to kill you."

"But he said he was sending me away."

"That was likely a ruse. I'm thinking if you hadn't run, the only place you would have found yourself going would have been to an early grave."

She went as still as a rabbit caught in the open as the knowledge sank in. Against his neck, her lashes fluttered. Her whisper was just as shaky. "He was going to kill me."

"Yes." Of that he had no doubt.

She took a slow breath. "I never thought about that."

He had. Ever since he'd seen that wanted poster, he hadn't
thought of much else. It was why he'd had to prepare and then
get her out of town. With a bounty that high and so seemingly
easy a target, every bounty hunter in the West would be hunting her. Some experienced. Some not. It was the inexperi-
enced ones that made him sweat. Pair excitable men with
loaded guns, and accidents often happened. He'd talked to
Cougar about his concerns, and he and the others had agreed.
Right now, the best thing to do was to ensconce Mimi and the
kids in Bentley's cabin and pray the sky stayed dry.

"You really weren't going to give me up?"

"No."

"Why?"

"Because what's mine stays mine."

She went still in his arms. Not stiff like before, but still,
like a rabbit facing down a wolf. Against his arm her ribs
expanded and contracted with a short breath, and he knew
if the moon were brighter, and life kinder, he'd be able to
see that slight flush along her cheekbones and that betraying hunger in her eyes. But life wasn't kind, and he couldn't
see, but he could feel, and she was wound tighter than a
Sunday clock. "Just relax."

"Why?"

"So that I can take advantage of you while you're unsuspecting and vulnerable, of course."

Her chuckle was weak but there.

"Do that again."

"What?"

"Laugh."

"I can't do it on command."

"That's a shame. You have a very pretty laugh."

And very pretty eyes and breasts and hips. But more attractive than all of that was her mind.

"Thank you."

"For what?"

"For making me feel special."

"You are."

She turned in his lap. She had to feel his cock hard against her thigh. She didn't balk and he didn't push. He just waited. He didn't have to wait long. After a soft expulsion of breath, her head tipped back and her gaze met his. Shadowed with mystery and redolent with an undefined emotion, her eyes held him enthralled even as her hands slid slowly up his chest and over his shoulders. So slowly that he held his breath, anticipation embracing his desire as delicately as her arms embraced his neck. She was something, his Mimi. Sweet. Intelligent. Passionate. Her tongue slid over her lips, leaving them glistening in pink temptation. Damn, he wanted to taste her. This time when her nails sank into his skin, they sent little bites of fire nipping down his spine.

"Make me feel special tonight, Jackson," she whispered. "Please."

Those hot bites settled into glowing embers of heat. "Why?"

She blinked. "Because I can't be a fool again. I have to know if this is real."

"You're no fool."

Her eyes, those beautiful eyes, narrowed. "You don't know how I feel."

But he would. Brushing the hair off her face, it was his turn to whisper. "Show me."

Her torso moved against his in a slow, intimate caress. Her breasts, soft and full beneath her clothes, dragged erotically against his chest. He could feel her nipples beneath her blouse. He wanted to rip her blouse open, lower her camisole, cover them with his mouth. Show her how she made him burn. Make her burn in return.

"I feel wild," she groaned.

So did he. "Good."

That got him a frown. "I don't like it."

She would. He'd make sure she would, because there was nothing more important than this bond between them. This wildness. Placing his hands on her hips, he angled her closer. "Then I'll like it enough for the both of us and wait for you to catch up."

His reward was a burst of laughter. With a flick she knocked his hat off. Combing her fingers through his hair, she found the leather tie. With three tugs, she had it free. "Why do you tie it back?"

"For the same reason you do."

Her smile bussed his throat as she sprinkled tiny kisses up to his jaw. "Somehow, I don't think you're worried about being tarred a loose woman."

It was his turn to laugh. "No. I'm just too lazy to comb out the knots."

"That I believe."

"Come here and stop teasing me, woman."

"You mean like this?" More of those butterfly kisses dusted his jawline.

"Exactly like that." Grabbing her hips he lifted her up and turned her so she straddled him. His cock notched against her pussy. Her satisfaction was expressed in the moan that whispered over his cheek. Wrapping his fingers in her hair, he tipped her head back. "Now kiss me like you missed me."

That was the easiest order Mimi had ever followed. Mac hadn't liked kissing. Or caressing. He hadn't liked anything soft. She hadn't ever missed Mac, but Jackson was different. She ached for him.

Like this, they were almost of a height, and it was easy to tilt her head just enough, to part her lips just enough, to lean forward just enough. To tease. To tempt. Not just him, but herself. She'd waited so long for this. It almost felt too good to be true.

"Do it."

The order whispered into her mouth, mingling with her desire, pushing it higher, drawing her in, forcing the connection. Completing the union. Completing them.

Her moan echoed his. She turned her head, or maybe he turned it for her. She wasn't sure. Didn't care. All that mattered was this kiss. This man. Fire arced from him to her and then back again. Lightning danced over her skin, burning her from the outside in, all that intensity focusing on the points of their connection. Her lips, her breasts, her pussy.

"I want you."

The words were dragged from her heart, breathed into his mouth. Felt in her soul. His answer was a growl. Or maybe it was a yes. She took it as a yes, plucking at the buttons on his shirt, whimpering in frustration when they wouldn't give, moaning in satisfaction when her fingers found warm skin.

"Yes. Just like that. Sing for me."

When his big hand cupped her breast, she forgot to breathe. When his thumb brushed over the sensitive tip, she found it again, high and sweet.

With a growl he dragged her hard over his cock, rocking her pussy against his length so hard it almost hurt. She tried to pull back. He wouldn't let her. "Don't fight it. Feel me. How hard I am for you."

"I can't—"

Before she could finish the thought, discomfort became pleasure. Fire. Oh, my God, he was fire.

"I've never felt like this before."

His growled "Good" blended with the passion.

She rocked harder. So did he. It wasn't fast enough. Hard enough. She needed to feel him. Just him. Male to female. Skin to skin. She stopped tugging at the buttons and started ripping them instead. His hands caught hers. "Slow down."

"I want you."

"And you'll have me. Just wait."

His hands were between them, tugging. She didn't want to wait. She bit his shoulder out of sheer frustration.

He laughed. And even that was good. Suddenly his hands were between her thighs, brushing and tugging.

"Hurry."

"Lift up."

She did, and then she had her wish. Skin on skin. Hard to wet. Cock to pussy. It was bliss.

"Yessssss."

"Look at me."

His hand on the back of her neck gave her no choice. His hand on her hip gave her no option. With a steady push, he parted her.

She should have been scared. It'd been a long time, and he was big, much bigger than her husband. But she wasn't. She gloried in the burn, in the possession. "More."

"Easy. We have time."

She didn't want time. She wanted him. "Now."

Bending her knees, she forced him deeper. Her flesh gave under the force. Shock went through her in a shudder.

"Damn it."

She didn't care. "I don't care."

He was in her, stretching her. The pain was part of the completion. She needed it to wipe the past clean. She needed him.

"Don't move."

She couldn't if she wanted to.

"It didn't have to be like that."

Yes. It did. "I wanted it."

"Open your dress."

She did, her fingers all thumbs. With a jerk of his chin he ordered, "Take out your breast."

The night air was cool on her overheated flesh. Her nipple beaded. She knew he was looking at her. "Make it harder," he commanded.

Rolling the nipple between her thumb and forefinger, she made it ache. His hand slipped under her skirts. Parting her slick lips with slow deliberation, he centered his thumb on that throbbing point that begged for attention. She could feel him watching her reaction as he drew slow circles on the sensitive tip. She knew and reveled in it. She didn't hide anything.

"Offer it to me."

His voice was a sultry rasp. His tongue the perfect torment. Hot, wet heat surrounded her nipple. Sparks sizzled along her skin. The fire burned high. The knot in her stomach coiled tighter and tighter. The pressure built. It was too much. It wasn't enough.

"More," she whispered.

"Yes," he groaned back. His thumb kept working that sensitive spot as he worked his hips in small pulses. Opening her more. Preparing her.

"Please."

"Easy."

No. She didn't know what she needed, but it was close.

Very close. She needed it. She needed it . . . Digging her nails into his chest, she begged. "Now."

"Yes, now." Leaning back, he balanced her on his cock, switching his hands to her hips. Lifting her. His cock slid along her sensitive tissues. She couldn't bear it.

"So good."

"Yes."

He drove back into her. Once. Twice. And then again and again. Carefully at first, but then harder as his control slipped and it was her turn to growl.

"Don't stop."

"Hell no."

The coil was tightening and hot. So tight. She needed something. It was too much.

"Jackson."

Leaning forward, he growled seductively in her ear. A dark angel demanding his due. "Beg me."

Shivers raced down her spine. Chills arced outward from her center. His thumb worked her sensitive spot as hard as his cock worked her pussy. Oh, God. Oh, God. She needed more. Just a little more.

"Jackson!"

Raking her nails down his chest, she growled right back. "Please, Jackson. I need you. Please."

"Son of a bitch."

His thumb left her clit. His fingers dug into her hips. He lifted her up and dropped her down. He plundered her pussy the way he plundered her mouth. Totally and completely, without anything held back. It was wild. It was crazy. It was almost perfect.

"Come for me. Let go."

She couldn't form the words, describe the sensation. "I don't know—"

On an "I do" he pumped hard and fast, catching her clit between his thumb and forefinger, teasing and caressing in rhythm until her breath deserted her and she was dangling on the edge of a cliff.

Just when she thought she couldn't take any more, the coil exploded, and she convulsed. It was only his hand over her mouth that kept her scream contained, but nothing could contain the pleasure that pulsed within her, gripping him with every stroke. Three more strokes and he pulsed high inside her, flooding her with his pleasure, binding them with satisfaction. Slowly, she came down off the spiral. Just as slowly he removed his hand from her mouth.

She slid her arms around his neck. He slid his around her waist.

His forehead dropped to hers. "Damn, woman."

"Damn, man."

"I think we might be in trouble here."

Twelve

Trouble found them a week later. It came sneaking through the woods, four men deep. It came the way trouble does, with no warning.

Tony noticed the riders first. In the middle of playing tag, he stopped dead and hollered, "Riders!"

Pushing aside the sheet she was hanging, Mimi searched for the children. They knew what to do if strangers approached. They'd practiced it. Not only because of Mac but because, out here, strangers often meant danger.

Tony was standing in the middle of the yard. Kevin and Melinda Sue were chasing each other nearby.

When Tony's warning sank in, Kevin stopped so fast Melinda Sue slammed into his back.

Oblivious to the potential danger, she crowed, "Tag! You're it. You're it."

Kevin might have been slower to realize something was

wrong, but he was faster to react. "Come on, Melinda Sue, run."

He bolted toward the house. Just as they'd practiced. Melinda Sue stayed behind. "Tony! Hurry."

Mimi dropped the laundry and screamed, "Jackson!"

But Jackson was hunting. Calling for him was as useless as the bell they'd bought to summon help. It sat on the ground beside the steps, too heavy to lift. They hadn't had time to set it up, because covering the well had been a greater priority, or so they'd thought at the time.

They were on their own. Hiking up her skirts, she ran for the house, shouting for Tony to run as she did.

He stood frozen in the middle of the yard, staring at the approaching men. She couldn't leave him there. Changing direction, she hiked her skirts up higher and ran faster. She had to get to Tony first. She could hear Melinda Sue yelling at Tony. She could see her tugging at his arm. She could see the riders coming hard, but she couldn't move fast enough. Everything she did was so slow. So very, very slow.

She screamed Jackson's name again like a talisman. Desperately hoping that maybe, maybe he was close enough to hear. That he'd come back and make this a bad dream. Picturing his face, she held it close in her mind, keeping her screams inside now because she didn't have the breath to spare. She had to get to Tony.

By the grace of God, she reached Tony first. Grabbing him by the arm, she whirled him around.

"Listen to me, Tony. You've got to snap out of it. You've got to get Melinda Sue to the house." He just stood there. She slapped him across the face. He blinked.

Please. Let him be here with me now. "Get in the house, Tony. Lock the doors, just like we practiced."

Her handprint stood out in stark relief on his cheek. "Mimi—"

"Just run!"

With a nod, he grabbed Melinda Sue and, half dragging, half carrying her, ran for the house. Mimi spun back around. The riders were almost upon them. She saw pounding hooves, bearded faces with beady eyes, and guns. Oh, my God, so many guns.

The riders spread out around her. She ran in front of them, waving her arms, trying to scare the horses in order to buy the children time. The horses were too well trained to spook. The men too in control. All she could do was stand there waving her arms in a futile distraction and pray the children made it to the house.

Suddenly, a shot rang out. She whirled around so fast her skirts twisted around her legs, tripping her. She bumped into a horse. The impact knocked her forward. When she caught her balance, she saw Kevin standing on the porch, one of Jackson's revolvers in his hand. Tony and Melinda Sue were almost to the house.

"Kevin, no!"

Either he couldn't hear her or he was too angry to care. The riders pulled up the horses. The one in front drew his gun and took aim. She followed the trajectory. Dear God, he was going to shoot Kevin. What kind of man shot a child? She spun in a circle, looking for anything. Spotting a rock, she grabbed it and threw it as hard as she could. It hit the gunman on the side of the head. The shot went wild.

Cupping her hands around her mouth, she screamed, "Get in the house, Kevin. Get in the house!"

Tony made it to the steps. Tossing Melinda Sue to Kevin, he grabbed the gun out of his hand and shoved him to the door. Then he started running back. To her.

"No, no, no, no, no."

From behind her came a bit of advice. "If you don't want him dead, then I suggest you tell him to put the gun down." She didn't turn around to look at the man speaking. She didn't dare break eye contact with Tony.

"Tony, put down the gun." She didn't think he'd do it. He had that same wild look in his eyes she'd seen before at Mac's. It was bloodlust.

"Put it down, Tony. They'll kill us if you don't."

He didn't lower the barrel. "They'll kill us if we do."

She held out her arms wide as if through sheer force of will she could keep the gunmen behind her and Tony safe. "No, they won't. At least not until they get what they came for."

"Smart girl."

And that fast, she remembered him. He was one of Mac's flunkies. A nobody in his operation. She briefly turned to the leader. "Shut up, Rob."

The barrel wavered. Tony was considering it, at least. "Please, Tony."

The metallic cock of a hammer echoed in her ear, and the cold press of iron bruised the back of her head. She stood very, very still.

"Do it, son, or I'll blow her brains out right here."

"Please, Tony." They couldn't die like this. "Please."

Tony placed the gun on the ground. He looked so much like Mac right then with that hate in his eyes. If she'd ever doubted the rumors of Tony being Mac's son, she didn't anymore. She kept her tone even, but she couldn't do anything about how her voice shook. "Go in the house now, Tony."

"Stay right where you are."

Tony looked to her for direction. With a motion of her

hand she indicated for him to stay. One of the riders took a position beside Tony. The other one rode around the back of the house.

She turned to the two flanking her and pointed toward the man. She didn't recognize any of them. "Where is he going?"

"Just making sure there's no surprises."

"There's nobody here except us." She thought he smiled. It was hard to tell behind the grimy beard. "I don't have any reason to lie," she told him.

He rested his arm across the saddle horn. Even to her untrained eye, she could tell he took much better care of his guns than he did of his appearance. His sleeve was stained and filthy.

"You don't exactly have a reason to tell the truth."

"What do you want?"

He looked her over from head to toe. "I think we both know what I want."

It spoke to the depth of her terror that she hoped he was just here for rape. That hope was short lived.

"You've led me a merry chase. Quite frankly, it's an embarrassment that you managed to get this far."

"You shouldn't be embarrassed about things you can't help. You're either born smart or you're not."

The kick came so fast she didn't see it, let alone have a chance to avoid it. There was a sense of impact, pain, and then a network of stars exploded behind her right eye. Clutching her cheek, she stumbled backward, but she didn't fall. She would be damned before she'd fall.

"Mimi!" Tony stepped forward.

Eyes watering, she waved him back. "I'm all right. Just stay there."

He teetered on indecision.

Rob tapped the barrel of his revolver on the iron of the saddle horn. Once, twice. Three times. "You won't be all right for long if you don't give Mac what belongs to him."

"I don't know what you're talking about."

"You might lie to Mac and get away with it, but I know better."

He kept tapping that barrel. Over and over. The metallic click resonated in her head like a countdown.

The throbbing in Mimi's cheek was nothing compared to the anger in her heart. She'd been taking crap from men like this for her whole life.

"You don't know anything about me."

"I know you're going to be dead if you don't tell me what I want to know."

She wanted to spit in his face. She wanted to take that gun he kept dangling as a threat and blow his brains out. "By your logic, the longer I hold out, the longer I'm likely to live."

The other man leaned forward in his saddle and spit. "For my part, I'm hoping she holds out a long time."

He made her skin crawl with his beady eyes and snaggle-toothed leer.

"Go to hell."

"I guess she told you." The leader smiled. His whole face disappeared inside the filth of his beard when he did. She suppressed her shudder through their laughter. Every time their horses shifted, she shifted, too, trying to keep herself between them and Tony, but there were three of them and only one of her, and eventually she and Tony were surrounded.

Had Jackson heard the shots? Was he on his way?

"Mimi?" Tony asked.

"Just stand behind me, Tony. We'll figure this out."

A series of crashes came from the house, followed by a high-pitched scream. "Mellie!" She spun around. "Tell them to leave her alone."

"I doubt they'd hear me from here."

Balling her hands into fists, she swallowed back panic. "Please."

Rob shrugged and kept tapping that gun. "You can end all this. Just tell me where the box is."

Giving him the box wouldn't gain her anything. What she'd said to him held. Her best chance of survival lay in dragging this out. Or bluffing. There was always bluffing.

More crashes came from the house.

What were they doing in there? "I don't have the box here."

"Where is it?"

She licked her lips. "I won't tell you until I see Melinda Sue and Kevin and make sure they're all right."

"It's your own hide you ought to be looking out for."

She shrugged. "If anything happens to the children, I'm not going to want to live."

He didn't respond immediately. Just kept tapping that muzzle. His horse stomped his foot. A fly buzzed by. Time crawled.

"They all say that."

"They aren't all me."

"You'll reconsider, just like them," Snaggletooth sneered.

Ignoring him, she kept her gaze locked with Rob's. She'd learned from Mac that the secret to a good bluff was the resolution with which you backed it.

Rob huffed and backed his horse up a couple steps. "Fine." Putting his hand to his mouth, he hollered, "Donald, bring those kids out here."

It seemed an eternity before a man came around the side of the house riding his horse, Melinda Sue propped up in front of him. She was squirming and kicking, but her little muscles were no match.

Kevin walked beside the horse, clothes torn, hair falling in his eyes, but his head was still high and his glare was still strong. They hadn't defeated him. It was up to her to keep it that way.

"See. They're fine. Breathing and everything."

Jackson, where are you?

The echo of a gunshot bounced across the hills. The buck Jackson had a bead on sprung to the left and vanished into the bush. Another gunshot followed that one. It was hard to tell the direction the shooting was coming from, but a hunter didn't space shots that way, and those reports were from different guns. There was nothing between here and town except Bentley's place.

Shit.

Spinning around, Jackson retraced his steps, sprinting back toward Lady. Branches slapped at his face and brambles tore at his clothes. He leapt over logs and splashed through streams, one thought driving him on.

Mimi.

Little Lady was standing right where he left her, munching on grass. When he broke into the clearing, her head snapped up.

"Hup-hup."

She tossed her head and trotted toward him.

Grabbing the rein and the horn with practiced smoothness, he leapt into the saddle, keeping his rifle clear. The little mare was in motion before he even had a chance to squeeze with his knees. And she was heading home.

"Good girl."

Lying low over her neck, he urged her on, cursing when the terrain forced her to slow, pulling back on the reins when they got close to the edge of the woods. He leapt off, dropping the left rein, knowing Lady would wait because he'd trained her that way. He reached into the saddlebag and pulled out his spyglass. The ten feet to the edge of the woods felt like ten miles.

Resting his rifle against a tree trunk, Jackson quietly pulled open the spyglass. Keeping the lens shaded in the foliage to prevent reflection, he surveyed the house. The indistinguishable figures in the distance took on sickening clarity. Four well-armed men dressed in dark clothing on horseback surrounded Mimi, Kevin, and Tony in the yard. From the glint of sunlight on steel, he knew weapons were drawn. A heavyset rider was holding Melinda Sue up in front of him. She was kicking and swinging for all she was worth.

Just riding in wasn't an option.

Stay calm, Mimi.

So much for the connection between them. Mimi was suddenly swinging at the man holding Melinda Sue. He heard the child scream. He saw Mimi go down in a tumble of skirts. The whites of her petticoat flashed beneath the horse's legs. She might've tripped. She might've been kicked.

It didn't really matter. These men were going to pay.

Men's shouts piggybacked on Melinda Sue's screams. Chaos ensued. For an instant the horses stepped aside. Kevin was on the ground. Tony was struggling against the hold Mimi had on his arms. He followed the trajectory of the boy's gaze. A gun lay on the ground a little left and in front of him.

"Don't do it." But his whisper didn't carry. With a wrench, Tony broke free. Dropping the spyglass, Jackson grabbed up his rifle, rested it on a branch, and took aim. On a prayer that turned into a curse he pulled the trigger. One of the men went down. More shouts as the men spun their horses around, looking for the source. Shifting his aim to the skinny man with the brown bowler hat, Jackson pulled the trigger. At the last second, his target moved. The man jerked but didn't fall. The son of a bitch who held Melinda Sue jerked his horse around in Jackson's direction, holding Melinda Sue up like a shield before him.

Jackson spat. "Bastard."

And then things got ugly. Tony had the gun and he was pointing at the bandit in the brown hat.

"Damn it, son," he whispered.

Any doubt that Tony would pull the trigger ended in the next second. Bowler Man jerked and fell off his horse. The report came a split second later. There was no chance to pick off another target. Not without risking hitting Melinda Sue. Instead, Jackson laid down a rapid-fire offense, relying on intimidation rather than accuracy to scatter the bandits.

Whoever the bandits were, they had experience. They didn't panic. Instead, they laid down a hail of bullets of their own. Diving behind a log, Jackson covered his head. A couple of bullets came close, one chipping the bark off the log. As soon as the bullets stopped, he jumped up. Just in time to see them gallop away, Melinda Sue dangling from the side like a tiny human shield. Mimi and Kevin ran screaming after them. Tony just stood there with the revolver in his hand, as helpless as Jackson. Grabbing his rifle and his spyglass, Jackson sprang into the saddle and followed.

The only use the gang would have for Melinda Sue was as a shield. Most likely as soon as they got to what they thought was a safe distance, they'd drop her, knowing whatever posse was following would be forced to pick her up, giving them the time they needed to get away. It was a good plan, but it wouldn't save them.

Nobody touched his family and lived.

It was dark by the time Jackson got back to the house. Light leaked from the cracks in the building, bleeding out into the barren yard. From the looks of things, every lamp in the house was lit. Bracing his palms on the saddle horn, he stretched his tired muscles. Little Lady plodded toward the house. It was a measure of the grueling pace they'd set that she wasn't dancing at the thought of oats and a comfortable stall. And it'd all been for nothing. The riders weren't amateurs. They knew how to throw a trail. And they hadn't discarded Melinda Sue. There were only a couple reasons why they wouldn't have dumped her by the side of the trail. Only one made sense. Melinda Sue was a bargaining chip.

"Shit." Lady flicked her ears. Swatting a mosquito on his neck, Jackson said it again. And again, because, damn it, that little girl was out there at the mercy of scum, probably scared, probably hungry—he swatted another bug—probably being eaten alive, and he couldn't do a thing about it tonight. Because he hadn't known what he should have. Because he'd been distracted by big blue eyes, a penchant for sass, and a passionate nature. Because he hadn't taken seriously the threat Mac posed.

The heavy bar scraped against the door as it was lifted. With a roll of his eyes, he pulled Lady up at the hitching rail. Now Mimi took precautions. Too little too late. With a heavy sigh, he dismounted. The door swung open and light spilled into the yard. Mimi, Kevin, and Tony spilled out right along with it, rushing onto the porch, coming to a halt at the top of the stairs, where they huddled. No one put into words the question he could see in their faces.

Hooking the stirrup over the horn, he loosened the cinch. Lady groaned in relief. "What'd you do with the bodies?" he asked wearily.

"Pried the cover off the well and threw them in," Kevin answered grimly.

That was fitting. Snakes should dwell with snakes. "We'll have to blow it or they'll take to stinking."

Mimi held a lantern high. The light cast her face in ghastly shadows. Her right cheek was swollen and black and blue, distorting her expression. "Where is she?"

"I don't know."

If the post hadn't been there to catch her, she would've fallen. Leaning heavily, she asked, "How could you not know?"

The question trembled under the weight of her fear. He ripped the cinch strap out of the ring on Lady's saddle. The leather hissed and slapped as it came free. "We're going to have to talk about that."

Tony came down the stairs. "I can take care of Lady."

After a second, Jackson placed the reins in the boy's hand. "I'm obliged." Before Tony could lead Lady away, Jackson put a hand on his shoulder and stopped him. "That was good shooting this afternoon, son."

Tony didn't look at him. "I didn't save Melinda Sue."

"No, you didn't, but neither did I."

That brought his head up. There were dark circles under his eyes. The rims were swollen. He'd been crying. "You'll learn, son, that not all battles are won in a minute. What's important is nobody died here today, and we've got tomorrow to settle up."

"But Melinda—"

"Will be fine." He'd make sure of it.

"But they have her."

"And I'll be discussing that with them shortly."

"I'm coming with you when you do," Kevin growled, his hands balled into fists. He hadn't cried.

"No. You aren't."

Kevin just set his jaw. Mimi came forward and quietly put her arm around his shoulders. There was an unnatural quiet about her. The kind some soldiers got after battle.

"How will you find them?" Tony asked.

Jackson cut a glance at Mimi. She was staring out into the night, as if Melinda Sue might appear any moment. "I have a feeling I'm not going to have to."

"But—"

"Kevin," Jackson interrupted, "go help Tony take care of Lady. Be sure to rub her down and give her an extra portion of oats. She put in some miles today. And give that new mule some oats, too."

Kevin didn't move.

Mimi blinked and then put her hand on his back. "Do as you're told, Kevin."

Instead of moving, he glanced over his shoulder at her.

Giving him a little push, she added, "I'll be fine."

After another hesitation, he joined Tony.

As the two boys led the tired mare toward the barn, Jackson dropped all pretense. Taking Mimi's arm, he escorted her up the stairs. "You and I need to talk."

Thirteen

Jackson released Mimi as soon as they got in the kitchen. With a kick of his foot, he closed the door. The moist air of the evening faded to the homey smell of stew and beeswax. She didn't turn around. As he stood there debating his options, she said quietly, "I'm not going to fight you."

He wanted someone to fight. He wanted to win. Melinda Sue was out there somewhere, facing he didn't know what. Grabbing his hat off his head, he tossed it on the chair. It landed on the right spindle, neat as a pin. Tonight, it gave him no satisfaction. Running his hand through his hair, he snapped, "You picked a hell of a time to become cooperative."

"I'm sorry."

He rubbed his hand over the back of his neck. "Did you recognize any of them?"

"The leader, Rob. He was someone who ran errands for Mac's foreman. No one important."

She stood there, back to him, shoulders bent and arms hugging her waist, passively prepared to accept whatever punishment he decided to hand out. He wanted to punch something. Not because she wouldn't give him a fight but because she just looked so . . . damned defeated.

"Come here."

She didn't move.

And suddenly he had something to do. It was only a step to take her in his arms. But it was a big step, because he couldn't remember a time in his life when he'd felt somebody's pain so keenly that it cut the legs out from under every other emotion. His frustration, his anger, his resentment . . . And his hurt, he realized, because somewhere along the line, he'd thought he'd had her trust.

Mimi stood stiffly in his arms, not resisting. Not encouraging. Just standing there. Probably because she didn't know what he planned, and honestly, if she'd asked him what he intended to do, he wouldn't have had an answer. But once she was in his arms, it was the most natural thing in the world to turn her, to tuck her into his chest, and to just . . . hold her.

Resting his chin on the top of her head, he sighed. "I'll get her back."

The hitch to her shoulders could have been either a sob or a shrug. He didn't know which. It really didn't matter.

"I know you'll try."

He tipped her face up with the side of his hand. Gently brushing her bruised cheek with his thumb, he asked, "What did I say?"

Tears filled her eyes, hovered on her lashes. "Will you bring her home the same as she was before?"

She was asking him to tell her they wouldn't harm Melinda Sue. He wanted to lie, but all he had was the grim truth. "I can't promise that."

That one was a sob. A deep, wrenching spasm that convulsed her shoulders.

The tears spilled over, staining her cheeks before pooling between his thumb and her chin, spreading out, sealing their connection. "Honey. I'm not playing hero. Before coming home, I stopped by Rivers Bend and telegraphed for help. You can believe me. I'll get her back."

Stepping back, she shook her head. Whether negating the reality or negating her ability to handle it, he didn't know.

"Please." Waving her hands, as if she had a prayer of warding him off, she choked out, "Please, don't."

Don't what? Don't tell the truth? Don't hold her? Don't comfort her? Don't care? He was long past all those don'ts.

He pulled her close. "Too late. I'm already doing."

Pressing her face into his chest, she whispered, "I failed her, Jackson." Her fingers clenched into a fist against his chest. "She's got to be so scared."

"She's a tough little thing."

Mimi shook her head. "You don't understand. She's so fragile."

Wrapping her braid around his hand, Jackson tugged her head back. She still wouldn't look him in the eyes. Shame did not become her. "Are we talking about the same child?"

"I know you look at her now, but she's just beginning to find her feet and I'm so scared that this time she won't be able to come back."

"This time?"

"She sees herself as bad."

"How is that even possible? She's four years old."

Tears dripped from the corners of her eyes. Her cheeks were flushed and blotchy, her eyes red and swollen. The bruise was starting to turn. She did not cry prettily. He didn't care.

"They're here because of her. Because of what she did. But she's just a child and she was just being a child."

"Anyone would know that." Jackson wiped a tear away with the pad of his thumb.

"Not Mac. Mac will never understand." She shook her head vehemently. Scrubbing at her cheeks, she swore, "I had to take them with me. Mac would've killed them. Just out of spite."

Mac was a real charmer. "How long ago was that?"

"A year."

She'd been on the run for a year with three children?

"Most men would have given up by now."

"Mac is a possessive man."

"And he thinks he owns you."

It wasn't a question.

"Yes." She glanced away. "He's crazy that way."

That he found easy to believe. Any man that had Mimi and threw her away was a fool.

"So you saved the children from him."

She nodded. "But I don't know what I'm doing. I thought it would be different. I thought I could be different." She wiped at her cheeks, scrubbing away the tears, before whispering, "I thought I *would* be different."

"How?"

"I thought we'd work together. The four of us against the world. I didn't realize there'd be so many decisions I'd have to make alone or that they'd have so many needs."

"They're children."

She nodded and bit her lips. "It was easier in Boston. Things were more . . . organized."

She looked at him, her shattered heart in her eyes. "A mother wouldn't have let them take her, Jackson."

"A mother would do exactly what you did. She would survive so she could fight another day."

She was shaking her head before he finished. "I should have stopped them."

"If I couldn't stop them with a rifle full of bullets, what could you have done?"

She just looked at him, lips quivering, tears dripping, shaking her head helplessly. "I told you, I don't know how to do this, and now those men have Melinda Sue and she's never going to be the same."

He gently wiped the last of the tears from her cheeks, being careful to avoid the bruise. "You still don't understand, do you? I'm going to get her back, or I'm going to die trying. That being the case, don't you think I should know what I'm getting into?"

She took a step back. He let her, but just until she ran into the barrier of his linked hands. She folded her palms together in a position of prayer and pressed the tips of her fingers against her lips. Her eyes closed slowly.

"I love her, too, you know," he informed her when she opened her eyes.

"You don't even know her."

"I know she's a lot like you. Full of light and smiles."

She blinked and straightened, her lips parting in shock. "You can't possibly think that she's . . . that I'm . . . ? I mean, we look nothing alike."

He dismissed that nonsense with a wave of his hand. "I know she's not yours, but I would like to know why she thinks she's bad."

"Mac had a lot of women friends and he liked to loan them jewelry to wear. The happier he was with them, the shinier the jewelry."

"Not the loyal type, huh?"

Her mouth twisted. "No. Not at all."

She reached behind her for a chair. "I need to sit down."

She was looking pale. He helped her into the seat.

"Tell me what happened, Mimi, that day you took the box and decided to run."

"That day, I'm not sure how, Melinda Sue got into the safe. I don't know how or when she figured out the combination—probably from spying on Mac—but she opened it."

He could see Melinda Sue doing that. The cherubic charm masked the mind of a master thief. "She is an intelligent little thing."

Mimi's nod was distracted, her focus clearly on that night. "She wanted to try on the necklace." She cut him a glance. "She liked to play princess, you see."

He nodded, and she continued.

"However, once she got the safe open, she told me she heard something in the next room." Pushing her hair off her face, Mimi explained. "It was Mac. He was furious." Horror ghosted her voice along with the memory. "We heard her screams, but then they stopped."

His fists clenched. If Mac didn't come looking for Mimi, Jackson was going to go looking for him. The bastard had hurt Mimi. Melinda Sue. The boys. He wouldn't leave him out there as a threat. "And?"

"When we got to the room, we could see why. Mac was choking and cursing her, shaking her like a rag doll. I tried to pull her free, but he was too strong. But then Kevin grabbed a big vase and hit him on the head." Licking her lips, her gaze met his again. "He fell and didn't get up."

"Good."

"I knew we only had a little time, but we needed money, so I grabbed the box from the safe and"—she shrugged—"we ran."

"Just like that."

She nodded. "Just like that."

"Shit." A vulnerable young woman and three kids alone in the West? It was a wonder she hadn't been raped and killed. "You were lucky."

"Not any longer." Gripping the table, she whispered, "As soon as Mac gets the book, he's going to kill us."

"Where is it?"

She let go of the table. "What makes you think I have it here?"

Jackson held out his hand. She placed hers in his. Her skin was pale and delicate against his suntanned flesh. Smooth where his was scarred and calloused. He helped her to her feet. "You wouldn't trust anything that important too far from your side."

"You know me too well."

She didn't seem too happy about it. "That bother you?" he asked as she headed to the back left corner of the cabin.

Without looking at him she said, "I haven't decided yet."

She hadn't decided . . . "Well, let me know when you do."

With a shake of her head, she knelt. He expected her to pull up the floorboard. Instead, she slid one of the wallboards sideways, hesitated, and then reached under the floor and pulled something out. Turning around, she brushed off something square wrapped in brown oilcloth. "Before the snakes and the well, I wouldn't have hesitated to reach in there."

"Sometimes, there's a lot to be said for ignorance."

"Yes. I miss it."

"Well, lucky for you, I never had it to miss." He held out his hand. She gave him the box but didn't release it.

"Being fearless got you a snakebite."

"And a pretty woman." He gave a little tug. "You can let go of it now."

She did, still looking nervous. "I don't know why I'm so reluctant, but the darn thing's been terrifying me for so long, I feel like I'm giving up a part of me."

He slid a finger down her cheek, tracing a tear track. "I told you down in that well, Mimi, that I'd keep you safe."

Clasping her hands in front of her, she leaned into his hand. "I know."

"Try believing it."

Her response was a wobbly smile. "I'll work on it."

"Succeed."

She rolled her eyes. Jackson unwrapped the box. It was an innocuous enough–looking thing. Wooden, about nine inches on a side, with black chipped paint. He opened the lid. A long, low whistle escaped him. He lifted the necklace out of the box. The diamonds were of such quality that even in that low light they sprang to life. The center pendant practically defined fire. "It's easy to see why she took this. It's a beautiful piece."

It was. Mimi had often admired it on her husband's mistresses' necks. "Yes. Every time Mac gave it to a new mistress, Melinda Sue pouted. She wanted it for when she played princess."

Jackson dropped it back into the black wooden box with an utter disregard for its value. The little brown leather journal he treated with far more deference.

"It doesn't look like much, does it?"

"Hmm." He was fully engrossed. She had to assume from the fact that he read the first few pages and skipped to the middle before quickly heading to the end that he understood what he was looking at. He closed the book with a snap. "Mac must want this very badly."

"He does."

He tapped the cover. "The information here would make him a very rich man for a very long time. Give him unlimited power."

"It's a blackmail list, isn't it?"

"Of some very important people, I'm sure. These are some damning secrets."

Rubbing her forehead, she fought a sob. "And he has Melinda Sue."

He looked up. "Mac?"

"Yes."

He shook his head. "I don't think he does."

"What?" she gasped. "He has to have her."

It was inconceivable that Rob had taken Melinda Sue for any other reason than ransom. Knowing Rob needed Melinda Sue alive to make a trade was the only thing keeping Mimi sane.

Jackson held up the book. "Mac wouldn't risk letting this fall into the hands of an intermediary. His power comes from the fact that he's the only one who knows what these secrets are, but anyone having possession of this book would have all the leverage that he has."

"I didn't think of that." Rubbing her arms, she whispered, "He's just always been so powerful. Nobody ever challenges him."

"A man in his position is always being challenged. Just staying alive is a delicate balance in his particular game."

"He's not a very educated man, but he is very, very cunning." And mean. Horribly, viciously mean.

Jackson nodded. "I know the type."

The awful emptiness inside threatened to suck her into the abyss. Her hands felt clammy. Her skin oddly cold. "So if Rob didn't take Melinda Sue to get the book, why did he take her?"

Jackson put the book back in the box and pulled out the necklace. It glittered in the lamplight. "I'm guessing for this."

Understanding came slowly. "They don't know about the book."

"I don't think so. Mac wouldn't advertise the book's existence. It's too valuable. But he could safely put out a bounty for whoever could bring him you and the necklace. That would be a reasonable compromise to get what he wants."

She licked her lips. "Because only Mac and I know the book and the necklace were together."

"Exactly."

She perked up. "So we can just give them the necklace in exchange for Melinda Sue."

"We could do that."

God darn it. He was always raining on her parade. Folding her arms across her chest, she snapped, angry that this couldn't go simply. "Why do I hear a 'but'?"

"Probably because there is one."

It didn't take Mimi but a second to figure it out. "He knows Mac and how vindictive he is. He knows he'll never give up looking for us, but if he succeeds in finding us and we tell him about Rob taking the necklace then he'll know he was betrayed." The cold emptiness sank deeper, right along with understanding. She stumbled back a step. Jackson caught her hand, steadying her. His expression was stony as he absorbed her fear. "Rob's going to kill us no matter what, isn't he?"

"Who's going to kill us?" Kevin asked from the doorway. Behind him Tony stood, the only indication he'd overheard was the pallor of his complexion.

Oh, dear God. She stood. "I didn't mean for you to hear that."

"You're always hiding things from us!" Kevin yelled, his green eyes narrowed in anger. "And look what happened." He made a slashing motion of his hand. "Everything's a mess, and now Melinda Sue is gone and they're going to kill us."

She didn't have anything to say to that. But she wanted to. She wanted to say so much. She wanted to have the answers so badly. In the end, she did the only thing she could do. She opened her arms. After a few seconds, Tony walked in. On the way he grabbed Kevin's arm and dragged him along. "Don't be a jackass."

She hugged them tightly. She didn't care that Kevin stood as stiff as a board and that only Tony hugged her back. She tried not to think about the space that was empty where Melinda Sue should be. For now, this was what they had.

Kevin whispered, "I don't want to die."

She squeezed him tighter. "Neither do I."

"No one's going to die."

Jackson said that with so much conviction Mimi almost believed him. Almost. The man just inspired faith.

"How do you know?" Tony asked.

Jackson smiled and ruffled his hair. "You know how when you're playing marbles and the big agate is on the line? And you're wagering high because you know you can make that trick shot? Because it's what you do?"

Tony nodded.

"Well, son, this is what I do."

"But you're just one man," Mimi murmured. Her lover. Her friend.

Jackson smiled that devil's smile, hooked his hand behind her head, drew her up on the balls of her feet, and right there, in front of the children, kissed her until her toes curled.

As he ended the kiss in a slow detangling of swirling emotion, he whispered, "Not hardly."

Grabbing his plate from the table, he headed to the stew pot. Mimi knew she should move, but all she could do was stare after him while Tony and Kevin stared at her.

"Wow," Kevin said.

"Yeah."

That about summed it up.

The explanation for that "Not hardly" arrived the next morning bright and early in the form of four men, all decked out in metal. Metal guns, metal rifles, metal bullets, and metal knives. They meant business. And when Jackson came out of the barn, blond hair shining in the light, he meant business, too. He looked like an avenging angel. Wiping her hands on her apron, she greeted her guests. "Good morning, Clint and Cougar." She nodded to the two men she didn't recognize. "Good morning, gentlemen."

Cougar tipped his hat. "Good morning, Mimi. These two gentlemen here are Asa MacIntyre and Elijah. They volunteered to help us settle this little matter."

Asa had the coldest gray eyes but a warm smile. "Nice to meet you."

"Nice to meet you, too."

Whoever said that green eyes were friendly had never

met Elijah. The man was ice through and through. Beyond
a nod of his head, he didn't acknowledge her. She didn't ask
his last name.

"Why don't you make us some coffee, Mimi?"

She couldn't even take offense at Clint's suggestion.
These men had come to rescue Melinda Sue, ready to die if
need be. They'd come because Jackson had asked them to.
They'd come because she needed them.

"I'll have it ready in a minute."

She looked back through the window as soon as she
went inside. The men were engrossed in conversation.
Clearly they had just been waiting for her to go in the house
to get down to work. Did they worry she'd faint if she heard
their plans? Did they really think she cared what their plans
involved as long as they brought Melinda Sue home?

"So how many do you think there are?" Clint asked.

"I think they're just down to the two," Jackson answered. "I can't see them wanting to share the profits any
more than they have to."

"Makes sense," Asa said. The way Jackson saw it, Asa
had been a lawman long enough to know.

With a wave of his hand, Elijah pointed to the dirt.
"Where'd you lose him? Draw me a map."

Elijah knew this area like the back of his hand. He'd
wandered for years after his wife died. And more, before
he met her, when he lived as an outlaw. If there was a place
to hide out in the vicinity, Elijah would know it. Jackson
quickly sketched out the area where he'd lost all sign of
the kidnappers.

Elijah took the stick and motioned to the bend in the
river. "There's a cave right here. More of a crawlspace stuck

between some rocks, but it's a good place to hide. The water covers your tracks, and it's not visible unless you know where to look."

Son of a bitch! Jackson ran his hand through his hair. "You mean they were right under my nose?"

Elijah didn't smile and didn't tease. "Likely. There's not really any other place to hide within a mile."

It was hard to believe that there had once been a time when Elijah was the first to smile and the longest to laugh. His wife had brought that out in him, and when she died, she had taken his joy with her. "So, that's where they're hiding."

"I doubt they're still there. The place is as buggy as all get-out. They'll be out in the open by now. Likely here in this clearing." He made a mark on the other side of the narrow river.

"Scratching their butts off," Asa added with grim humor.

A smile ghosted Elijah's lips. "Yup."

Jackson would have smiled, too, but if they were scratching, so was Melinda Sue.

"How do you know they'll be there?" Cougar asked.

Elijah shrugged. "It's where I would be."

Jackson sat back. "That's good enough for me."

"Do we have a plan?" Cougar asked. "Or are we just going to wing it?"

Clint looked at his cousin. "*We* aren't going to do anything. *You* are going to escort Mimi and the children back to Cattle Crossing."

Cougar reared back and shook his head. "The hell I am."

Jackson loved Cougar like a brother and he understood his drive to be out in the middle of things, but this time he was going to have to sit it out. "The hell you won't. You have a wife about to give birth. She needs you. You can't afford to take this chance right now."

Elijah nodded.

Jackson took Cougar's growl as agreement. "Besides, I need someone like you to make sure they get to Cattle Crossing safely."

Cougar cocked an eyebrow at Jackson. "Like me?"

"Tough as nails and deadly."

"Are you expecting trouble?" It was typical Cougar that he perked up at the prospect.

"Yes."

"Any chance these guys are working with Mac and just waiting for him to show?"

"No." He was sure of that on a gut level. "Mac wouldn't trust anyone with that ledger."

Cougar smiled and fondled his knife. "A shame. I was looking forward to making his acquaintance."

"No more eager than I am." Every time Jackson thought of the scars on Tony's back, his blood boiled. "I've a feeling he's the person that whipped the crap out of Tony."

"The hell you say. He beat that boy?"

"No," Jackson corrected. "He whipped that boy."

Clint cursed. Elijah tossed the stick in the dirt. Asa shook his head. "Some people just need a slow death."

"Amen."

"Anybody have any ideas of how we want to handle this?"

"I've got a few."

Elijah was always the first to speak up when it came to vengeance. And fortunately, vengeance was something he was an authority on.

Jackson took a sip of his coffee. "We're listening."

* * *

They rode out an hour later, four strong men armed to the teeth determined to rescue a little girl. Wrapping her arms around herself, Mimi hugged her fears tight, keeping herself from screaming for Jackson to come back. Keeping herself from running after him. This uncertainty crippled her usual optimism.

What if Melinda Sue was already dead? What if she wasn't? What if only some of them came back? What if none of them did? How could she ever face their wives?

The easy confidence with which they rode made her want to smack them. Doing the right thing wasn't always enough. Being strong didn't always win the day. And sometimes good didn't always win over evil.

Cougar came out of the house carrying her satchel. As always when he got close, she took a step backward. It wasn't that she feared him; it was just that he was so big, so intense, so intimidating. Beyond the cock of his eyebrow, he didn't acknowledge the distance.

"Are you ready to go?"

She supposed. "Do you have the book?"

He raised the satchel.

"Are you sure it's safe enough in there?"

"It's as safe there as anyplace. Bushwhackers aren't shy about searching your person or your possessions."

"It just makes me nervous."

"I can understand why."

She glanced after Jackson again. Despite her efforts to keep him in sight, the woods swallowed him up.

"Are they going to be all right?"

"They know what they're doing."

It wasn't an answer. She bit her lip. "Are you really sure you don't want to go with them?"

"I've got to admit the pull of a guaranteed fight is tempting, but seeing as how you're so important to Jackson, I'm going to resist and concentrate on getting you home."

She looked toward the awkwardly built house. "I thought this was home."

Cougar scoffed. "That's not home. That's just where you went to ground."

"I tried to make it a home."

Shaking his head, he waved for her to precede him. The boys were coming out of the barn with the mule. "One thing Mara taught me is that home isn't a place. It's a feeling, and I've got a feeling your home just left."

Fourteen

~⟶~

The kidnappers were right where Elijah predicted they'd be. Waiting for dawn to attack had left Jackson with a hair-trigger temper and a lust for blood, but now that the time had arrived, nothing but cold, calm determination ruled his actions. Jackson inched a little closer to the edge of the outcropping he was lying on and angled the spyglass to see through the leaves. He was wrong about one thing. There were more of them. Two more, to be exact. The sound of a mourning dove blended with chirps of robins and the raucous scream of blue jays. Common woodland sounds that blended with the warm sun, the light breeze, and the soft, puffy clouds. Only a few would recognize the signal that a predator was in place. Clint repeated the signal.

Looking at the crew, Jackson wondered if all these precautions were necessary. From the way they were lounging about, it was clear they weren't expecting trouble. Did they think their position was secure? Even the guard, leaning against a tree, was paying more attention to the dirt under his fingernails than a potential attack.

There was nothing Jackson appreciated more than the enemy making his work easier.

Being careful not to dislodge any rocks, Jackson swept the area again. He didn't see Melinda Sue anywhere. His stomach knotted. On the third sweep, an out-of-place bit of blue caught his attention. He centered in.

There she was, lying on the ground, scrunched up half under a log, her feet and hands bound. He couldn't be sure from this far away, but he was pretty sure from her body language that she was crying. And why shouldn't she be? The poor kid was just four years old. In the last twenty-four hours, she'd seen two men killed, watched her family terrorized, and been dragged off by the men who'd attacked her family. She had every right to cry. But not for long. Soon she'd be safe and sound.

Jackson imitated a crow cawing four times to alert the posse to how many enemies there were. He waited five seconds and followed up with one more. That was the important one. That one announced Melinda was alive. Closing his eyes for a second, he let the relief flow through him. She was alive. Asa responded with the chattering of a squirrel.

The leader, Rob, lifted his head. Did he suspect something? Signaling wasn't all that uncommon for Indians or anyone else used to working together. An experienced outdoorsman might detect the slight difference between human imitation and the real thing. Jackson prided himself on his crow imitation, but Asa's squirrel could use work. When this was over, he'd rib him about it. That should be worth a few beers and a couple laughs. For all his laid-back ways, Asa was the most uptight man Jackson knew when it came to getting things right.

After a couple minutes of milling about nervously, the man settled down. Another signal came through. This time a two-toned call of a bobwhite quail. Damn!

Swinging the spyglass to the left and then the right, Jackson spotted the reason for the warning. A mini army of eight was trooping through the woods led by a heavy-set, ruddy-faced, dark-haired man with beefy hands. He dwarfed the horse he was riding. Rob lumbered to his feet. He was clearly nervous. If the rider was Mac, Jackson's theory just got shot to hell.

Jackson swept the perimeter again. It took him a long, tense minute to find them, but the newcomers hadn't arrived unprotected. The big guy'd brought at least two sharpshooters. This wasn't a friendly visit. Those men on the perimeter were here for business. And Melinda Sue was directly in the line of fire.

Fuck. This was a complication they hadn't anticipated.

Elijah signaled once. It wasn't one of the predetermined signals. *What the hell are you up to, Elijah?* There was nothing to do but wait to find out and provide cover when needed.

Hang in there, Melinda Sue.

The big guy rode into the campsite. His entourage fanned out.

The campsite exploded into action. The guards shouted and whipped out their revolvers. It was too late. The big guy's henchmen had the drop on them. Angry voices carried up the rise. The bandits' leader was gesturing emphatically. Whatever he was saying, the big guy wasn't buying it. With a gesture and an order that carried in tone, he put an end to Rob's protestations. The clearing settled into a tense silence. Even the birds quieted.

Watching the interaction, Jackson almost missed a

movement down by the log sheltering Melinda. Shifting his position so he could get a better look, he made out Elijah's broad-shouldered silhouette belly crawling across the forest floor. Son of a bitch!

Melinda Sue stiffened, thumb stuck in her mouth. He knew Elijah was talking to her. Elijah with the cold voice and cold eyes trying to sweet-talk a terrified little girl? Jackson grabbed up his rifle and quietly cocked the hammer, setting it beside him before picking up the spyglass again. If Melinda Sue panicked and screamed, all hell was going to break loose.

Listen to him, sprout.

To his surprise, she didn't scream and actually appeared to pay attention. With a tiny nod, she pulled her thumb out of her mouth and began inching out a little from the log, her progress hindered by her bonds. Every few seconds, she stopped and slowed down, clearly following orders. God bless Elijah and his sneaky-ass ways.

Now all they needed was time. Tensions were high. He panned over to the big guy. From the way he was looking down his nose, it was clear he didn't have any respect for Rob. In a matter of moments bullets were going to be flying. A quick check revealed the sharpshooters still had their rifles trained on the kidnappers. They weren't paying attention to where Melinda Sue sheltered, but that wouldn't last. Movement always drew attention. The big guy dismounted.

Come on, sprout. Keep going.

Little by little she crept toward the foot of the log, not changing her body language, just creeping along, periodically stopping when Elijah signaled.

Come on.

A holler snapped his attention around. The standstill

had escalated into a pushing match. The next thing in line after insults were bullets.

Let's go, Elijah. Get her out of there!

Signaling his intent to the rest of his crew, Jackson drew a bead on the two sharpshooters. Clint would have to handle the campsite. Marking his angle, he sighted his target, selecting the shooter whose actions were most likely to draw fire in Melinda Sue's direction. Switching to his rifle, he braced the barrel on the rock outcropping and carefully took aim. Finger on the trigger, he again silently urged Melinda Sue to hurry.

Come on!

She was almost to the bottom of the log. The hardest thing he'd ever done was to not pull the trigger. The urge to step in battled with the prudence of keeping his position secret. The sentry's focus was on the men arguing.

Just a little more, sprout . . .

In the next second, all hell broke loose. Rob went for his gun. He was surprisingly fast, but the big guy was faster, kicking it out of his hand. Rob had another, but before he could fire, a red stain blossomed on his chest. The report came a split second later. From up in the hills, the sharpshooters weighed in. Screaming, men dropped or dove for cover.

The battle was on, with Melinda Sue in the middle of it.

Shit!

Before Jackson could squeeze off a shot, his target switched positions. Damn it! He checked on Melinda Sue again. He was just in time to see her reach the end of the log. Elijah grabbed her foot and hauled her around the corner.

Fuck, that man was cold. In the middle of a gunfight, he lay there on the ground, calmly sliced the little girl's bonds, and then showed her how to belly crawl. And did it all as if bullets weren't peppering the air and ground around them. Jackson covered their retreat, ready to take out any threat, not relaxing until they became indistinguishable from the foliage. Then he turned his attention back to the battle.

The gunfight was over. A short and sweet execution and Melinda Sue's kidnappers were dead with the exception of one. The lone survivor knelt on the ground, fingers laced behind his neck, blood dripping from a wound on his head. Words were exchanged. The big guy approached. The prisoner waved toward where Melinda Sue had been crouched. Without looking, the big guy shook his head. Pulling his knife, the big guy grabbed the man's hair, tilted his head back, and held the knife to his neck while the survivor sniveled and begged, before, finally, slashing his throat. Blood arced through the air and poured down the man's shirt. The big guy smiled.

With his foot in the dying man's chest, he pushed him over. The man lay where he'd fallen, twitching twice before finally lying still.

Jackson had seen a lot of cold-blooded killers in his time, but this was different. Mainly because it wasn't cold. The big guy had clearly savored his victim's terror. More and more, Jackson was beginning to believe the big guy was Mac. It boggled his mind that Mimi had been shackled to him. Jackson couldn't imagine Mimi's optimistic, happy, nurturing self with a coldhearted brute like this.

Watching the big guy clean his knife on the dead man's pants, it was too easy to imagine this man whipping Tony, terrifying Kevin, or abusing Melinda Sue.

In the aftermath of the massacre, men gradually wandered into the clearing, talking, joking, smoking, generally relaxed. Jackson counted ten in all. Mac didn't travel light, but he also didn't travel smart. This wasn't Boston, where he controlled the authorities and repercussions were more predictable. Out here no one was safe. Especially after a gun battle. Gunshots attracted scavengers. Men who wanted to either profit from the death or profit from a body's death. The one thing no one did after a gun battle was let down their guard.

Doing so was a greenhorn mistake. One that he and the others would be sure to take full advantage of. Seating his rifle in the saddle scabbard and grabbing extra bullets for his revolvers, Jackson started working his way down to the clearing, being careful to stay out of sight.

Even though he couldn't see, he knew the exact moment Melinda Sue's escape was discovered. The yelling was immediate, followed quickly by cursing. He assumed everyone was pointing the finger and assigning blame. The next step would be searching. He faded back into the brush. It was a fair bet Clint and Asa were doing the same.

Mac's men fanned out in pursuit of the little girl. Jackson palmed his knife. This fight was going to be personal. Heading down into the ravine, he wove between the trees like a ghost.

The heat beat down on him as he worked his way through the woods. Around him, men called for Melinda Sue, utilizing endearments that ran the gamut from "honey" to "dear child" to "sweet thing." It was a waste of time. Elijah had Melinda Sue safe. But it was kind of them to reveal their positions.

He came upon his first target. Jackson drew the knife across his throat, holding him tightly through the shock, and then eased him down as acceptance came.

Taking the dead man's guns, he placed them quietly to the side. The knife he stuck in his own waistband. Stepping over the body, he continued on. One down, so many more to go. It was convenient for them to all show up like this. Some would say too convenient, but he believed the devil took care of his own. And if a man didn't think too hard on whose side he was fighting, the job got done.

The big guy was like a bull lumbering through a china shop, making his way through the woods. The singsong voice he used to entice Melinda Sue out of hiding made Jackson's skin crawl.

"Where are you, little girl? It's me, Mac. You remember me, don't you? I've come to save you." His tone dropped to cajoling. "You were always my favorite, Melinda Sue." There was a pause. Then, "I have those candies you like right here in my pocket."

Bastard.

Jackson waited until the man passed before stepping up behind him. Jackson shifted his weight to the balls of his feet. "Hello, Mac."

Mac spun around, hands out to his sides, looking for all the world like a big bear. "Who the fuck are you?"

"My name's Jackson Montgomery." He rolled up his right sleeve.

Mac spat to the side in contempt. "Get the hell out of here before I call my men."

A squirrel chattered. A mourning dove sang.

Jackson smiled.

"Go ahead," Jackson said encouragingly, rolling up his left sleeve. "Call them."

Mac did. Nothing happened.

"You see." Jackson smiled. "I have friends, too."

He watched the understanding flicker in Mac's eyes. Studied his change of position to a wide-legged, stooped crouch.

"Do you think I'm going to wrestle you?"

"A pretty boy like you wouldn't stand a chance." Spitting into his palm, Mac rubbed his hands together.

Jackson smiled. "So I'm told. No sense competing without a prize." Reaching into his pocket, Jackson pulled out the necklace. Even in the dappled sunlight of the forest, it sparkled like happiness.

"That's my necklace."

"It's mine now."

"The hell it is."

Jackson dropped the necklace into his pocket. "You want it? Come take it from me."

With a growl, Mac lunged forward. Jackson held his ground, letting him charge, waiting until the last second to spin to the side and out of his path. Mac stumbled. Jackson followed him forward, bringing his elbow down in the middle of the spine just below his neck. Mac went down and rolled over, scrambling to his knees.

"How did that feel, Mac?" Jackson taunted. "Good? Bad? Has it been so long since you've lost a fight that you've forgotten what it feels like to lose? To be the mouse rather than the cat?"

Mac struggled to his feet. "I'll show you who's the cat."

With a shake of his arm, Mac dropped a wicked-looking knife into his hand. Lunging forward, he drove it at Jackson's stomach. Jackson barely evaded the strike. Mac was faster than his bulk would imply.

Tossing the knife from hand to hand, Mac growled, "Come here, you bastard."

Those robin calls coming in succession were signals. From the count so far, there were two left at most. Clint and Asa could handle them. Mac was all his.

"Tell me something, Mac," Jackson goaded, wanting the

other man so mad he'd pop a blood vessel. "Do you also pull the wings off flies and boast about all the fights you've won when you get to the saloon?"

"Why don't you come here and find out, pretty boy?"

Jackson smiled. He didn't mind when men underestimated him because of his looks. "You like the way I look? Well, I'm sorry. You're not my type."

"I don't like a goddamn thing about you. Give me my necklace!"

Keeping Mac in his sights, he took the necklace out of his pocket again and hung it on a tree branch to his left. "Come get it."

Jackson didn't think it was possible for the man's face to get any redder. "Fuck you."

He charged in again. Jackson danced back. As he'd told the boys, it wasn't always size that mattered in a fight. Quickness, agility, and strategy often carried the day.

The fight was vicious but short. Mac never laid a hand on him. When Mac was panting and wheezing, Jackson kicked the knife out of his hand. It went sailing. The incredulity on Mac's face as it landed in the bushes made him smile.

Jackson walked around him, balancing on the balls of his feet, ready for the lunge that was sure to come. Mac fought like a man who'd been in the city too long. His muscles had softened and turned to fat. He wouldn't last long in this heat. He was already winded.

"How are you feeling?" Jackson taunted. "Getting scared, big man?"

"Who the hell are you?" Mac rasped.

"I told you. I'm Jackson Montgomery."

"What do you want?"

"I came to settle the score."

Breathing heavily, Mac wiped his brow and brushed aside the comment. "Give me my necklace."

"Give me my vengeance," Jackson snarled right back.

"For what?"

Jackson's first punch landed in Mac's stomach, sinking deep and doubling him over. "For Tony."

The next punch caught him in a kidney. "For Kevin."

The third he drove into the other kidney. "For Melinda Sue."

The last blow went to his throat, crushing his windpipe. As the big man crumpled to the ground, eyes wide, trying to gasp for air that wasn't ever going to come, Jackson looked him in the eyes. "For Mimi Banfield."

Mac jerked and grabbed his throat. His mouth worked and his chest heaved. His eyes bulged and his face shaded a ghastly blue. With complete dispassion, Jackson watched the life leave Mac's body.

"We had time. You could've made him suffer more."

Jackson turned to find Elijah surveying the dead man with his usual impassivity.

Untangling the necklace from the branch, Jackson shrugged. "I could've, but there's only so much energy I've got to waste on that piece of shit." He dropped the necklace in his pocket and buttoned it in. "Where's Melinda Sue?"

"She's bandaging Cougar's boo-boo."

Jackson raised his eyebrow. "I thought we sent Cougar home."

Elijah shrugged. "When did Cougar ever follow orders? He dropped off your crew and pony expressed it back, switching horses on the fly to cut that three hours down to one and a half. Said he didn't trust us to handle this."

"How badly was he hurt?"

"A thorn scratched the back of his hand. Melinda Sue's not buying his argument that it's a long way from his heart."

"She's a character."

"She'll give Gray a run for his money."

Those two together was a heck of a thought. "Jenna loves her."

"Jenna loves all children."

"It's a shame she'll never have any of her own."

"I don't think she sees any difference between adopted and her own. That woman is all heart. Like Nidia."

Jackson had long suspected the taciturn Elijah was sweet on the former prostitute, now saloon owner. "Is Jenna still insisting on an open friendship?"

A small smile ghosted Elijah's lips. "She refuses to listen to Nidia when she says that a friendship between them cannot be. That a former whorehouse owner and a respectable woman should not associate."

"Nidia saved Brenna and Gray. Jenna will take the head off anyone who dares question her friendship with the woman who saved her children's lives."

"Tell Nidia that."

"Why don't you?"

The group's debt to Nidia and Elijah was huge. Jackson handed the necklace to Elijah.

The other man dangled it off his fingers like he was holding a rattlesnake. The diamonds glittered and flashed. "What am I supposed to do with this?"

"Give it to Nidia."

"What's Nidia going to do with it?"

"Break it into pieces? Create a nest egg?"

Elijah waited.

"Buy some happiness?" Jackson asked.

"That woman is too damn scared to buy happiness."

Jackson shrugged. "Maybe she needs somebody to teach it to her."

Elijah tried to give it back. "This is Mimi's and the kids'."

"Mimi doesn't want it."

"She may change her mind."

"She won't, but if it worries you, I'll ask her again."

With a snort of exasperation, Clint walked up and glanced at the necklace. "We owe you for the Rev. And you owe her. Take this and call the debt settled."

Elijah shook his head. "She's going to call me something."

Clint pushed his hand back. "You should marry her, you know."

Elijah's expression went cold. "I have a wife."

"Had. She died."

Elijah slammed the door on the conversation with a cold "Yeah, she did."

Clint crooked his brow but let it go. With a wave, he indicated Jackson's hands. "A bit pissed, were you?"

Jackson followed his gaze. The knuckles were bruised and split. "A little."

"You could have spared your knuckles and just slit his throat."

"I wanted him to know why he was dying."

Elijah snorted. "You've always got to make it personal, Jackson."

He shrugged. "Because it is."

Elijah tucked the necklace into a pocket.

"You'll give it to Nidia?" Jackson asked.

He nodded. "When the time is right."

"What's wrong with now?"

"She'd run."

"She could go far away and start a new life for herself with that," Clint interjected.

Elijah shook his head. "She needs to find herself here. Otherwise, she'll spend her whole life running."

Jackson and Clint shared a look. Elijah was definitely sweet on Nidia.

"What happened to Asa?" Jackson asked.

As if his name were an incantation, Asa stepped out of the woods, with several saddlebags slung over his shoulders.

Clint adjusted his black hat against the bright sun. "Thought we'd lost you."

"I had business to take care of."

"What kind of business?"

Asa dumped the saddlebags on the ground, separating out the expensive, elaborately tooled one.

"Mac's?" Jackson asked.

"Yes."

"Don't tell me there's another book."

Asa shook his head. "No."

"What's in there, then?"

Asa pulled out a piece of paper and waved it back and forth. "I think, gentlemen, this is what we commonly refer to as a key."

There was one person Jackson had to see before he could relax. Leaving the others to clean up the site, he headed back to where they'd staked the horses. The strength of the sun hit him like a fist as soon as he stepped into the clearing by the remuda. Taking off his Stetson, he wiped his brow with his sleeve. Damn, it was hot. Lady whickered a greeting. Her bridle jangled as she tossed her head. Patting the side of her neck, he surveyed the camp.

Cougar was sitting down on a rock. Melinda Sue was standing in front of him in the remnants of her blue dress, the one she loved so much, holding his big, sloppily bandaged hand in her tiny ones and, from the sound of things, lecturing him about how he had to be more careful in the future.

Jackson took a breath. And then another. He'd thought she'd be traumatized by the experience, but it looked for all the world that she'd taken it in stride. He wished he could say the same.

Cougar nudged Melinda Sue's arm and pointed. The little girl turned. For a moment she just stood there, a tattered princess bathed in sunlight, no words. No expressions.

Stepping away from the horses, Jackson smiled. "Hey there, sprout."

She stared at him a minute more, unnaturally silent. Maybe two. Her lower lip started to quiver. Tears shimmered in her eyes, brimmed, and then overflowed. Poured down her cheeks. A sob jerked her body.

Son of a bitch.

Kneeling, he opened his arms. She ran into them, her mouth open on a silent scream of his name. He caught her up, holding her close, burying his face in her hair. Her tiny arms wrapped around his neck. Her tears dripped on his skin, each one tearing out his heart. Little girls shouldn't know such fear. "Don't cry, sprout."

"You founded me," she whispered, as if just saying it might make him disappear.

Squeezing her tightly, he gave her a hug. "I came licketysplit."

She nodded. "They hurted Mimi."

"I know. She's all right."

She rubbed her snotty nose on his shirt. Sticking her right arm out, Melinda Sue sniffed. "They hurted me, too."

Three bruises in the shape of fingerprints marred the pale flesh of her forearm. Each one hurt his heart. She was so tiny. "I'm sorry."

"Mr. Cougar said they're deaded."

"They are." Her arm was still stuck out in front of him.

As if he were particularly slow, she instructed him from the vicinity of his neck, "You have to kiss them better."

"Of course." He dutifully kissed each mark. Over her shoulder, he could see Cougar's smile. "There. All better?"

She nodded. Another tear dripped onto his chest.

"Then why the tears?"

There was a long silence before she confessed. "I was scared you wouldn't come."

Pulling back, he asked, "Why would you think that?"

"Because I was bad. I didn't run like Mimi said." The confession came out in a barely audible whisper.

Mimi's words came back to haunt him. Until now, he hadn't understood. *She's so very fragile.*

"Sprout, look at me."

Very slowly, she lifted her face. Tears left muddy tracks on her rosy cheeks. He wiped them away with the pad on his thumb. She sniffed again.

"Are you paying attention? Because this is very important."

The remnants of her pigtails bounced as she nodded.

"I will never allow anyone to steal you away. Not ever, for any reason. You could be the baddest little girl in the whole wide world, and I would always find you. All you have to do is sit back and wait."

She wiped her nose with the back of her hand, leaving another smudge. "Even if I touched your knife on accident?"

He made a mental note to revisit the safety rules of the house. "No matter what." He crossed his heart. "I promise."

The tension seeped out of her body. Slumping forward, she popped her thumb in her mouth and snuggled into his chest. "Can we goes home now?"

Jackson stood, supporting her with a hand on her back and one under her hips. "You bet."

Cougar gathered up his gear and looked at the sky. "Might want to wait until after we get some food and rest."

Melinda Sue sucked her thumb and nodded. As Jackson attempted to set her up on Lady, she clung to him, squeezing his neck tightly as she whispered, "I love you, Mr. Jackson."

Patting her back, he whispered right back. "I love you, too, sprout."

Fifteen

The waiting was interminable. Mimi stood on the back porch of Jenna and Clint's big house and watched the children playing hoops in the yard. Tony and Kevin were thrilled with the new game and determined to develop their skills, while Gray, Jenna and Clint's adopted son, watched and gave advice.

She didn't know what to make of Gray. It wasn't the big knife he wore on his narrow hips—clearly an emulation of his father and his uncle Cougar—that made her nervous. It was more that aura of intense energy that surrounded him, combined with those too-old eyes with which he surveyed everything. If she didn't know he was Jenna's son, she'd swear he was a warlock. What she hadn't decided was whether he was a friendly one. That had bothered her. Tony and Kevin hadn't had that many friends, but they'd had more than their fair share of rejection. Gray had the look of

a boy who could be quite cutting. Her fears turned out to be
for nothing.

Tony had found a kindred spirit in Gray. And vice versa.
They were close in age and understood each other. The
way they looked at the world was compatible, too. They
both saw it as something to be conquered and managed.
And since neither of them smiled much, neither worried the
other was mad when they were just being quiet.

Kevin had also found a friend in Jenna's adopted daughter. Brenna was another unique child. Red haired with
wide-set green eyes. The bond between her and Gray was
so strong, they often seemed to communicate without
words. And yet, she'd attached herself to Kevin. Mimi
wasn't surprised. There was something about that boy that
people loved. She liked to think it was his enthusiasm and
fighting spirit. Heaven knows she found it endearing,
though his enthusiasm for Gray's knife did worry her. He
was completely enthralled with it, and he'd taken to putting
a stick in his belt loop in imitation. And they'd only been
here a day. Two more and he might be wearing one of his
own. That was a scary thought.

On the other hand, it was good to see him looking up to
someone. There was so much of what most children took
for granted that her three didn't have. Parents. Stability. A
community. Sighing, she rubbed her hands on her arms.
She watched them run after the hoop, chasing it with a
stick, trying to keep it going long enough to attempt more
intricate tricks. They looked so carefree, laughing and
playing, swapping suggestions and encouragement. For the
first time since she could remember, they were just being
children. One prayer answered. With a sigh, she went back
to studying the road, the way she had since they'd arrived
the previous afternoon. With a greed she wasn't ashamed

of, she wanted her second prayer answered. She wanted Jackson and Melinda Sue home.

Jenna came out onto the porch wiping her hands on her apron. She smelled like vanilla and sugar. It suited her. "Bri is finally down for her nap. I swear it's unfair how she just nods right off for Clint but makes me sing ten lullabies before she'll even consider closing her eyes . . ." Her voice trailed off as her gaze followed Mimi's. "They'll be back, Mimi. They wouldn't have chanced attacking last night and risked Melinda Sue getting caught in the crossfire. They would have waited for this morning."

"How did you know what I was thinking?"

Jenna's smile was gentle. "Well, I could claim to have magical abilities, or it could just be common sense that you're staring down the road so hard because you want to see your daughter and your man riding up it."

Mimi smiled wryly. "Am I that obvious?"

"No more so than me. I miss Clint, too."

And Clint was gone because of her. She owed this woman, this family, so much. "Thank you for letting us stay here."

"It's been my pleasure."

Mimi placed her hand on Jenna's forearm. There was strength in that softness. "If there's anything I can do to repay you, let me know."

A light flush touched Jenna's cheeks. Her gaze locked on the children. "I heard you were making some . . . intimate clothing for Sunny and Red."

"You heard?"

"At the restaurant. They were bragging on how they would be beautiful and drive the men wild."

"I'm sorry."

"Why?" She frowned at her and then chuckled. "Oh. I wasn't embarrassed. It's more that I'm intrigued."

Mimi did a quick assessment. "You're a stunning woman. I could make you something beautiful if you'd let me."

"Do you really think you could?" Licking her lips, Jenna confessed, "Our anniversary is coming up. I'd love to surprise Clint with something . . . special."

This was comfortable ground. "You mean sexy."

Jenna's blush bloomed to rival the bright red roses running rampant in front of the porch. "Yes." She rubbed her thigh. "I have scars . . ."

Clint had to have seen those scars a hundred times over. "And you worry because . . . ?"

"I don't want to look like a pig's ear posing as a silk purse."

As if that could ever happen. "I promise you, you will look lushly desirable, and not one bit foolish."

"You're sure?"

Oh, she was sure. "Very sure. This is my one talent and I take great pride in it."

"Then it's a deal." Jenna held out her hand. "But I'm quite sure it's not your only talent."

Mimi took her hand. "Good."

Jenna didn't immediately release her. With a squeeze and a pat, she added, "I do promise you they'll be back."

"How do you know?"

"When you're married to one of the McKinnleys, you do a lot of waiting and a lot of worrying."

"I'm not married to Jackson."

"Not yet."

Mimi's stupid heart did a hard thump at the possibility. Outwardly, she rolled her eyes. "We haven't known each other very long."

Jenna dismissed that with a wave of her hand. "I know

couples that have known each other a long time and others who just up and knew from the get-go that they were meant to be, so I don't think time has a lot to do with it."

"I think I'm meant to be—"

She didn't get to finish the thought, as Kevin spotted Jenna and hollered, "Miz Jenna! Watch me!"

Jenna moaned good-naturedly. "I've been discovered."

So she had. The children just lit up seeing her on the porch. Even Tony smiled in a way he didn't ever smile at Mimi. She felt a swift pang of jealousy.

His happy "Miz Jenna!" didn't ease the sting.

Jenna said, "If you all come on in, I've got cookies."

She didn't have to say it twice. They came rushing.

"There is milk in the cool box. Be sure to have some."

Gray came up at a slower pace. He stopped. His hair was long like Cougar's. He was definitely all Indian, with those deep brown eyes and darker skin. He looked at her for a moment before continuing up the steps. As he passed, he said, "You don't have to worry. He will return."

A chill went down Mimi's spine. So much self-possession in so young a boy was eerie. Following him into the house, she asked Jenna, "Does he know, or is he just guessing?"

Jenna shrugged. "I've never been able to figure that out, but he does inspire belief, doesn't he?"

"Yes."

Jenna shook out her apron. Flour puffed. She waved it away.

"You're lucky to have such wonderful children."

Jenna nodded. "That I am, but I'll tell you a secret: I'd love to have more. There's just something about the sound of children in the house that makes me happy."

"Tony and Kevin love it here."

Jenna looked at her. "Of course they do. We've got cookies and other children to play with. What's not to love?"

Mimi sighed. "There's more to it than that. You have stability. You have a home. You know what to do—"

Frowning, Jenna interrupted her. "What are you trying to say?"

"I'm not a good parent."

"How can you say that? You've been—"

It was Mimi's turn to interrupt. And when she did, it was like a dam broke deep down inside and the truth spilled out in a rapid tumble of words. "You don't understand, Jenna. I don't enjoy it. I feel like I've been thrown somewhere in time way ahead of myself, and I'm in this place where I'm just struggling and drowning. And I don't think I'm doing well for myself. I don't think I'm doing well for them. I don't think I'm doing well for anyone and I'm just . . ." She pushed the feeling away with a quick gesture. "I'm just drowning."

Jenna placed her hand on Mimi's arm and squeezed lightly. "Oh, Mimi, we all feel this way from time to time."

"I feel this way all the time."

There was a long pause. Jenna smoothed her hair. "How old are you?"

"I turned nineteen last month."

"Nineteen," she repeated. "And how old is Tony?"

"He's ten."

"And the others?"

"Kevin's eight and Melinda Sue is four."

"You have been just tossed into the deep end of the lake, haven't you?"

"I know." She licked her lips. It felt so wrong to confess this, but so right, too. "My whole life, I've been paying for other people's crimes, trying to live up to strict ideals. I have never even had a chance to decide for sure what I might want to be."

"And now you're a mother."

"This is going to sound crazy, but I never planned to be a mother. I just wanted to get them out of Mac's house."

"Clint told me about Mac, but not anything about his house. Is it what I think it is?"

"Probably. At the time, when I thought I was married to Mac, I just gave it a lot of fancy names to make it more palatable, but when you boil down to it, it's just a fancy whorehouse."

Jenna put her hands up. "Wait! Back up. What do you mean, when you *thought* you were married to Mac?"

Ouch. Had she really let that slip? "It's a long story."

Jenna wasn't one whit deterred. "Then let me get some milk and cookies and we can go on the porch and have a snack while you tell it."

Jenna didn't give Mimi time to protest, gathering up cookies and large glasses of cool milk on a tray, some-how twisting her arm with smiles and gentle nudges until she was seated out on the porch in one of the two rocking chairs, accepting a glass of milk and a plate of cookies.

"For such a nice woman you're amazingly persuasive," Mimi muttered.

Taking her seat, Jenna smiled her soft smile and arched her brows at her. "Where do you think Gray gets it from?" Picking up a cookie, she took a bite. Waving it in the air, she ordered, "Now, spill."

Fifteen minutes later the cookie tray was empty and she'd spilled everything. Truth be told, it felt more like an-other purge, and Mimi couldn't even say why she felt better for it, but she did.

Jenna, tapping her fingers against her glass, glanced over at the children. "Just a whorehouse?"

"Yes."

"Sounds like a hell house to me. The life that monster would have condemned those children to doesn't even bear thinking about."

"No, it doesn't."

Jenna toasted her with the empty milk glass. "You saved them."

"Not on purpose. Taking them with me was more of a panicked impulse than anything I thought out."

Jenna dismissed that notion with a wave of her hand. "Sometimes doing the right thing just happens. Doesn't make it any less right. At least that's what Clint says."

"I suppose." It was a lot better way of looking at it than the way she did.

Jenna leaned back in the chair and set it to rocking with a push of her foot. After a moment, she asked, "If you weren't a mother, Mimi, what would you want to do?"

"I think I'd like to be courted by a nice man. To flirt."

"You'd like to be young."

Very much so. "Yes. I'd really like to make a decision that's based just on what I want or need or . . . I don't even know how to explain it." She tried to fill in the blank with a wave of her hand. "I want to have a time in my life where I make a choice because I want to."

To her surprise, Jenna nodded. "I can really understand that. Before I married Clint, I was married to a very, very bad man. And before I was married to that very, very bad man, I was living under the roof of a very, very strict father. I think the only thing I knew really well was how to be afraid."

Mimi blinked. "I just can't even imagine you being afraid."

Jenna smiled. "That was Clint's gift to me. We married because of Brianna. Because I wanted children so badly and I couldn't have them, and then somebody just left her on my doorstep." Her smile was soft with remembered wonder. "She was clearly half Indian, with this wild hair that stuck straight up. I was widowed, crippled, and running my restaurant. Nobody in their right mind would give her to me, but Clint made it happen. And then he gave me more."

Blowing out a breath, she shook her head. "I was a mess when he married me. I didn't even know how to *be* me, but I've flourished in this marriage. I love Clint, and I love my life, but getting here wasn't easy. I gave Clint some black moments. Through it all, though, he's loved me as I am, with all my flaws, asking nothing in return except that I let myself love him as he is."

"And you do?"

She nodded. "Loving like that, being loved like that, is the greatest gift."

It was so easy to see why Clint loved Jenna and was so fiercely protective of her. There was an innocence about her, a purity of soul that just demanded protection, but there was also an inexhaustible strength that promised an emotional haven.

"Clint's a very lucky man."

Jenna grinned cheekily. "Yes, he is. But I've wandered off my point." Jenna sighed and grimaced. "I know what you mean in regard to wanting to be in charge of your life. There was a point when I had to make a choice and it *scared* me, but I did it. It was the first time I'd ever done it, and to this day that decision was the hardest yet the best one I've ever made."

The kids came out and plunked down on the porch,

cookies in one hand and milk in the other. Kevin looked up. For approval?

"Are you having a good time?" she asked.

Kevin grinned and nodded. To Jenna, he announced, "I love it here."

Mimi's heart caught. She couldn't provide him with this.

Jenna smiled. "And I love having you here."

And she did. Mimi could see it. Jenna was a natural mother. She exuded warmth and hugs and happiness. She was comfortable with who she was. She was comfortable in that role.

Tony took a bite of his cookie and then another one, as if he thought the first one wasn't big enough. "Melinda Sue is going to be mad she missed out on these cookies."

"I set some aside for her."

Jenna said it so simply, as if there was no doubt in her mind Melinda Sue would be back. Mimi was grateful.

Gray glanced over. "Where'd you hide them?"

"Oh, no, I'm not telling you that."

He shrugged as if it was no matter.

Jenna feigned offense. "And don't you even think about ferreting them out."

On another shrug, he said, "We can always make more."

Mimi had to admire his nonchalance.

Jenna shook her head. "Yes, we could, but I think it would be nice to have something special for her when she comes home. She's had quite the adventure."

Gray looked off into the distance. With a nod, he pronounced, "She'll like that."

"You don't even know her," Tony said, the next cookie lined up for devouring.

Gray glanced at him and raised a brow. "What's not to like about cookies?"

He had a point. Kevin handed her a cookie. Even though she was full, Mimi took a bite. The rich sweetness spread across her tongue. The cookie would taste even better if Jackson and Mellie would appear on the horizon.

Gray tapped her shoulder.

She turned. He pointed to the right. "They'll be coming from that way when they come."

There was nothing to do except say "thank you" and change her position.

That evening, Mimi was back sitting on the porch steps, listening to the sound of the crickets chirping, watching the bats fly by in their erratic patterns, and swatting the mosquitoes that ventured forth. She looked up at the sky. The stars were big tonight but the moon not so much. It was starting to wane but still bright enough to illuminate the landscape, which was why she was out here watching the horizon in between trying to break the coded names in Mac's book.

Over and over she ran her finger over the names. It was so frustrating. There was something about the mixture of letters and numbers that teased her. There was a pattern to the combinations. She could almost see it . . . but just when she thought she had it, it disappeared.

Turning up the lantern at her side, she gave it another try. As soon as she did, the moths came flying in, fluttering about and getting in her hair. She quickly turned it back down. Reading outside at night was definitely a balancing act.

The children were inside playing poker with Jenna, using twigs as chips. Even little Brianna was throwing a card into the mix now and then. They'd invited her to join in, but she was too worried to be social. She didn't have the confidence that everyone else did that the men would bring Melinda Sue back. What if Jackson was wrong? What if Mac had found her? What if he'd ridden into a trap? She knew Mac, how devious and evil he was. He'd shown her too many times how much he enjoyed tricking people and then making them suffer. What if he'd done that to Jackson and his friends? Mac knew important people everywhere.

Hearing the front door squeak, she turned. Kevin came out to join her.

"Are you all done playing cards?"

He shrugged and dropped into the rocker beside her. "I lost the entire pot."

"But you had so many sticks!"

"I put it all on one thing." He frowned and rested his arm on his knee, hand dangling. With the other hand he gestured. "I was sure I was going to win."

"A lot of gamblers feel that way."

"I don't like gambling."

"I see." It was a relief to know there were some risks Kevin didn't enjoy.

"Gray's good at it, though."

"Gray's older and I imagine Clint taught him a lot."

Kevin frowned and picked at the tear on the knee of his pants. He obviously had something on his mind.

"Gray said that Clint and Jenna adopted him."

Her stomach fell a little. "Yes."

He cut her a glance. "I don't know who my father is."

"I don't know who mine is, either."

That surprised him.

"Does it bother you?"

"It used to bother me a lot."

"And now?"

Her first instinct was to lie, but she owed him better. "To

be honest, it still does. Sometimes, I'd walk around the town where I grew up, looking at all the different men to see if I could see my face in theirs."

"How come your mother didn't tell you who your daddy was?"

How many times had she asked that question herself? "I don't know." She shrugged. "She's not a woman who thinks the past matters."

"But your father's the present."

She shrugged. "There was nothing I could do about it, so, finally, I just accepted if he'd wanted to be in my life he would have been."

Kevin fell silent again, grinding the toe of his worn leather shoe into the porch boards. She waited patiently for him to speak his mind. Finally, he looked up.

"I like it here."

It was almost a challenge. Her stomach dropped again. "I know."

Another long pause and then, "Do you think if we asked her nicely Jenna and Clint would adopt us?"

"You want to be adopted?"

"Not just me." He made an inclusive circling motion with his hand. "All of us. You, me, Tony, and Melinda Sue." Excitement vibrated through him. "We could all stay here. Together."

Oh, Kevin. "I'm too old to be adopted."

"Then maybe you could marry Jackson and just stay near."

Her heart did a ker-thump at the thought. "That's not likely, but if we did, wouldn't you like to live with me and Jackson?"

He frowned. "I hadn't thought of that. I just thought we're family and we'd find a family together."

She didn't know what to do with that. Apparently, he didn't see her as a mother any more than she saw herself that way. "How does Tony feel?"

"Tony wants us to stay together."

"I see." She was trying so hard to be a mother to them and she'd failed so thoroughly. It was a crushing revelation.

He scuffed his heel across the porch. Fussed with a bit of dust on the arm of the rocker. "Do you think they found Melinda Sue?"

"I'm sure they did."

"Then why aren't they here?"

"They're probably waiting for daylight to travel." It was the most plausible lie she could think of.

He shot it down with irrefutable logic. "The moon's bright enough."

"They might be too tired."

He agreed, albeit reluctantly, before adding, "I think Melinda Sue would like it here, too."

She wasn't sure why he was pushing so hard to create his family here. "Did Jenna say something to you?"

"No, but she adopted Brenna and Gray and Bri. She might like us, too. Melinda Sue can be a pain, but Tony and I could keep her quiet."

So much angst packed into one sentence.

"Keeping Melinda Sue quiet is quite the tall order."

"Yeah." He kicked his foot and frowned. "She'd probably ruin everything."

Mimi's heart twisted at the defeated acceptance in the statement. "Did you have a family, Kevin? You know, before we met?"

The shake of his head ended on a shrug. "Sort of. My aunt took care of me, and she was, well, you know where she worked."

Unfortunately, she did.

"My mother's dead." Hunching his shoulders as if to soften the blow of memory, he continued. "Before we went to live at Mac's, she tried to find me a pa. She brought a few men home, but . . ." He scuffed his heel across the chair rung. "They always got mean, and after a week or so they'd leave."

"But your aunt kept trying. She loved you."

He nodded. "After a while, I wished she'd stop." He shrugged. "And then she did."

Silence again. This time when the door opened, Tony came out loaded down with cookies. He handed one to Mimi before he sat down on her other side. "What are you all talking about?"

Kevin cast her a quick warning look. "Just this and that."

He nodded and took a bite of the cookie. "Mrs. Jenna makes good cookies."

"Yes, she does a lot of things well."

"I like her."

"I like her, too."

"Mr. McKinnley's a little scary, though."

"Gray doesn't think so," Kevin taunted.

"Gray's known Clint longer." Mimi swatted a mosquito. "Do you like this town, Tony?"

"The people we've met are nice."

"Maybe when things get better we can come back here and stay."

Tony looked at her. "Things never get better."

He was too young to be so negative, but then again whenever had he been given a reason to be positive?

"It would be nice to be able to stay in one spot, though," Tony admitted.

"I liked it at the other house," Mimi said.

"Yeah, it was nice," Tony said, "but there's more to do here in town."

Kevin perked up, obviously remembering something. "Mrs. Jenna said tomorrow we can eat at her restaurant."

"It's the same food as here," Tony pointed out with all the arrogance of his two-year advantage.

"Yeah, but it's in a restaurant!"

"It sounds exciting to me," Mimi agreed before a squabble could break out.

"Do you like being in town, Mimi?" Kevin asked.

"Yes. I grew up in the city. The mercantile was just a block away, and there was always somebody to talk to, something to do."

"Did you have a lot of friends?" Kevin asked.

"My situation was difficult." Had they never really talked about this before? She guessed not. It was always so busy. First with trying to protect them in Mac's house, then trying to get them out, and then trying to keep them alive. Afterward, there just hadn't been a lot of time for conversation. "Do you remember what it was like when we lived at Mac's? How people used to assume things about you because of where we lived?"

Tony nodded and Kevin brushed the bottom of his pants off. "Yep."

"Well, I lived in a little house in town with my mother, but everybody knew my mother hadn't been married to my father. That in itself might not have been so horrible, but my mother wasn't happy. She didn't like how her life turned out, so she liked to make rules for everybody around her to follow. People tried to be friends with her, but . . . I don't know." She spread her hands helplessly. "I thought sometimes that she resented them for wanting to be her friend."

"So they didn't talk to you, either?"

She shook her head. "And if they did, she would tell me whether I could talk to them or not. It was difficult." There was no way to explain how her mother seemed to believe that everybody in the world had an ulterior motive and that they were best just staying away from the world. She'd felt very alone growing up. Even to this day, she still wasn't sure she knew how to make friends.

"I always thought having a mother would be fun, but doesn't seem like it was much fun for you."

She spread her hands wide again. "I think family is just like anything else. I think you have to know how to make it work."

"I don't know how to make it work," Tony confessed.

"Then we're all just going to have to do the same thing. We're going to have to imitate people who do. If we copy people who know what they're doing, then we can't go wrong, right?"

Tony shifted position. "Like Mrs. Mara and Mr. Cougar."

"Exactly."

"Like Mrs. Jenna and Mr. Clint."

"Yeah. They really know what they're doing," Tony agreed before adding, "Gray, Brenna, and Brianna are happy. Gray said Mr. Clint is teaching him to shoot."

There was envy in his voice, and what could she tell him? That maybe Clint would teach him to shoot, too, when she didn't even know if they were going to be here? "I'm sure we'll have opportunities to learn all the things that we want to do."

Kevin took the book out of her hand and flipped the pages. "Have you figured it out yet?"

She shook her head. "I think I should be able to see it, but I can't."

"What happens if we figure out who the people are in this book?"

"I don't know."

Tony sighed and held out his hand for the book. "There's a lot you don't know."

She didn't need him to tell her that. "Well, I think that's pretty much how it's going to be for a while. I'm not going to always know and we're just going to have to wing it."

Neither boy looked thrilled, and how could she blame them? They'd finally had a taste of what they'd been missing and now they wanted it for themselves.

"We'll figure it out."

Both boys nodded. Tony handed her back the book. "Hopefully sooner rather than later."

"Yes." Looking down the trail, hoping against hope to see Jackson ride in on Little Lady, Melinda Sue safely in front of him, Mimi felt the same weariness and insecurity reflected in Tony's voice. "Definitely sooner."

Sixteen

~~~~~~~~~~

There was nothing better, Jackson decided, than coming home and witnessing your woman light up like the sun cresting the horizon when she saw you.

"I hope Jenna's got breakfast cooking," Elijah said, rubbing his stomach. "If I don't eat something soon, I'm going to waste away."

Clint snorted. "It's going to take more than a day without a meal for you to disappear."

Elijah grunted. Clint smiled. Jackson nudged Melinda Sue, who was dozing on the saddle in front of him.

"Do you see Mimi, Melinda Sue?"

The little girl snapped up straight. "Where?"

He pointed. "Right there on the porch."

She rubbed her eyes, spotted Mimi, and started waving her arms. "Mimi! Mimi!"

As if Mimi hadn't already seen her there. As if she

wasn't coming down off the porch, skirts raised, showing a delectable bit of ankle.

"Mimi!"

Mimi was already running across the dew-wet lawn toward him, her joy leading the way.

"Put me down," Melinda Sue ordered, kicking her feet. "Put me down."

The front door banged open. Out came Kevin, Tony, and Gray. Behind them, Jenna holding a squirming little Brianna. At nearly two, she was a handful.

"Don't kick while I put you down. You'll hurt Lady."

She switched kicking for wiggling. "Hurry!"

Holding on to Melinda Sue's arm, he carefully lowered her to the ground. Lady flicked her ears at the commotion but held her manners. He owed her an extra measure of oats for her patience of late. As soon as Melinda Sue's feet hit the ground, she took off, racing across the grass.

"Melinda Sue!" Scooping up the girl, Mimi gave her a big hug, holding her tightly, spinning in a circle. Over the little girl's shoulder, her eyes asked a question. He shook his head and mouthed a "no." They hadn't hurt her.

Mimi hugged Melinda Sue again, tears shimmering in her eyes. "I was so worried about you!"

Wrapping her legs around Mimi's waist, cupping her cheeks in her hands, and shoving her face close, Melinda Sue announced, "Me and Mr. Jackson had adventures."

"I can't wait to hear about them." Satisfied with Melinda Sue's health, Mimi turned her attention to him. "But first let me thank Mr. Montgomery for bringing you home."

Shifting sideways, Melinda Sue beamed at him. "Mr. Jackson says I can be bad all I want, and he'll always bring me home."

That got him a raised brow. "He did, huh?"

"That wasn't exactly the agreement."

Melinda stuck her lip out. "Was, too." To Mimi she whispered loud enough for everyone to hear, "He loves me."

Clint and Elijah laughed out loud.

Jackson had a hard time containing his own laughter. "Dang it, Melinda Sue, you're not supposed to just blurt out a man's secrets like that."

Melinda Sue was completely unrepentant. "It's all right. I loves you, too."

Mimi laughed, grinned, and shook her head.

Clint nudged his horse toward the house. "I'm going to leave you to it. You all are making me hungry to greet my wife."

Urging his horse into a trot, slapping hands with Gray as he went by, he headed for the porch. With consummate grace, he leapt off in front of a waiting Jenna. She kissed him with the same passion that Jackson wanted to kiss Mimi with, but Clint and Jenna were married and had privileges he did not. Yet.

Elijah cleared his throat. "I'm going to wash up. If I'm not mistaken, that's bacon cooking."

Mimi just shook her head, and she kept on smiling and kept on coming. Jackson kneed Lady forward, more than happy to meet her halfway.

The boys caught up with her before he did. Excited to see the boys, Melinda Sue squealed and wiggled. Mimi handed her over to Tony, who twirled her around and pelted her with questions the little girl was happy to answer.

Smoothing her hair, Mimi took six more steps toward him and then stopped. Holding her hands out in invitation, she tossed the ball into his court.

She was so beautiful in the soft morning light. The flush from exertion brought out the blue of her eyes and the soft strands of blonde streaking her hair. She stood there, breasts heaving slightly, lips parted, waiting for him to reach her. When he did, she placed her hand on his thigh and stepped in. Her gaze searched his. His searched hers.

She spoke first. "You look tired."

"You look beautiful."

She opened her mouth, to protest, he was sure. He cut her off. "Just say thank you."

"I can't stop smiling. You're so beautiful."

"Men aren't beautiful."

She tossed his own words back at him. "Just say thank you."

Even dead tired, the woman could make him laugh. "Anyone ever told you, you've got more sass than ten people?"

"Only ten? I must be slipping."

Chuckling, he shook his head. "Come here."

He held out his hand. She grabbed his forearm.

Kicking his foot out of the stirrup, he ordered, "Put your foot in the stirrup."

She did, catching her skirt and almost slipping, but he lifted her out of trouble. When she landed across his lap, palms braced against his chest, she laughed. There'd never been a better sound to come home to than that.

He leaned in. "I said come here."

She stretched up. He tasted her laugh before her kiss. Sweet joy, then passion. Brushing his lips across her forehead, he confessed, "I might be in trouble here."

She looked at him, and there was just so much emotion in her eyes, it spilled over into her hug.

"You trying to break my ribs, woman?"

"I was so worried you weren't going to come home," she

whispered, checking him over for injuries. She found the bruise on his shoulder and the one on his ribs. He shook his head at her frown. "Bruises, nothing more. I'm fine."

"And the men who took Mellie?"

"They're not a problem anymore."

Her teeth sank into her lower lip. "They're dead?"

"You don't need to fear them anymore."

He was stopped from filling her in about Mac by the boys coming up. There was always later. Smiling, he ruffled Kevin's hair and shook Tony's hand. "Hey there, you two. Did you hold down the fort while I was gone?"

Kevin stood straight. "We did."

"Good to know I have you to depend on."

Both boys stood a little taller. He wasn't so old that he couldn't remember how tall praise could make a man feel, no matter what the age. "Thank you."

A little pressure from his knee sent Lady ambling forward.

The boys strolled alongside them, pelting him with questions.

"Was there a fight?"

"Did anybody get hurt?"

He managed to get in a "no" and a "yes" before they hit him with, "Did you kill anybody?"

The "of course" died on his tongue as Mimi shook her head. "Shouldn't you boys first be asking if Mr. Montgomery is all right?" she said.

Tony snorted. "I know he's all right—otherwise you'd be looking at his wounds."

Jackson couldn't tell if her snort covered laughter or disgust as she complained, "I'd like to think I'd wait until he got off the horse."

Laughter, Jackson decided. It was definitely laughter.

Kevin was just as quick to retort, "Not hardly. You don't have much in the way of patience."

That stung her. He could tell.

"Harrumph."

"Mimi's got plenty of patience when she needs it, but mostly she's always hurrying because you all have things you feel you need . . . right"—he mimicked Kevin's whine when he wanted something—"now."

Kevin rolled his eyes. "I don't sound like that."

Jackson hid his grin again. "My mistake."

Melinda Sue squirmed in Tony's arms. "I want to get down."

It wasn't hard to tell why. She'd spotted Gray on the porch. He stood there as he always did, with that aura around him that most people shied away from. Not Melinda Sue, though. She did slow down when she got within four feet, walking until she got a bit closer, and then she just stopped and stared at him.

He folded his arms across his chest and stared back. He was obviously intent on intimidating the child. She studied him, tilting her head to the side. He tilted his head back, looking down his nose at her arrogance. Undeterred, she put her hands on her hips and took a couple steps closer, smudged dress, cockeyed pigtails, and all. They stared like that for a good thirty seconds. It was Melinda Sue who put an end to the competition. With a nod of her head she declared, "I like you."

Gray raised his eyebrows, mustering even more disdain. He might as well have saved himself the effort. Ignoring all of his body language, she ascended the stairs and squared off toe to toe, and then, to Gray's shock, she hugged him. He unfolded his arms, whether to push her away or hug her wasn't clear. In the end he just stood there, arms out, and got hugged.

That was more than Brenna could stand. Brenna had laid claim to Gray ever since they'd met behind the saloon a year back. Ignoring Gray's shake of his head, she came closer and demanded, "Stop that!"

If the red of Brenna's hair showed her temper, the tone of her voice declared war.

Melinda Sue blinked her big blue eyes up at Gray. "Are you going to let her hurt me?"

Gray blinked and frowned at Brenna. "No."

"Can I hurt her?"

This time the "no" was stronger. Melinda Sue pouted. Gray finally figured out what to do with his arms. He gave her a quick hug. Brenna scowled.

Jackson chuckled and whispered in Mimi's ear. "That is not going to be the last time two girls fight over that boy."

She nodded.

Though he was too far away to hear the whisper, Clint was obviously of the same mind. "We're going to have our hands full over the next few years."

Gray untangled himself from Melinda Sue. She was not pleased. Her lower lip puffed out. Declaring, "I didn't want to be your friend anyway," she stomped off.

Watching her, Clint grinned. "And so are you."

Jenna saved the day. "Melinda Sue, do you by any chance like butter cookies?"

Melinda Sue stopped. "Cookies?"

Jenna nodded. "I just happen to have a very special plate of cookies saved just for you."

Her expression cleared. "Just for me?"

Jenna nodded. "Just for you, and I even have some nice milk in the cold box to go with them."

Melinda Sue's smile broke out. "I love cookies."

Jenna held out her hand. Melinda Sue took it without a bit of hesitation.

"Then why don't you come with me? Today, we'll let the boys do the work while we go have a snack."

Over her shoulder, Melinda Sue stuck her tongue out at Kevin and Tony, who just rolled their eyes. Brenna seemed content to have Melinda Sue gone, whereas Gray just shook his head and observed, "That one gets her way too much."

"Keeping her contained is kind of like trying to harness a tornado," Jackson agreed. Little Lady stopped at the hitching post. The boys grabbed the reins.

"Are you ready to get down?" he asked Mimi, who contentedly snuggled against him.

Mimi's head nodded yes, but her body said no. Somewhere over the course of their short ride, the curves of her body had melted into the planes of his, as if they were one. Not only did it feel good, it felt right. In the past he'd had an abstract idea of what it would be like to have a woman greet him the way Jenna and Mara greeted their husbands. How it would feel to have somebody light up like Elizabeth did when she saw Asa. To have someone to verbally spar with the way Brad did with his Evie. And now he knew. He hadn't even been close.

"You're going to have to let go."

She sighed. "You're so bossy."

He grinned and kicked his foot out of the stirrup. "Hold on to my arm."

"See. Bossy."

"I see." He saw the fullness of her breasts straining the bodice of her favorite blue dress. He saw the smudges under her eyes that spoke of lack of sleep. He saw the pallor of her skin and the concern clinging to the edges of her smile.

"What do you see?" she asked as he lowered her to the ground.

"I see that you were worried about me."

She wrinkled her nose. "Maybe a little."

He grinned at the grudging admission, slung his leg over the saddle, and hopped off. As soon as his boots hit the ground, he said, "Maybe more than a little."

Elijah, who'd been trailing behind and observing, as was his wont, pulled his horse up to the post and dismounted in time to hear Clint tease, "Young love."

Elijah snorted. "Is that what we're calling it?"

Mimi blushed a bright red.

"No one said anything about love," Jackson retorted. If possible Mimi's blush deepened.

With a wave of his hand, Clint indicated the two of them. "That's because no one felt the need to state the obvious."

Elijah laughed.

Mimi groaned.

And Jackson sighed. That cat was neatly out of the bag. Jamming his hat down on his head, he grabbed Mimi's hand and all but dragged her up the steps. "I want a cookie."

Mimi tried the cookies. She also tried the ham dinner that Jenna had prepared. And now, sitting around the McKinnleys' dining room table, she was adding a cup of coffee to the mix in an effort to calm her nerves. None of her efforts succeeded. With the children around they hadn't had any time at all to talk about what had happened with the kidnappers. And she knew from the looks that the men were exchanging that something else had gone on out there. Something bigger than the kidnappers being dead. If they didn't tell her soon, she was going to explode.

"Can you tell me again why we're waiting for Asa?"

"Because Elizabeth will want to be in on this," Jackson explained.

"And," Clint pointed out dryly, "he's not giving us a choice."

"And we need the Rev," Elijah said, adding cream to his coffee. "We definitely need the Rev."

"Why?" Why, why, why? The question repeated in her mind. "Are you trying to drive me crazy?"

Jackson's hand sought hers under the table. "I told you, you have nothing to worry about." Lacing his fingers between hers, he squeezed gently. She wanted to take comfort from that, but she couldn't. It was like they all were part of an exclusive club complete with its own special language. And she wasn't a member.

"I understand all of you have been together for a long time and you've built up this big understanding of how you all work, but I've only known you all for three weeks, and, trust me, that's not enough time for that much faith."

Jackson had the gall to cock an eyebrow at her. "You're breaking my heart."

She dug her fingers threateningly into his hand. "If I had a rug beater in hand right now . . ."

"You'd do what?"

She sighed and relented. "I'd have the cleanest darn house in town."

And he might have a dent in his head.

Jenna shook her head while Clint just sat over there smiling. Through the window, Mimi could see Elijah outside smoking. At the other end, Jenna clucked her tongue. "You're as bad as Melinda Sue."

Sitting back in her chair, she grumbled, "Well, just how long does it take to get here?"

"Asa and Elizabeth do have the baby."

"And Evie can't make it anywhere on time to save her life."

Clint nodded. "That's true. And the Rev isn't much better. Hell, the man was literally late for his own funeral."

"How is that even possible?"

"You've got to know the Rev."

The knowing looks the group shared only made her feel more the outsider. Which just irritated her more. Tapping her fingers on the table, she muttered, "So you're telling me I've just got to be patient?"

"It is a virtue."

She cut Jackson a glare. "You can say that all you want; it's still not going to make it one of mine."

"Not all surprises are bad," Jenna pointed out.

"Well, this one had better be a doozy."

Finally, they were all here, minus Cougar and Mara. Even if there hadn't been complications with her pregnancy, Mara was just too far along to be risking bouncing around in a buckboard by night. The children were all in bed, and to avoid the chance of being overheard, they all moved out to the front yard. Clint had built a fire to keep the bugs away. It was rather cozy sitting on the chairs that were set up outside, watching the fire dance and listening to it crackle. It might even have been romantic except for the fact that anxiety was eating her up from the inside out.

Asa finally broke the silence. "Just how well did you know your husband?" he asked.

"About five minutes ago I would've answered 'Too well,' but from the tone of your voice I think the correct response would be 'Not well enough.'"

Brad tipped his hat back. "I did some research. He is an interesting man. He wasn't overly educated, but his belief that everybody was out to get him made him highly skilled in some areas. That code that encrypts the names in his book is pretty sophisticated. But that he chose to protect that information in a box in his house was pretty careless."

"What do mean you did research?"

"My father was a prominent minister back East. He has connections with a lot of people. He sent me a telegraph."

Mimi shrugged. "I didn't know much about his business life. He sometimes had parties at the house that I hosted, but I don't know what he did when he left the house."

"Apparently," Brad said, "your husband spent a lot of time keeping tabs on a lot of people with the intent of blackmailing them."

"These men are very powerful," Jackson added.

Mimi nodded. "That makes sense. Mac could leave the house with an insurmountable problem and be back two hours later with it solved. What always struck me about that was how unemotional he was about the problems when they happened and when they were solved."

"As I said, very powerful men."

Brad turned his coffee cup. "Normally, it would be a mistake to blackmail so many powerful men. Except Mac was smart enough to stagger his demands. He seemed to have a knack for knowing how to get what he wanted without ever applying too much pressure.

"Sort of like a mild bout of gout," Brad elaborated.

Mimi laughed along with everyone else. When the laughter ended, however, the stress came back. "All I want to know is whether his contacts can reach out here."

"They could, but that won't be a problem."

"Why not?"

Asa pulled a piece of paper out of his pocket. "He left you an inheritance."

The paper rustled in the breeze. Reality hit in a paralyzing rush. She couldn't breathe, couldn't reach for it. "He *is* really dead? You're sure?"

Elijah's deep drawl blended with the roaring in her ears. "Not many who mess with what's Jackson's live to regret it."

"Jackson?"

"Oh, my Lord, catch her!" Jenna cried.

The world tilted and she was pitching into the roaring black. Just as suddenly it righted and she was pulled up close to a hard chest. "Come here, honey."

Jackson. Thank goodness. Something to hold on to. Beneath her cheek, she could hear the steady rhythm of his heartbeat. She placed her hand over it, anchoring herself through touch and sound. Closing her eyes, she breathed in his scent.

"Jackson." Forcing her eyes open, Mimi clutched his arm and asked again.

"Yes."

She looked into his eyes. The truth was always in Jackson's eyes. "Spell it out for me."

"He's dead. I killed him."

"Why?"

"Because of what he did to you and the children. Because he needed it."

The roaring started to subside. Mac was dead. Truly

dead. Licking her lips, she whispered, "Thank you." And then, "I'm free."

His fingers in a steeple, Brad looked at her. "Not quite."

It didn't really matter what new thing they'd dreamed up to complicate this issue. Nothing could be as bad as Mac. "I'm not going to let you rain on my happiness. Mac is dead. It's time to throw a party."

"Not yet."

Asa handed her the paper. She opened it up, the letters and numbers on it meaning nothing to her. "I don't understand what this is."

"That"—he pointed to the code—"is the key to your freedom. Without that, you'd never be safe."

"All right. But how do I use it?"

"With that key we can decipher all the names in that book. And with the names we can return whatever he's holding over these people to the rightful owners."

"They're words on a page—how can we return them?"

"First off, anonymously. Nobody knows who you are. Nobody knows who's read that book. And that's important. That's why the children are here. Because if one word of this gets out, and anyone in the book does find out who we are, they might decide to take protective measures."

"You mean kill us?"

Would it ever end?

"They'll have to go through me to get to you," Jackson said.

She patted his hand absently, her mind spinning. "You do realize, when you say that, it's not a comfort? I don't want you dead."

"Good to know."

"I don't know how you can joke in the middle of all this.

You do realize by coming here I signed your death warrant?"

Elijah shook his head. "Ma'am, those Easterners? They have to get to the end of a very long line. We haven't exactly been slackers when it comes to collecting enemies."

"So what is the plan?" She knew them well enough to know they had a plan.

It was Brad who answered. "We're going to take the key and the book and decode all the names. And we'll rip out the pages in that book and send them anonymously to the owners with the message saying that Mac is dead and it's over."

"They can consider it an early Christmas present."

"A very early Christmas present."

"I'm sure it will be appreciated."

"Why can't we just let it alone and not do anything?" Mimi asked. "Burn the book and move on."

"Because those men know the information is out there. It's only logical that Mac kept some sort of record. They're going to want to control that information once they know of Mac's death."

"And most on that list have the money and influence to hunt anyone down."

"The best chance you've got is to give them back what's theirs and hand them their lives back. Make it clear that's what's happening and keep an eye out."

"What if they aren't satisfied?" Mimi asked, not really wanting the answer.

"Then we'll deal with them," Elijah said with chilling dispassion.

"But I don't think it will come to that. Businessmen understand a good deal."

"Are you all right with this, Mimi?" Jenna asked. "After all, this is your life."

She weighed her options. "Yes."

Jackson's thumb brushed her lips in a parody of a kiss. Tingles raced down her spine. She wished the others gone.

"It's settled, then?" Asa asked.

She nodded. "Yes."

"Good."

"Well, now, since that's settled," the Reverend said, "I'd like to discuss something else." Everyone looked at him. Mimi was the only one foolish enough to ask, "What?"

The Rev lounged back in his chair, looking for all the world like a lean, basking lion. Making a temple of his fingers, he considered Mimi and Jackson. "I'd like to talk about you and Jackson continuing to live in sin."

Mimi's stomach did a flip-flop. Jackson's thumb stilled. Her "I don't know what you mean" was weak even to her own ears.

In contrast, Jackson's "That's none of your business, Rev" was cold and hard.

The Rev just smiled. "I can't rightly do that, Jackson. I've been approached by the good ladies of the town. They're worried about the children."

It was the nightmare of her life. The one that wouldn't go away. Mimi clenched her hands together. "I haven't done anything wrong."

It wasn't a complete lie. In the eyes of the church, maybe she'd sinned, but in her heart, absolutely not.

Jenna stood up. "Brad, you stop this."

Elijah tossed his cigarette into the fire. "I didn't think immortal souls were your realm of expertise, Rev."

Jackson put his hand over hers. His thumb drew calming circles on the back. Mimi was grateful for the support.

Brad cocked an eyebrow at him. The blond hair falling over his brow gave him a distinctly unpreacherly look. "Just like in any profession, a man has to know it from all angles."

Jackson cocked his head. "And you've got sin covered?"

"I'm a married man. These days you'd have to ask my wife how well my sin is doing."

Everyone turned to Evie. She threw up her hands.

"You know I can't answer a question like that! I'm a preacher's wife."

Mimi didn't know whether to laugh or cry. Jackson didn't seem to have the same ambivalence. Getting to his feet, he growled. "I don't think I want to hear where this conversation is going."

Everyone else stood, too. Firelight danced across their features. Outside the circle of light, darkness encroached.

The Rev pulled his hat down over his brow. "It was heading in the direction of marriage."

"Whose?"

"Yours."

"Why?"

"Because, quite frankly," Brad said, "we're a bit worried you won't have the common sense to see what's standing in front of you."

"So you're ambushing me?"

Mimi couldn't tell if Jackson was mad or amused. But for herself, she was mortified.

Evie spread her hands and shrugged. There wasn't a lick of apology in the gesture. "It seemed prudent."

"For what it's worth," Elizabeth offered, "I'm thinking of it as surprise encouragement."

Jackson rolled his eyes. "You would. Did it ever occur to any of you jackasses that I might not want to get married?"

If the ground could conveniently open up a giant hole in front of her in that moment, Mimi would have dove in headfirst. They were backing Jackson into a corner. Forcing him to do something he clearly didn't want to do. It was humiliating. It was demeaning. The nice thing about being all grown up, though, was she no longer had to sit and tolerate being the butt of people's jokes.

"Excuse me." Turning, she just started walking.

"Mimi!" Jenna called. "Don't go."

She wasn't going to stay. Letting the faint moonlight guide her, she headed into the woods. A mosquito promptly bit her neck. She cursed and slapped it. Another came at her. She decided to run for it. Deeper into the woods. Away from the house. Away from the painful, humiliating reality that while they were teasing Jackson, she had pathetically been holding her breath, waiting for him to propose. Hoping it had been his idea. Wanting it to be.

The only fool tonight had been her.

Seventeen

⟨⟨⟨∾⟩⟩⟩

"Have you lost your damned mind?" Jackson demanded, running his hand through his hair, making note of the direction Mimi had bolted.

Brad sighed. "Maybe."

"In his defense," Elizabeth said, "that didn't go at all like we'd planned."

Asa held up his hands. "I had nothing to do with it."

"Me either," Elijah said.

Jackson looked at Brad. "But you did?"

Brad looked at Evie and blew out a breath. "I lost a bet."

It didn't take a genius to figure out what kind of bet it'd been. If he had any doubts Evie's blush dispelled them. "You sabotaged my proposal and ran my potential bride off into the night, because of a bet?"

"You were going to propose?" Jenna gasped.

"Well, why didn't you say something?" Evie snapped.

"Probably because it was none of our business," Brad interjected, catching Evie's hand and pulling her down.

"But if I'd known he had the sense God gave a gnat, I wouldn't have interfered," she muttered, leaning against his chest.

Jackson grabbed up a couple blankets from the chairs. "Good to know, and when I get back tomorrow, you can explain that to Mimi."

"Tomorrow?" Asa asked with an arch of his brow.

Pulling his hat down, Jackson muttered, "After all your help, I'm thinking she's going to take a heap of persuading to see me as any sort of husbandly prospect."

It wasn't hard to find her. She'd pretty much run in a straight line until she'd run into a tree. And then she'd sort of crumpled. She was still crumpled, sitting against the base, knees drawn up to her chest, pretending she didn't know he was standing there looking at her.

"Are you going to make me stand here all night?"

She sighed but didn't lift her head. "I'm actually hoping that if I ignore you long enough, you'll go away."

"Not going to happen." Squatting down in front of her, Jackson tipped her chin up with the tip of his finger. Her face was red and her cheeks blotchy. Damn. She'd been crying. Next time he saw Brad he was going to kick his ass. "Look at me, honey."

It took her a minute, but when she finally did, the misery in her eyes broke his heart. Very quietly he said, "I never give up."

She licked her lips. "You should."

Brushing his thumb across the moist skin, he asked, "Why?"

Her shrug was more like a hunch. "I'm sorry they did that to you."

"Why?"

Her head snapped up. "Can't you find anything else to say but 'why'?"

"Yup." He had a whole lot to say. "And as soon as you answer that, we can get to it."

"Maybe I don't want to."

Standing, he shook out a blanket.

"What are you doing?"

"Settling in. Looks like it's going to be a while."

She just stared at him. "You're crazy."

"And handsome." Sitting down on the blanket, he ran a finger down her nose. "It's a good idea to sprinkle some compliments in with your insults."

She swatted his hand away. "It's not an insult if it's true."

With a pat of his hand he indicated the blanket. "Come here."

"No."

With a tug, he tumbled her to his side. He needed to hold her.

"Yes."

She sat stiffly in his arms. Taking the second blanket, he wrapped it around her shoulders, cocooning them together. "There's no point in fighting it, you know. I've been away from you for three days. I'm pretty determined to cuddle."

"Why?"

"Because I missed you." He rubbed his chin across the top of her head. "See how easy it is to answer a simple question?"

"It depends on the question."

Turning, he leaned back against the tree. Pulling her with him, he draped her across his lap. Her full hips cushioned his cock. Her soft breasts pressed against his chest. His forearm settled neatly into the curve of her waist. She smelled like vanilla. He missed the honeysuckle. Resting his head against the tree, he savored the moment. "Damn, you feel good."

"Sweet-talking won't get you anywhere."

"Then I won't try it. It's time you answered my question, Mimi."

"Your friends tried to force you into marrying me. I don't want a man humiliated into marrying me."

Tilting his head to the side, he studied her expression. "Have you met me?"

"Those were your friends."

"Who took it upon themselves to stick their noses where they didn't belong. They'll apologize tomorrow."

She dropped her head to his chest. "Could this get any worse?"

"Give me a minute, and we'll see."

Her chuckle was weak but there.

He could work with that. "In the interest of my plans for the night going well, I'm going to sum things up. My friends are opinionated but good-hearted. They like you. They like me. In their eyes one plus one makes two."

"And in yours?"

"I don't have the patience for addition. I just know what I want."

She tilted her head back. Moonlight caressed her face. She was so achingly beautiful. "And what is that?"

"You."

She froze.

He shrugged. "The Rev stole my thunder."

"You don't have to say that."

"Honey, I don't have to do anything. I'm Jackson Montgomery."

That got the smile he was looking for. "Are you ever serious?"

"All the time. Just no one seems to notice."

Her hand opened over his heart. "I've noticed."

"Yes." He waited to see what she would do. She didn't speak for the longest moment. It could have been seconds or minutes. It felt like hours. There was a mosquito buzzing his ear. He didn't swat it. He didn't want to disrupt the moment. He felt the instant she reached a decision. The tension in her muscles subsided and she released her breath in a long, drawn-out sigh.

Finally, she said, "I like how I feel in your arms."

"How is that?"

Instead of answering, she pushed away from his chest and straddled his lap. "I'd much rather show you."

He glanced down at her hands braced against his shoulders. "Are you worried I'm going to resist?"

"You have a contrary side."

"True." His hands came up to the buttons of her dress. "I'm not crazy and only a crazy man would turn down an offer like that."

The first button gave easily. The second was a bit more stubborn. When the third parted, he had access to the sensitive skin of her nape. He took full advantage, drawing little circles over the exposed flesh. Her shiver went straight to his cock. "Don't you agree?"

"Yes."

The goose bumps that sprang up in the aftermath inspired him. "Turn around."

"I thought I was showing *you*."

"Give me about two minutes and you'll be showing me all sorts of things."

It wasn't easy to turn around on command when her skirts were wrapped around her legs, a log was wedged against her thigh, and desire was sapping the coordination from her muscles, but Mimi managed it. Not cleanly, and not without laughing, but in the end she was sitting on Jackson's lap with her back to his chest and her hands braced on his knees.

"In my head that went a lot smoother," Jackson confessed, still chuckling.

She liked that about Jackson. For all that intensity he could laugh at himself. She shook her hair out of her eyes. "In mine, too. I'm afraid I'm not going to make a living as a femme fatale."

"If you were any more 'fatale,' this would be over before it started."

Yes. Yes, it would. The proof pressed against her buttocks. The passion that hummed between them thrummed in a tangible connection. Wherever they touched, there was potential. Whenever they moved, there was pleasure. Between her thighs, his cock throbbed. On her back his fingers brushed tantalizingly as he unbuttoned her bodice.

"What are you doing?"

"What does it feel like?"

"It feels like you're teasing."

"Now, why would I do that?"

"Because you like to hear me moan."

"I do enjoy that. Do you like this?"

"This" was a light drag of his nails down her back.

Goose bumps sprang up along the path. Her shiver was hard and long. His chuckle was low and deep.

He did it again, and this time when the shiver hit, his

lips were there to capture it. Warm, moist, and teasing, they gathered that pleasure and then spread it further, raining gentle kisses down her back, cherishing her as button by button new territory was revealed.

He didn't have to tell her to kneel. She didn't have to ask him to continue. In this dance they were in perfect sync. Desire feeding desire. Passion spiking need. And the need . . .

Oh, she ached with the need. Her breasts tingled for his touch, her pussy throbbed for his possession, and her skin begged for his caress. It was torture just kneeling there, letting him paint his appreciation on her skin in kisses too light, caresses too fleeting to satisfy. It was also bliss. She never wanted it to stop.

"Beautiful siren."

"Yes." He made her feel beautiful, desirable. He made her feel so much. She didn't know how to contain it. But she did know how to show it.

His palms swept up her back and then around her shoulders before sliding down her arms. Her bodice went with them, revealing her breasts to the night and his enjoyment. Her nipples peaked. Her breasts ached.

"Jackson," she whispered.

His lips brushed her ear. "Tell me. Tell me what you need."

"I need you to touch me."

"Where?"

"Here." Taking his hands, she dragged them to her breasts, sighing in relief as he cupped the full curves, whimpering when his thumb and forefinger found the sensitive tips.

"Yes. Oh, yes."

Rough and deep, his "yes" echoed hers.

For endless moments he held her there in breathless anticipation, making her focus, making her want, before he finally—finally—pinched ever so lightly. Once. Twice. And then he pinched harder, longer, catching those splintery sensations of anticipation and binding them into bolts of pleasure that ripped through her reserves. Squirming on his lap, she moaned and trembled, closing her eyes so she could feel it more. She wanted everything. She wanted it all.

"More."

"Always."

She wanted him to give her everything, and she wanted to give it back. The excitement, the passion, the pleasure. The love. And, oh, yes, she wanted to give him love. Arching into his hands, she reached behind her and worked the buttons free from his pants. And then she had him in her hand. Smooth silk over hard steel. A promise waiting to be delivered.

His touch on her breasts grew rougher. Her hand on his cock gentler, teasing and tempting, drawing another growl from his throat, trying to drive him past the point of no return.

She wanted him to take her, hard and rough, so fully and completely that she couldn't tell where he began and she left off. She wanted him. She needed him. His teeth pressed against her skin between her shoulder and neck, lingered. Dropping down she ground her pussy against his groin, rocking against him, seducing him as he was seducing her.

"Shit, yeah."

He bit and she screamed. The bite stung, her skin burned, and deep within her the coil tightened.

"Jackson!"

"Yes."

His hand at the base of her neck pushed her forward. How could he do this to her? Make her crazy with lust, so needy she whimpered and arched her back when he tossed her skirts over her back, offering him everything with a spread of her thighs. With a loud rip, he tore her pantaloons in half. The soft material drifted down her thighs as he came over her.

She felt small and vulnerable and feminine kneeling there before him, completely exposed. She imagined she could feel the heat of his skin. The memory of how he felt was nothing compared to the reality when the broad thick head of his manhood snugged home. She couldn't help stiffening.

"Easy, now. You know you can take me."

She nodded. "I know, but—"

But there was always that first moment when she struggled before pain became pleasure.

"No buts. I've got you."

And he did. His fingers parted her folds, sliding through the slick heat until they found her swollen clit. He was gentle at first, teasing and tempting as he had her nipples, seducing her past her fears and luring her back into that mindless fire where she only wanted to burn. With him. Just him. Beneath the surface, she could feel the wild waiting. And she wanted it.

"Jackson."

"Yes."

"Please."

With his knee he pushed her thighs wider. With his cock he parted her further. His fingers plucked her clit, stretching and twisting, giving her the more she needed as desire spiraled. The coil tightened and reality faded until there was only this moment. This need.

The smack on her ass took her by surprise. The sting blended with the pleasure. She jumped and he pushed. Her muscles surrendered and his cock forged deep. She screamed and for the first time he let her.

"Sing for me, baby."

And she did. Over and over, riding the pulsing pleasure, struggling to take more, always more, rejoicing when he gave it, welcoming him deeper until she felt he touched her very soul.

It was too much. Digging her fingers into the blanket, she tried to hold on, but she couldn't. This was Jackson. This was them and when he touched that spot now, and growled, she surrendered, body and soul. Screaming again as he pulsed high within her, her name a rough whisper in her ear. His, a soft expulsion of her breath.

She collapsed on the blanket. He followed her down, still hard within her. She wiggled. He chuckled. "Stop tempting me, woman. I've got this one night without kids to interrupt and I intend to get my cuddle."

She slapped a mosquito on her arm. "You and the mosquitoes."

"Hmm." He wiped one off her shoulder. "I'm beginning to suspect a conspiracy."

Rolling on his back, he patted his shoulder. She'd never received a more welcome invitation. Scooting over, she settled into his arms. He pulled the blanket up. It was the most natural thing in the world to snuggle into his side, to cup his cock in her hand, to listen to his heart beat. To be sheltered in his arms. Mimi lay there for a time, and let her mind wander. As it always did, it roamed back to her childhood and the tightrope of guilt her mother made her walk. And for the first time, she realized it didn't matter. Her mother had done what she'd thought best, but Mimi was no longer that girl who felt she had to atone for her existence. Over the last year, she'd found her purpose.

Propping up on his elbow, Jackson leaned over her. His hair caressed her breast; his thumb stroked her cheek. "A penny for your thoughts."

She couldn't see his face, but she felt his smile. "I was thinking I like it here."

"Here in Cattle Crossing or here in my arms?"

"Both, but mostly the latter."

"Not missing the children?"

She shook her head. "I'm a bit jealous of Jenna—she makes mothering look so easy—but I'm beginning to also accept I don't have to be everything to Melinda Sue and the boys. I'm not their mother, but I can be most things and it will be all right. Not their mother, but something close."

"So you worked that out. Good."

She touched his smile. "I'm a slow learner."

"I won't argue that."

"Based on what?"

"Based on the fact you can't see when a man is head over heels in love with you."

"What?" She couldn't have heard him right.

"Don't sound so shocked." He tipped her mouth close. "I love you. That being the case, Mimi Banfield, would you do me the honor of being my wife, my partner, my love for all the rest of your days?"

It was all her daydreams come together, sprinkled with fairy dust and touched with magic. But a younger her could never have known what to do with a man like Jackson. She would have run, she would have fought, she would have let fear destroy everything.

"Are you sure?" she asked, just to be fair. "The kids come, too."

"I'm always sure, and I wouldn't have it any other way."

Because he sounded so arrogant she teased, "Good. Then you can tell them they're stuck with us."

"I'm not expecting complaints."

"Not even from Kevin?"

"Nope."

"What makes you so sure?"

"He loves you and trusts me. Besides, I promised him a rifle of his own."

"So you bribed him."

He cocked an eyebrow at her. "Any complaints?"

She shook her head. "Not a one."

"What about you? Are you sure?" he asked. "Do you think you can give up Bentley's Folly to become the wife of a struggling rancher?"

"You won't be struggling for long." Of that, she was sure. "And yes, I'm looking forward to it."

"It'll be just us. Pa's taking a liking to California."

She tried to cock her eyebrow, failed, so just settled for cocking her head. "Are you trying to talk me out of it?"

"Nope." With the lightest of touches, he stroked his finger down her cheek. The familiar caress was as compelling as a kiss. "Just making sure you're sure."

She leaned into his touch. Instantly, his fingers opened, offering her support. "Sure? No, I can think of a million reasons why you're making a mistake."

"But?"

Turning her head, she pressed her lips into his palm. "But if you're determined to make it, I would be honored to be your wife, your partner, and your love."

"Why?"

She smiled softly and cupped his face in her hands. This kind of insecurity she knew how to handle, because he'd taught her. "Because I love you. I love you with my body, my heart, and all my soul. I've loved you since you dropped into that hellish well cracking jokes, and it's only grown since. It used to scare me, but now it thrills me and I can't imagine the future without you in it." Kissing him softly, she asked, "How was that?"

Hooking his arm around her neck, he shook his head and pulled her closer. "It sounds like I've got my work cut out for me."

She smiled and breathed into his kiss, "You can handle it."

They were all there. Standing at the altar with his best man, Clint, Jackson looked around the church, decorated in white and green, and felt at peace. With the exception of his father, who'd sent a congratulatory telegram, all the people he'd known for his life were there. People he'd breakfasted with, worked with, laughed with, and fought over pie with. His friends and his family, in the form of the McKinnleys, the Swansons, and the MacIntyres. His life told through the faces of the people he loved. A sense of continuity that he appreciated now that he was adding another face, another facet. It was good.

The organist began to play. The soft music floated through the space, quieting the chatter.

Jackson stood up straighter.

Brad, holding his Bible, leaned over. "You sure about this?"

He'd never been more sure. "Absolutely."

"Still got time to run," Clint teased.

"Shut up, Clint."

The other man chuckled. From the front row, Jenna

hushed him. The music stopped. Everyone turned expectantly. The organist launched into the wedding march. Jackson, along with everyone else, held his breath, waiting for that first glimpse of the bride.

The double doors in the back opened. Melinda Sue strolled through the door, looking like a pink angel in her new dress, tossing rose petals to the right and left. Behind her, Mimi walked down the aisle, Tony and Kevin, looking uncomfortable yet dapper in their new suits, on either side.

Jackson had never seen a more beautiful bride. The light green dress hugged Mimi's figure before flaring out in a lace-drenched skirt. Her hair was pulled back in a fancy twist that showed off the length of her neck, and an ornately braided crown of daisies circled her head, giving her the appearance of an ethereal princess. She walked down the aisle as if she didn't have a care in the world. Head up, chin level, eyes straight ahead, her bouquet of white roses held loosely in her hand. When she reached the altar, he held out his hand. Without hesitation, she took it. Ignoring protocol and everyone waiting, he asked her the same question that'd been asked of him. "Are you sure?"

Her smile softened and she stroked her thumb across the back of his hand. "Absolutely."

"Still got time to run," Clint offered.

Mimi didn't hesitate. "Shut up, Clint."

Clint chuckled. "For sure she's your woman."

Yes, she was. Bringing Mimi's hand to his lips, Jackson pressed a kiss to the back and smiled into her eyes. Together they turned to the Reverend.

"We're ready."

About the Author

Before becoming a full-time writer, **Sarah McCarty** traveled extensively. She would bring a pencil and paper with her to sketch out her stories and, in the process, discovered the joy of writing. Today, Sarah is the *New York Times* bestselling author of more than a dozen novels, including the Promise series, and is best known for her historical and paranormal romance novels.

CONNECT ONLINE

sarahmccarty.net